VIVA CITY FC BOOK FOUR

KIRU TAYE

I0582794

FIRST PUBLISHED IN Great Britain in 2025 by
LOVE AFRICA PRESS
103 Reaver House, 12 East Street, Epsom KT17 1HX
www.loveafricapress.com[1]

Home of African Love Stories

• • • •

Available in eBook and paperback

---

1.   http://www.loveafricapress.com

OTHER BOOKS BY KIRU TAYE

1

Xandra: Killer of Kings

Osagie: Bad Santa

Rough Diamond

Tough Alliance

Trophy Wife

Mistletoe Mafia

Royal House of Saene Series

His Captive Princess

The Tainted Prince

The Future King

Saving Her Guard

Screwdriver

Viva City FC Books

Against the Run of Play

Offside Trap

Wives and Girlfriends Vol 1

Others

Haunted

Outcast

Sacrifice

Black Soul

Scar's Redemption

Viva City FC Books

Game of Two Halves by Unoma Nwankwor
Against the Run of Play by Kiru Taye
Beyond the Touchline by Unoma Nwankwor
Offside Trap by Kiru Taye

Offside TRAP

Viva City FC Book Four

KIRU TAYE

Playlist

Wild World ~ Maxi Priest
Anxiety ~ Doechii
Only For a While ~ Anita Baker
Terms and Conditions ~ Mahalia
Let Me Love You ~ Ne-Yo
I Know Love ~ Maxi Priest
Next to Me ~ Emeli Sande
Stamina ~ Tiwa Savage, Ayra Starr, Young Jonn
Hallelujah ~ Kevin Olusola
Best of Me ~ Maxi Priest
Check ~ FLO
Listen on Spotify[1]

---

1. https://open.spotify.com/playlist/31pQE4I70uuANlSUUs-

BzTe?si=POhmYm3LTAa5qcJ1Q2hdaA

Blurb

The thing about an offside trap? You don't see it coming ...

Diaye Zambo is one of the best defenders in the English Premier league. But now, it's not a striker dogging his heels, it's one scandal after the other. Forced onto the sidelines both professionally and personally, while no team wants to touch him with a ten-foot pole, his life can't get any lower. A stint in Nigeria, back home to see his grandmother, seems like the only thing he can do as the fates decide his future.

Oseki 'Seki' Asemote is a compassionate nurse, juggling two jobs to stay afloat and keep her family together. The last thing she has time for is a hot-headed football player from the UK who thinks the sun shines out of his arse. But Diaye is her employer's grandson, and she'll keep the peace for her, even if the too-hot man makes her want to pull her hair out in the same breath as her knickers.

Then providence shines—Viva City FC wants Diaye on their team ... but this offer comes with strings. He has to prove his days of scandal are behind him, for example, by taking a wife.

There's no way Diaye will turn his back on playing football, and if it comes with the noose of marriage, he will bite down. According to his grandma, Seki's the perfect candidate. If she marries him, she gets an all-expenses-paid opportunity to study for her master's degree in England, which will set her and her family up for a better life.

A marriage of convenience, on paper, shouldn't be hard. But real-life is another matter, when your spouse gets under your skin and in your blood. Suddenly, the opposition is neither on the pitch nor on the sidelines. It's in their hearts as passion and feelings get involved. This is supposed to be play-acting for a few years, and the first rule is not to succumb. What happens when off-side is now on-side, and pretend starts to look too real?

Step into the thrilling world of professional footballers in the Viva City FC Books series!

Diaye

"*Kinky Zambo! Kinky Zambo!*"

The words slither into my mind, the chant like the hiss of a poisonous snake. With a shake of my head, I try to dislodge the loud noise from the spectators and concentrate on the solidity of the ground beneath my feet and the other sounds of the stadium.

Thousands of eyes stare at me, a sea of indistinct faces, as I brace myself to defend against the league's best. The environment feels unfamiliar, taut with the smell of grass and exertion.

Swiping the stinging sweat off my eyes, I track the opposition's powerful forward, who is bypassing our midfield and heading towards our back four. A low hum of anticipation vibrates through the crowd, a tangible wave of tension washing over me.

Normally, the electric atmosphere generated by the cheering fans, and their passionate support, gives me a boost. I was born for moments like this. The feel of the perfectly manicured grass beneath my cleats, the thunderous roar of the spectators, and the unwavering focus required to be the last line of defence, holding my team together. Playing in Europe's elite leagues proves I've reached the pinnacle. I made it to the top. In some circles, I'm classed as football royalty with a father who is a former footballer and is still involved in the world of sports.

However, today is turning out to be less than lacklustre.

My team bosses haven't been making great decisions all season. To be fair, nothing has gone right for me this year. Bad things happen in threes, right? Well, this has been a total clusterfuck.

First, I find out my fiancée, Phoebe, is cheating and break up with her. Then she spreads lies about me in the media to cover up her actions. The headlines are etched in my mind:

"Bedroom Scandal Rocks Zambo! Fiancée's shocking claims shake his off-field reputation!"

As if it isn't bad enough, my team coach drops me from the regular lineup and as team captain because of the scandal. And my bum has been warming the reserve benches since February.

But finally, I'm playing—a sub—but still on the pitch for the second half of a crucial match. And they don't get much bigger than this one.

The season's title decider.

We're playing against our biggest rival, and we need to win to secure the Premier League title.

To be fair, we've won this title a few times before along with the Champions' League and FA Cup, but this feeling never gets old. I need to make space on my cabinet for this season's trophy.

But today is not going our way, a symptom of the second half of the season which we should have dominated but haven't. We've been playing catchup, in second place on the league table. The game is currently drawn at nil-nil. The opposition will be happy with a draw. If it stays this way, we've lost the EPL title.

Of course, it doesn't help when I can't seem to get my head in the game. The mocking boos each time I have possession of the ball are distracting. My legendary ability to focus on the task at hand has deserted me. How can I concentrate on football when I've been falsely accused publicly, and I can't even defend myself in the public arena?

The match is unravelling in a series of near-misses and defensive blunders. A misplaced pass here, a failed interception there. Our attackers miss the cues from our midfield, when they're not downright offside. So many stops and starts, tactics our rivals are using to disrupt our flow. It seems to be working.

We are in disarray, and I can almost feel the premiership title slipping from our grasp.

Frustration coils tightly in my chest as I attempt to keep up with the opposition's relentless attacks. We know their strategies well, having played against them numerous times. Yet, familiarity is a double-edged sword. They know our moves, too.

Usually, I'm at the heart of the defence in centre-back, organising the rest of the team. Today, I'm in the right-back position and someone else is team captain.

Blocking another advance, I clear the ball to a midfielder and try to suppress the anxiety gnawing at me.

The opposition surges forward—wave after wave of relentless attack. The clock is winding down, every second feeling heavier than the last.

A precise through-ball cuts through the defensive line. I react, launching myself into a last-ditch sliding tackle. My studs scrape the turf, my body stretching to meet the ball. For a moment, time suspends—the crowd inhales, the air electric. I make contact, deflecting the ball just enough to send it rolling away. I stumble. The net ripples. Goal.

The referee's whistle cuts through the chaos. The match is over.

I push myself up, muscles aching, frustration coursing through me like fire. I clench my fists, looking toward my teammates, their faces a mixture of exhaustion and disbelief.

The scoreline is one-nil.

Yet, my team, Bishampton United FC, has lost the title race.

I watch the opposition celebrate, the stadium divided between deafening cheers and the stunned silence of our supporters.

I fought with everything I had, but tonight, victory slipped through my fingers because of a rookie mistake. My tackle didn't clear the ball. It sent it into the net. Our net. I hang my head, chest heaving, defeated and broken.

The battle is lost, and the season is over.

• • • •

AS MUCH AS I LOVE PLAYING a team sport, suddenly, I can't bear anything but solitude right now. Those fibres knitted to form the backbone of my life—football and family—are unravelling, twisting and twining around my body, strangling me.

For the second time, events beyond my control have up-ended my life.

I feel afloat, unanchored, and lost. Drifting out on an ocean with no land in sight.

I don't know what to do. Whatever it is, I know I don't want the usual crowd around me.

Hence the reason I'm strolling through the expansive gardens of this house aimlessly.

The crunch of footsteps against the paved stone pathway makes me turn.

Mr O'Connell, my agent, is walking towards me with a kind smile on his face.

Although I'd rather be alone right now, I force a small smile on my face that feels more like a grimace. He is one of two people I trust wholeheartedly. I've known him for most of my life. But it wasn't until my mother, Esosa Zambo, passed away that he became my agent. Before that, my father was my personal manager. However, while my mother was sick with the effing c-word, she made me promise to sign with Mr O'Connell if anything happened to her. At the time, I'd thought it wouldn't come to pass. I'd expected her to make a full recovery, and I'd had no problems with my father overseeing my endorsement deals and public image.

Then the worst happened, turning my world upside down the first time around.

My mother lost her battle with cancer.

The overwhelming sadness at her loss returns, a crushing boulder on my chest, constricting my breath and squeezing the air from my lungs.

"Diaye, I want to talk to you."

Mr O places his hand around my shoulder and steers me towards the beach, which is a walking distance from his home worth millions in a very prestigious neighbourhood.

My African mother never allowed me to address him by his first name when she was alive. She would disapprove if I did so now. So, I fondly call him Mr O.

I nod and walk beside him, swallowing to shift the lump in my throat. I can't wallow in my misery in peace. It's the reason he invited me to stay at his house for a few days and the reason I accepted. Honestly, I'm not very good alone. I want privacy, not isolation.

Mr O is a few inches shorter, with grey hair around his temples against his otherwise dark hair. He has bright green eyes and a day's growth on his chin. He is well into his sixties, but has the energy of someone twenty years younger. Before he became an agent, he was a footballer and still maintains his fitness. He has successfully negotiated multi-million Euro sponsorship deals on my behalf over the years. Now, I suppose he's wishing he hadn't taken me on, because he has a publicity nightmare on his hands to sort out on my behalf.

He is a father figure, especially now my father is being a pain in the arse.

"I know you're having a tough time at the moment, and it feels as if everything is going against you," he says.

Well, it's not just a feeling, it's a fact.

My long-term girlfriend cheated on me and spread lies about me.

I scored an own goal for the first time in my career.

My team lost the Premiership title. Never mind how everyone conveniently forgets we would have lost the title regardless of the own goal.

The country coach dropped me from the national team.

To top it off, my father wants me to take back my cheating ex, Phoebe, and I'm not talking to him.

So yeah, I know everything is going against me.

But I don't say any of this to Mr O. He knows it all anyway. It's the reason I'm here instead of my million-pound flat, hiding from the media and nagging family members.

To be honest, I'm all talked out. It feels like I've been talking a lot, and no one is listening. Perhaps I should take a vow of silence. Maybe someone would listen then.

Perhaps I need to do some introspection and contemplation. Reassess my life.

I need to get my head right. Yet, I can't seem to get myself away from the spiralling negative thoughts.

We meander through the mature garden with trees, shrubs, and flowering plants. He pauses at a wooden bench in the corner separating the flower beds from the manicured green grass.

He lowers his body onto the bench and pats the seat beside him. I settle on the wooden slats, waiting for him to continue speaking.

"I spoke to Granger," he says eventually.

My body stiffens, and I expect bad news.

Granger is my club head coach. We haven't been getting along since he took over from the previous one. I would say he has it in for me. I would even say he's not a very good coach. The just-ended season—his first with the team—was our worst run of bad form since I started playing for the club. We have no new trophies. No FA cup. No Premiership. No Champions League, even though we finished second in the EPL.

Then again, I'm biased because he's tried to move me from my position in the centre back to midfield. I'm not a midfielder. I play my best game when I'm in defence cutting down the opposition. He's even stripped me of the team captain position.

So, I'm not expecting good news, although we're in the summer break and the new season doesn't start for another two months.

"I'll be honest with you. He wants to release you from your contract," he continues.

"What?" My stomach congeals and drops as my breath hitches.

The team ending my contract suddenly is not a good thing. Especially at the height of the controversy surrounding me right now. It means the next team won't offer a high price for me. It signals the beginning of the end of my career. I'm only twenty-five going on twenty-six, for goodness' sake. My career cannot be ending so abruptly. I don't want to end up playing in some obscure country. The English Premier League is the best football league in the world. As the most competitive and most unpredictable, it has financial backing and global reach. It attracts the best players and has high-quality teams.

I am one of, if not the best defender in the world, and I don't want to play football outside the EPL.

"I've spent my entire professional career with this team. I've been loyal to them, and this is how they want to treat me?" My tone sharpens as anger pitches through me and my booted foot bounces on the paved stone as I try to contain my agitation. "You can't let them end my contract early."

"Of course I won't let them do this to you," my agent says. "You know I negotiated the last contract for you. They can't break it without penalties. Granger knows it, even though he doesn't like it."

I let out the breath I didn't know I was holding.

"But the bugger is going to try to frustrate you by keeping you on the bench for the coming season, which doesn't do you any good."

"True." I nod. "I already spent too much time on the sidelines in the last season."

"That's what I thought. Therefore, I suggested they loan you out for the coming season."

"Loan? To an EPL club?"

"Not quite. I think you will be better off outside England for a while. Until the scandal dies down and someone else starts trending on social media. I've lined up some PR events and charity matches for you in West Africa."

I already know about the trip to a few countries in Africa over the summer, including my fatherland, Cameroon, and my motherland, Nigeria. My agent is deflecting, trying to soften me up before he lands the major blow. But I'm not buying it.

"Mr O, where am I going to play football next season?" My eyes narrow as I imagine being sent to some obscure league. Granger can be spiteful.

"It's a Serie A team."

"No! Is there no other club in the EPL..." I trail off as he shakes his head sadly.

I hang mine as my body trembles and my anxiety spikes. I breathe heavily, deeply, and fight to control it. To not break down in front of my agent. I have an irrational fear of change, or so my therapist says. It's always been there but got worse after my mother died.

Wonder why I stayed with the same club for a decade and never considered other top-tier clubs who were offering even bigger money.

Loyalty is one reason. Acute anxiety is the other.

"Diaye, it won't be so bad." He places his hand reassuringly on my back. "I will work to ensure you're back in the EPL by Mercato."

I exhale a heavy sigh. I can't wait for the January transfer window.

2

Diaye

Now that I've lost everything to you...

The first verse of Maxi Priest's 'Wild World' fills my head through the noise-cancelling headphones. From my first-class seat in the wide-body, twin-engine jet airliner, I stare out the window. Because of my fascination with aeroplanes, I can identify the class of airplane. In another life, I picture myself a pilot, gazing down at the world from a cockpit high above the earth.

Maybe I should become one in this life, since my footballing career has taken a nosedive.

But then, a lot of nice things turn bad out there.

The lyrics echo in my ears. Echo my experiences. My life. There seems to be a Maxi Priest song for every mood. My mother was a huge fan of his. Ironic really. As an adolescent boy, I preferred the likes of Ne-Yo and Rihanna instead of Mum's favourites, like Anita Baker, Maxwell, and Mr Priest. It wasn't until her passing that I started listening to these artistes and songs again.

This one is supposed to evoke a bittersweet and contemplative feeling. The soothing reggae tones carry a sense of heartfelt emotion, blending melancholy with warmth and hope.

On a different day, it should create a relaxed reflection on the complexities of parting ways and wishing the best for someone moving forward in life.

Except, today, I'm not exactly in the mood to wish my ex well. Certainly not without a shitload of sarcasm.

To be honest, when I think about her and what she did to me, I want to burn shit down and break bones.

But as my therapist, Olivia, reminds me, I'm a footballer, not a gangster, and I need to channel that energy elsewhere.

Sometimes, I can't believe my ex did what she did. Her actions were calculated and deceptive. The ultimate betrayal. Hell, I can't believe I allowed myself to be manipulated like that.

Now, I'm the one losing everything I worked hard for. Because of the disastrous season I—we've—had, Coach is shipping me off. The club management has agreed to loan me to an Italian Serie A club for the upcoming season.

Almost a decade I've dedicated to this club. One relationship failure, and I get shipped off. Like a child who gets sent to boarding school because his parents can't handle him.

Is football more about the WAGs than the actual players and what happens on the pitch? Why am I being punished because Phoebe's father is footballing royalty? I'm supposed to be ball royalty too, damn it!

Fuck that! Fuck *them*!

Never again. There will be no forgiving or forgetting.

Olivia says it takes time to heal. That I'm going through seven stages of grief.

I laughed when I heard this because I didn't get it then.

I think I get it now.

A state of shock and bargaining were the first two stages for me.

Now, my blood boils.

Then again, there are days when the world feels muted, colours seem washed out, and sounds are distant. Days when I want to shut everything and everyone out.

No. I am not in the mood for well-wishes and hope. But I continue listening to the song because I love Maxi Priest. He connects me to my mum, to the good old days, and I won't allow my shitty experiences to taint the music for me.

I won't lose the only thing that brings me relief, like I've lost everything else.

I refuse to think about how my life has turned bad recently. So, I shove the thought aside and focus on the view. Below, the clouds are a sea of fluffy white, drifting past.

I guess Olivia has a point. She thinks playing football outside the UK will do me good. That I won't have the usual triggers reminding me of the scandal.

It's also the reason I'm on this plane heading to Nigeria during the off-season instead of heading to a riviera or other holiday location and partying the summer away.

Mr O lined up a series of promotional events and charity matches for me through different cities in West Africa. Lagos, Abidjan, and Douala. The focus needs to pivot from the scandal to my soccer prowess.

The energy of the African fans is unmatched, their passion infectious. Colourful clothing, a riot of vibrant hues, the powerful vuvuzelas, and echoing chants light up any stadium, showcasing their boundless enthusiasm.

My trip to Abidjan was a whirlwind. The city welcomed me with open arms, embracing the energy and passion that define the spirit of its people. Matches played there were exhilarating, with fans cheering wildly, their voices creating a symphony of support reverberating through the stadium.

The promotional events allowed me to connect with the community, sharing moments that transcended beyond the pitch. Local children, full of dreams and aspirations, reminded me why I fell in love with football in the first place. Meeting them and seeing the joy on their faces as we played together gave me a renewed sense of purpose. It was a reminder of how football has the power to inspire and unite, even in the face of adversity.

As I left Abidjan and boarded the plane to Lagos, I reflected on the experiences which were contributing to healing the broken parts of me. The vibrant culture, the warmth of the people, and the electric atmosphere of the matches were a step in the right direction to mending the wounds inflicted by the scandal.

This journey isn't just about escaping the triggers back home. It's about rediscovering the joy of the game and the impact it can have on lives, including my own.

The flight has been smooth, but a heaviness hangs around me, a mixture of anticipation and uncertainty about what awaits me. The haunting thoughts of my broken-down relationship plague me.

The plane begins its descent, and I lean back, contemplating the city awaiting me. Lagos, vibrant and chaotic, a city of contrasts where the glamour of the elite rubs shoulders with the gritty realities of everyday life. Here, I hope to continue my journey to a place where I can find solace from the relentless scrutiny and criticism that has followed me.

As the plane touches down at Murtala Muhammed International Airport, I gather my belongings. Usually, I travel with an entourage including one or more of my half-siblings. But Will and Liam—mostly Will—attract paparazzi like flies to waste disposal site. Will doesn't know what incognito means, which is what I'm aiming for over the next few days, outside of the scheduled events. Sure, there are local reporters. But they were specially curated to ensure the spin is positive.

Wondering why my half-brothers have shortened versions of the same name? They are named after my father, William Zambo. Think of it, what you may.

Rumour has it, I was going to be William Zambo II. But my father was away when I was born, and my mother registered my birth with the names her mother chose. Hence, I am named after my maternal great-grandfather.

I adjust my baseball cap and sunglasses, hoping to remain inconspicuous amid the bustling crowd. I step off the aircraft, breathing in the warm, humid air that envelops me like a familiar embrace. It's different from the crisp, icy breeze of Leeds, the city of my birth and it reminds me of my origins, the roots I sometimes feel so distant from.

Navigating through the airport, I swiftly move past the throngs of travellers. I'm grateful for the VIP treatment arranged by my management team, allowing me to avoid the usual chaos of baggage claim and customs. I make my way to the arrivals lounge, where a chauffeur awaits me.

A tall man in casual clothes stands holding a sign with my name on it.

"Mr Zambo," he greets warmly, a smile spreading across his face. "Welcome to Lagos. My name is Chinedu, and I'll be your driver and personal assistant during this trip. Mr O'Connell arranged it all."

"Thank you, Chinedu," I reply, extending my hand for a firm handshake. "I appreciate it."

Chinedu takes my luggage and leads me to the sleek black car parked in a dedicated zone outside the terminal. As I slide into the back seat, I glance around at the bustling cityscape.

The car pulls away from the airport, and I settle into my seat, watching the city unfold before him.

Lagos is alive with energy. Street vendors hawking their goods, honking cars, and pedestrians weaving through the crowd. It's a city that never seems to rest, a stark contrast to the quiet, orderly streets of Leeds.

Chinedu drives with practiced ease, navigating the traffic with skill.

"How was your flight, sir?" he asks, glancing at me through the rear-view mirror.

"Good," I reply, my voice tinged with exhaustion. "Smooth, and not too long."

Chinedu nods. "Well, you're in Lagos now. We'll make sure you have a pleasant stay. Your hotel is not far from here, just a short drive."

As the car winds through the streets, my mind wanders to the events coming up. The charity matches are important to me, a chance to give back to the community and inspire the next generation of footballers. Nevertheless, the weight of my recent performance still lingers, a shadow casting doubt over my abilities.

The cityscape changes as we move further downtown. Towering buildings give way to bustling markets and residential neighbourhoods. Children play football in the streets, their laughter and shouts filling the air. I watch them with a sense of nostalgia. Scenes like these sparked my passion for the game many years ago.

We arrive at the hotel, a luxurious establishment nestled in the heart of the city. Chinedu parks the car and assists me with my luggage.

"I'll be here whenever you need me, sir," he said, handing me his card. "Just give me a call."

"Thank you, Chinedu," I say, pocketing the card. "Where can I change some money?"

"There's a Bureau de Change in the hotel lobby," he says.

"Great. Thank you." I enter the hotel, the cool air conditioning a welcome relief from the heat outside.

The receptionist greets me and hands me the room key. "Welcome, sir. We hope you enjoy your stay."

Afterwards, I stop by the currency exchange counter and change some Pounds Sterling in my wallet into Naira notes. He hands me a big brown envelope of cash, which I stuff into my backpack.

I make my way to my room, with the bellboy pushing the luggage trolley, my thoughts still a whirlwind of emotions. Once inside, I tip him generously and drop my bags. Then I collapse onto the bed, staring at the ceiling. The silence of the room is a stark contrast to the noise and chaos of the city

outside. I close my eyes, trying to shake off the fatigue clinging to me.

My phone buzzes, breaking the silence. I pick it up and
see a message from Mr O, reminding me of the schedule for
the upcoming days. I sigh, knowing despite the exhaustion,
I must keep moving, keep pushing forward. There are inter-
views, meet-and-greets, and matches to prepare for. The fans
in Lagos are excited to see me, and I can't let them down.

I decide to take a shower, hoping it will reinvigorate
me. As the warm water cascades over me, I think about the
match that led to my current state of disarray. The final whistle, the own goal, the split-second of silence in the stadium.
It replays in my mind like a broken record. I try to shake off
the memories, focusing instead on the opportunities ahead.

After the shower, I feel better. I dress in casual clothes
and make my way downstairs to the hotel restaurant, where I
hope to find some comfort in a good meal. The restaurant is
quiet, with only a few patrons scattered throughout. I find a
table by the window overlooking the city.

As I wait for my food, my thoughts drift to my maternal
grandmother. I haven't seen her in a few years. But I miss
her. Her comforting words and prayers for my wellbeing.
She could always make me smile, even in my dark moments
when I was a teen. I long to hear her voice. If I'm honest, I
haven't been a good grandson. I haven't kept in touch since
my mother died. She calls me sometimes. But it's been so
long since I spoke to her.

She lives a few hours away from here. I used to visit her
house in Sapele when my mother was still alive. Maybe if I
call her, she'll let me visit for a while.

But I hesitate about calling. What if she doesn't want to talk to me?

The waiter brings the food, and I thank them. But my mind is restless, and I can't eat.

I pull my phone out and scroll through until I find the last number I had for her. I press the call button, and it rings. With each ring tone, my stomach knots, and my turmoil increases. After a few seconds of no response, I'm about to hang up when someone answers it tentatively.

"Hello?"

A rhythmic lilt in the soft, unfamiliar voice sends shivers down my spine, my heart pounding like a drum against my ribs, heat flooding my cheeks.

The speaker is young, probably in their twenties, certainly younger than my almost eighty-year-old grandmother.

"Who is this?" I ask. My voice has a slight tremor, betraying my emotions. This is unlike me. I'm usually more controlled. More aloof. Yet as I wait for her response, each second feels like an eternity.

Perhaps I have the wrong number. It's been so long, and people change their phone numbers all the time. Disappointment settles on my shoulders like a heavy weight, and I swallow the lump in my throat.

"This is Seki," the person on the other end says in a calm tone, then pauses, creating a tension that makes my breath hitch. "Who is this?"

The name does not sound familiar. None of my maternal relatives have this name. None I'm aware of, anyway. So, I'm not about to reveal myself to a stranger. Not until I find out more.

"I think I have the wrong number," I say instead of answering her question.

"Oh. Who did you want to speak to?" she asks.

"I was trying to contact my grandmother, Mrs Aghoghovie."

"Your grandmother?" she gasps, and I can hear the shock in her voice.

"Yes, do you know her?" An awakening of hope kindles.

"Yes. I'm Seki. I help her around the house." There's a change to her tone, a hardening.

Relief washes over me, mingled with a touch of embarrassment. I didn't realise my grandmother's health had deteriorated to the point she needs a carer. She has always been a strong woman. Invincible. Undaunted. Then again, she's in her late seventies.

"I'm glad to hear she has help. Is she available?"

My mind races through memories of my grandmother, her gentle smile, and her unwavering support. I feel a renewed sense of anticipation and connection.

"No. When was the last time you spoke to her?"

There is full-on censure in her tone now. It's unmistakable, as if she suspects I haven't been a good grandson.

Heat rises through my neck even though I'm sitting in a cool, air-controlled restaurant. I tug at my collar, not liking her tone at all.

"Not that it's any of your business," I reply in an annoyed tone. "I've been meaning to call for a while, but life has been...busy." The words sound inadequate, even to my own ears.

I hear the sharp intake of breath, as if she is offended. I don't care. Who is she to judge me?

"Is my grandmother there or not?" I say in a sharp tone.

"I..." she trails off. "She's not here," she continues in a firmer tone.

"Then can I have a number where I can reach her?"

"No."

"What?" It's my turn to be shocked.

"I don't know who you are?"

"What do you mean? I told you already. Mrs Aghoghovie is my grandmother."

"So you say. But you can be a fraudster, a scammer, for all I know."

Anger flares through me, and my voice deepens in a harsh whisper, although I'm aware I'm in a public space.

"Are you having me on? Me, a fraudster? I think you're the fraudster. A thief. I bet you stole my grandmother's phone."

As soon as I say it, the potential horror of the situation floods through me. What if she stole the phone from Grandma? Why else would she have the phone number, even if she claims she works for Grandma? Why else would she prevent me from speaking to my grandmother?

"What—"

"If you don't put my grandmother on the phone in the next few minutes, I'm going to get the police on you. Be sure they can track you to wherever you are."

"You're not serious. You will not call the police on me." She chuckles derisively.

"Missy," I say in a sharp tone. I don't even know why I say it, but I like the sound of it. "My name is Diaye Zambo. You don't want to test me."

"Is that name supposed to mean something to me? Anyway, my name is Seki, not Missy." She sounds annoyed.

Okay. She has me stumped. Very few people on this planet don't recognise my name. I've been in the running for the Ballon D'or for several years. Not to mention how the recent scandals in my life have been feeding the tabloid, gossip bloggers and podcasters for some time. It seems I found one person who seems to live under a rock and without social media access, although they have a phone.

Still, I'm not impressed by her attitude.

"I don't care. Tell me how to reach my grandmother, or you will find out why my name means something!" I bite out.

This seems to give her pause, or she is taking my treat seriously. She doesn't speak for a few seconds.

"What will it be?" I push, not willing to give any ground.

"Fine, Mister. I'll tell her you called."

Did she call me Mister in that insolent tone?

The line disconnects.

More to the point. Did she just cut me off?

3

Seki

The rain pours down in relentless sheets, drumming on the roof of the taxi like a thousand impatient fingers. The windshield wipers struggle to keep up, swishing back and forth in a futile attempt to clear the glass.

"Oga driver, how far?" I ask in the Pidgin language everyone uses around here.

I lean back against the worn seat, my eyes scanning the blurred landscape outside. The traffic is at a standstill. A sea of red brake lights stretches into night, punctuated by the blare of horns and the rumble of idling engines.

"You don see am now." The driver, a middle-aged man with a grizzled beard, mutters in frustration while waving at the barely visible road via the windshield.

I let out a heavy exhale, pulling my sweater tighter around me as the damp chill seeps into the car. I can't even get out and walk. Not with the downpour. Some roads will be flooded. Hence the delays in traffic. Best to wait it out.

I'm going to be late returning from work placement, which isn't good. I'm a final year nursing student, and I'm currently doing my work placement at the Delta State University Teaching Hospital. When I started the course three years ago, I had to move away from home in Warri to Sapele. Because of how hard things were for my family, I got a job as well. Luckily, a family friend connected me to the lady whose house I stay in.

Iye. She is more than a landlady, the house more than just a place I lodge.

Mrs Aghoghovie is like a grandmother to me. We have no blood connection, but I've grown close to her in the since I moved in.

I cast a worried glance at the clock on the dashboard. We've been stuck in this jam for what feels like hours, inching forward at a snail's pace.

Iye will get worried because I'm usually home by now. I should call her.

My phone buzzes in my handbag, breaking the monotony of the rain and the honking horns. I fish it out, glancing at the screen. And don't recognise the number.

It's a foreign one starting with +44. A UK number. I recognise the country code because I have dreams of going to the UK to further my studies. But the cost of the international tuition fees alone means it's an aspiration that might never come to pass.

Still, I swipe to answer the call. "Hello?"

An unnerving silence hangs in the air for several seconds, interrupted only by the faint hum of the phone line and the occasional blare of car horns. I wonder if the call disconnected.

"Who is this?" an unfamiliar voice asks. It's a deep, raspy whisper, youthful yet undeniably English in its cadence. It pours over me like sun-warmed shea butter on my skin, lush and sensual, making every nerve tingle with awareness.

"This is Seki," I replied in perfect English, switching up from the local version. The words sound formal even to my own ears as I wait for their reaction. "And who is this?"

"I think I have the wrong number," he replies, sounding disappointed.

A mournful sigh escapes his lips, heavy with unspoken sorrow. It resonates within me, reminding me of the grief of losing my mother and evoking a powerful need to alleviate his distress. I can't see—or hear, in this case—someone in anguish and ignore them. It's a strength and perhaps a weakness too of mine. This is why I want to be a nurse.

"Oh. Who did you want to speak to?" I ask, keen to keep him on the line even if he was a wrong number.

"I was trying to contact my grandmother, Mrs Aghoghovie."

For a moment, I'm speechless, my mind racing. The connection between the mysterious caller and Mrs Aghoghovie is unexpected, and the realisation leaves me reeling. My heart pounds in my chest, each beat echoing the surprise coursing through me. "Your grandmother?"

"Yes, do you know her?" Hope tinges the caller's voice.

Yet I ignore it as my stomach hardens, and my suspicion rises.

I'm aware Iye has a grandson because there are photo albums of the boy when he was younger. But her grandson hasn't called or visited her since I moved into the house. Not to my knowledge. I'm close enough to Iye to be ninety-nine percent sure he hasn't called her in the past year. What kind of person would ignore their elderly grandmother for a whole year?

All the sympathy and attraction I have for his voice vanishes in an instant.

"Yes. I'm Seki. I help her around the house," I respond, my tone hardening slightly.

"I'm glad to hear she has help. Is she available?" he hesitates, as if he's ashamed.

He should be very ashamed. Anyone would think he died with his mother, the way he neglects his grandmother.

"No. When was the last time you spoke to her?"

See, I'm not usually this abrasive.

Let me not lie o.

Sometimes, I am a total nightmare to people who mess up. I fight to protect the people I love, and it's usually my mouth doing the fighting. It runs faster than my brain, especially when I'm annoyed like right now.

"Not that it's any of your business," the voice shoots back, sounding irritated. "But I've been meaning to call for a while, but life has been...busy."

A sharp intake of breath rushes into me, along with another dose of shock.

How dare he? I'm the one sitting here taking care of his grandmother. And he dares to say it is none of my business. After what Iye has done for me and my family. She *is* my business, whether he likes it or not.

"Is my grandmother there or not?" he demands before I can reply to his last rant.

"I..." I want to say I'm not at home. Instead, I say, "She's not here."

I don't have to be helpful to him since he's being rude.

Our chat goes back and forth. The man has the effrontery to ask for Iye's phone number and, of course, sounds shocked when I decline. Who does he think he is? He needs to learn some manners, *joh*.

The conversation deteriorates from there because neither of us is willing to give ground. If he chooses to be arrogant, he has met his match. I imply he could be a fraudster, which is a legit concern, in the current climate. Then he threatens to call the police on me.

Police! At first, I laugh at him because I think he's bluffing, and I'm prepared to call his bluff.

Then something in his tone changes when he calls me Missy and says his full name. It's deeper, unwavering, calm, and authoritative. The sound makes me sit up straight in the car seat and yet something melts inside of me. Heat flushes across my suddenly sensitive skin, and I shiver. I recognise my body's response.

Lust. Unadulterated desire.

His voice alone sends desire from my ears to my core.

With it comes anger. Because why am I attracted to the sound of Iye's grandson's voice? Never mind how he is an arrogant man who ignores his grandmother.

I can't help my retort when I pretend I don't know who he is and tell him his name means nothing to me. I hear his sharp inhale, and it seems to keep him silent for a while. Thank God!

But of course, I know the legendary footballer who has played Premiership football for a decade. Born in the UK to a former Cameroonian footballer father and a Nigerian mother, Iye's late daughter.

He has won almost every trophy in the UK and Europe at club level. If only the rest of his national team were as good, he would have won the World Cup by now.

A small smile tugs at the corner of my lips.

Look at me *yabbing* his national team as if they didn't perform better than my national team in the last World Cup.

You see what I mean about my bad mouth? At least this time, I don't open it.

Not when it sounds like I *don vex am well well*.

Oh, by the way, Pidgin is my language of choice. My language of internal recrimination.

When he threatens me again, I give in and tell him I will let Iye know he called.

Thankfully, the taxi is pulling up outside my—Iye's house, so I cut the call, glad to be rid of him. I settle the driver and get out of the car, hurrying to the pedestrian gate and knocking on the metal bars.

The rain has stopped, and the streetlamps are bright, which means we have electricity supply. We're in the GRA, a quiet residential suburb, which is considered the poshest part of the town. The residents contribute to maintain their local transformer, which means we have relatively fewer blackouts, unless something happens to the national grid.

The house is an old style two-level white house built in eighties, with six bedrooms in a main building including a staff annex. It remains pristine, having undergone several refurbishments. Green foliage hedge surrounds it, culminating at the wrought-iron gates where I stand. Beneath my shoes is the patterned concrete paving which runs across the drains on the side of the tarmacked street and leads to the driveway beyond the front gates.

The gateman in casual clothes approaches. He is visible through the gaps between the welded black metal rods of the gates.

"Seki, why you return late?" the gateman asks, dragging his feet to open the security barriers. He's dark-skinned and in his thirties and has worked for Iye longer than me. He acts as if he's my senior, which he is in age and service length. But he's not my supervisor, and I don't report to him. If anything, he answers to me as I'm the housekeeper and Iye's carer.

When I first moved in, he tried to behave as if he were my boss. But I soon put him in his place. He still tries it once in a while, like now. But unlucky for him, the phone call with Diaye already wound me up, and I'm not in the mood for his shenanigans.

I raise the phone in my hand and turn on the camera app and start recording a video. "Íruoghẹnẹ," I say his name disdainfully. "No vex me, you hear me so? Open this gate right now. Unless you want to explain to Madam why I'm standing outside in the rain at night."

"Ha. Person no fit joke with you again?" he tries to tease as he unlocks the heavy padlock and pulls the bolt back with a squeaky noise.

"Premium joker ... Mtcheew," I hiss with a hard expression and stomp past him in a hurry.

"Small madam, dis one way you dey vex like this. Wetin happen?" he calls out, the rattling metal hinges and locks resounding as he locks the gate.

I'm already half-way down the side of the house to the entrance I use and don't reply to him. He refers to me sometimes as Small Madam when he wants to appease me.

But he's right. I'm not usually this grouchy or easily provoked. But that Diaye person...

Which reminds me. Where is Iye?

The thought skitters through my minds as I enter the hallway. The concrete steps leading upstairs are to my left, and the door to the laundry room is to my right. Normally, I will go upstairs and drop my bag before going to see Iye. But during those times, I'm home before it gets too dark.

Now I hurry through the door ahead of me, able to hear the clatter of crockery before I reach the kitchen door.

"Iye, I'm back," I call out.

"Seki, is that you?" she replies, definitely from the kitchen.

"Yes, it is." I push the door open. "Iye, good evening."

She is wearing the long Ankara booboo I helped her put on this morning, her grey hair styled in a low cut. The tap is running in the stainless-steel sink, and the electric kettle is on-the-boil atop the laminate worktop.

"Evening, my dear." She reaches for the cupboard above her head.

But I hurry and intercept her and open the cabinet. "Let me help. What did you want to get?"

"Just the tea bags," she replies and moves aside so I can retrieve the box with her favourite brand of black tea.

"Is the flask empty?" I make fresh tea in the large flask for her every morning before I leave, so she can just pour when she needs some. Same way I prepare meals in advance so she can eat when she's hungry.

"Yes," she replies. "I wanted to make tea and have it with some bread."

I sigh. Íruoghẹnẹ is supposed to assist her in my absence. He didn't come to check if she was hungry this evening.

"Please go and sit down. I'll bring you the cup of tea, and I'll make your supper."

I dump my bag on the worktop so I can check the white deep freezer for an already cooked frozen meal. There's no time to cook from scratch. She needs to eat at regular intervals because of issues with her blood sugar.

"Okay." She moves towards the little table and chairs in the corner of the kitchen. She likes to sit there and chat with me while I prepare a meal. The long booboo swishes around her legs, but she stands instead of sitting. "Why are you late home? I was worried."

Turning to face her, I lean my back against the counter. "Iye, I'm sorry. You know how the traffic is on Shell Road. I think some areas were flooded because of the rain so we had to go through the back streets. It took longer than usual."

"I thought as much." She nods.

"I was going to call Íruoghẹnẹ to let you know the situation."

She gives me her phone to use while I'm out because mine stopped working and I haven't been able to replace it. The phone is Dual SIM Active, which means it accommodates her number and mine on the same phone and it can receive calls on both numbers at the same time.

"But I got another call," I continue. "Which reminds me. Your grandson called."

"You mean Omo Ovie?" She frowns.

"No. Not your step-grandson. *Your* grandson, Diaye."

"Hey, Diaye called? My Diaye?" Her eyes brighten, and a huge smile curls her lips.

"Yes."

"What did he say? Is he well?" She walks back towards me.

I put my arm around her shoulders and steer her to the padded chair.

"He's very well," I say. At least, he sounded like he had no problems on the phone. "Sit down and relax. I'll make you a cup of tea. Then you can chat to him yourself while I make your food."

"I can't wait." She's still grinning as she settles into the chair. Her excitement is palpable.

My heart warms at seeing the anticipation she exudes. I know she misses Diaye, who is her only surviving descendant since her daughter died. She didn't have other children. Although she has stepchildren. Her husband was a member of the king's cabinet who married several wives. Iye was the first wife. But she only had one child, a girl. Her husband married other women who gave him multiple male children.

So Iye has several step-grandchildren, but only Diaye is of her lineage.

I make her a cup of tea and put a small bowl of groundnuts in front of her. It's something to nibble while I make the food. Then I grab the phone from my bag, press to dial the last incoming number, and check it's ringing.

"Hello?"

The quick response and deep voice on the other end set my pulse racing.

"This is Seki." I swallow the lump in my throat. "Is this Diaye?"

"Yes. Is my grandmother there?"

"Yes. Hold on, let me pass the phone to her."

I hand the phone to Iye and make sure she has it to her ear. "Aghadiaye, is this you?"

I don't hear his response, but a smile splits her face. "It's so good to hear your voice."

Best to give them some privacy. So, I grab my bag and walk to my room to get changed.

4

Diaye

Ten days after I first arrived in Nigeria for the PR events, I'm in the country again, this time for personal reasons. I'm in the SUV with Chinedu, and we left Lagos for Sapele just before dawn, heading east on the Benin-Sagamu expressway. Chinedu mentioned when we drove past Sagamu minutes earlier. He's being quite chatty, a friendly guide. But I'm not saying much, withdrawn, contemplative.

On reflection, the past fortnight has been a success. Somewhat.

When I spoke to Grandma last week, I promised I would visit her once I completed my work schedule. Hence the reason for this road trip.

I'm done with the publicity tour, which Mr O arranged for me across several West African countries.

Positive images of me now outweigh photos of my ex online. There are pictures of me meeting African fans, playing the game I love with celebrities, and raising funds for local charities.

Mr O says it's a great start to repairing my public persona.

Although it does nothing to heal my private identity. The man in the mirror. My heart.

If anything, anything I've lost myself, faded away. It's weird, like the trauma of losing my mother all over again.

My days of boundless energy are gone, replaced by a quiet, withdrawn existence. The situation robbed me of the inclination to speak my truth, and my momentum vanished. I feel empty, shrunken, mourning the person I used to be. Someone I don't know if I can ever find or be again.

I can't be that person again because I can't trust anyone or invest myself the way I did with Phoebe.

The memory of Phoebe's betrayal and lies still stings. A sharp pain pierces my heart each time I think of her. A suffocating feeling grips me when I contemplate not playing for the club next season—a club that has been my home for over half my life.

All because her powerful father, a major player in the sports world, can and has exiled me because his daughter cried wolf. My life is in chaos once more. I hate chaos. It leaves me reeling and heartbroken.

I'm not ready to forgive or forget.

Usually at this time of the year, I'm on holiday at an exclusive resort in the Caribbean or the Mediterranean. Last summer, Phoebe and I spent a week in the Maldives, then spent another week in Saint Tropez with my family and hers.

Since our breakup, her family is not talking to me, and I'm not talking to mine.

An effing mess.

Chinedu exits the expressway and pulls into a spacious car park next to a service station outside Ore. He tells me it's a town in Ondo state. The quiet hum of the highway fades as he cut the engine.

Although I'm not hungry, I climb out of the vehicle to stretch my legs and use the restroom, appreciating the fresh air. Grey clouds partially obscure the sun, high in the sky, making the day pleasantly bright but not oppressively hot. My digital watch, with its bright LCD screen, displays a temperature of twenty-eight degrees Celsius.

The restaurant is a low brick building, painted olive-green and orange. The sound of cheerful chatter spills out from the open doors, along with the smell of freshly cooked food, which makes my stomach rumble. Neat, trimmed, green hedges border the concrete path from the car park.

Unable to resist the delicious aroma, I enter the establishment and order a plate of rice and beef stew. It should keep any hunger at bay for the rest of the trip.

Soon, we're back on the road, the rumble of the tyres almost a comforting sound. Motion is a good thing. It implies fluidity and momentum. Elements that help in football. Elements I need in my life.

Chinedu starts a conversation. This time about the ancient Benin kingdom. I tell him I studied some of it in history as a child because of my mother.

"Of course, you mother must have been from this area," he says.

"Yes, she was from Delta state," I reply.

"That's interesting. I'm from Delta state, too. From Anioma. What part of Delta is your mother from?"

"I don't really want to talk about my mother." The heaviness of grief returns and sits in my chest, constricting it.

"I'm sorry." He sighs, a sound thick with resignation. He's probably exhausted from my disinclination to chat and the one-sided conversations between us. But he leaves me be.

As part of Mr O's team, he knows about the scandal surrounding me. His job is to provide whatever I need until I get to my destination.

To break the silence in the car, Chinedu selects a lively talk radio station, the host's energetic voice filling the space with current events and opinions. After about two hours, the sights and sounds of Benin City explode around us — a vibrant tapestry of motion and noise as we drive south towards Sapele on the Benin-Warri Road.

I recall colourful markets and bustling streets from childhood trips to Benin City—driving through it now brings a poignant mix of joy and sadness. During the holidays, particularly around December, my mother immersed me in our Nigerian heritage with visits to family, vibrant cultural experiences, and the fragrant aromas of home-cooked meals. Travelling around the Benin-Sapele-Warri areas, I remember the sights of lush vegetation and the feel of the humid air on my skin.

Anticipation buzzes through me when I recognise the landmark leading into Sapele town. I know the address of my grandmother's house, but not how to get to it. Thankfully, Chinedu is street-savvy, and with the help of the Satnav, we arrive at the neighbourhood by mid-afternoon.

"That's the house," I say, and Chinedu stops the car outside the black metal gates, beeping the horn.

A white two-storey building with a flat roof stands proud inside the compound surrounded by trees and green hedges. The road is a yellowish-brown with patches of grass on the sidewalk.

My heart pounds a frantic rhythm in my chest, a mixture of excitement and apprehension. Years have passed, the memories fading, but the familiar scent of orange blossoms and damp earth brings it all back as I set foot in this place.

A stout dark-skinned man in a grey long-sleeved jersey shirt and dark trousers appears on the other side of the gates, and I recognise his familiar face.

I press the button to lower the window and pop my head out. "Íruoghẹnẹ, open the gates."

"Ah. Oga Diaye don come o!" he exclaims, his voice rich with warmth.

His face breaks into a wide smile as he unlocks the metal barriers and pulls them aside. It's a wonderful feeling to know he recognised me, considering I haven't been here for years. Not since my mother's funeral.

Chinedu drives into the compound and parks under the carport, where the gateman indicates. He runs back to close and lock the gates.

The air is hot and heavy with humidity when I step out, as if rain is imminent. Chinedu pops the boot open before walking to the back of the car.

Íruoghẹnẹ hurries towards us. He is in his thirties and has worked for my grandmother for about ten years.

"Íruoghẹnẹ, it's good to see you," I say, shaking the older man's hand firmly. "How have you been?"

"You don see us now," he replies, still beaming with a smile. "We haven't seen you for a long time. We missed you. Iye has missed you o."

The guilt gnaws at me, a familiar ache from being away so long.

"I missed everyone," I reply, my eyes tracing the recognisable contours of the house, every corner etched with memories. The front part-paved driveway where I used to kick balls with my friends when I was little. Some of my favourite memories are of this house.

A tinkly laugh, like wind chimes in a gentle breeze, peals through the air, drawing my eyes towards its source.

Two women emerge from the house, onto the veranda leading to the front yard. The older woman with the short grey hair and yellow midi dress has her head tilted to the side as she listens to whatever the young woman is saying to her. The two are giggling, whispering secrets. Like the closest of friends or family.

Yet, I know it can't be true because of the obvious age difference.

I recognise my grandmother. The other woman is much younger, about my age. She must be the girl I spoke to a fortnight ago, Grandma's housekeeper, Seki. They are certainly not family. So, they can't be friends, either, right?

Yet Seki's face is bright with animation as she continues talking and laughing with Grandma. She seems too chirpy, too sweet, like she's about to break into song as a character in a famous animated children's classic movie.

I wonder if her laughter is fake. If she's putting on an act because she knows I'm arriving today.

I know plenty of people who put on a mask every day and pretend to be what they're not. People who smile at those they hate, laugh at jokes that aren't funny, all while working to destroy the same people they laugh with.

Is Seki one of those fake people? Is the laughter all an act?

I can't tell as I walk across the front yard towards them.

My grandmother looks well and happy, from what I can see. Her face lights up as soon as she sees me, and she starts singing and dancing as I approach her with a grin on my face. I understand only some of the words. But the gist is, she's calling the community to welcome home a long-lost child.

"Iye, good evening," I greet as I stop in front of her.

Her response is to wrap her arms around me. The years of separation melt away in her embrace, and she holds me tight. I swear she's trying to lift me. But that's not going to happen because I'm probably more than twice her weight. So, I lift her off her feet, and she giggles before I put her down. It takes a full minute before she releases me to pull back. As if she's reluctant to let me go.

"Welcome home, my dearest grandson," she whispers, her voice cracking with emotion.

"Thank you, Grandma. It's good to be home."

I didn't know how much I needed to be here, to see her until right now. Until her embrace surrounded me, anchoring me.

The comforting warmth of the old house envelopes me, the scent of sun-baked stones in my nostrils, a familiar love settling deep in my bones. For the first time in years, I feel an overwhelming sense of belonging, truly at home.

As the shadows retreat from my mind, a sense of calm washes over me, and I breathe a little easier, the tension leaving my shoulders.

I turn to Chinedu, who is a step behind me while Íruoghẹnẹ carries some luggage inside. "Iye, this is Chinedu. He brought me from Lagos."

"Good evening, Ma," Chinedu greets and genuflects.

"You're welcome, my son," Grandma replies.

"I hope it's okay for him to stay for a few days," I say.

"Of course," Iye agrees. "Seki will prepare a room for him. Remember Seki? You spoke to her days ago."

"Yes, I remember her," I say. How can I forget the bold stranger who dared to challenge me over my infrequent visits to Grandma? Her sharp tone on the phone still echoes in my mind.

She's dressed in a pair of blue jeans and a yellow T-shirt, which matches Grandma's outfit. Coordinated outfits. How old is she? Five? I resist the urge to display my contempt at her attempt to impress me.

Her hair is in cornrows pulled together in a bunch at the back. Her face is smooth but without makeup, and her laughter has disappeared. She's nothing remarkable. Unsophisticated. Plain is the word.

The way her body fills out her clothes sends a jolt through my veins, though. Yes, I notice it. Her body is the epitome of my ideal—wide hips and thighs flowing into a tiny waist, a shape that's both powerful and graceful.

With effort, I tear my eyes away from her lower body and focus on her face. She lifts her chin, her dark eyebrows drawing together, her intelligent brown eyes locking with mine in a challenging stare.

Isn't she supposed to welcome me? She had no problem berating me on the phone. Now, she seems tongue-tied.

I should say hello to settle her unease, but I don't. Why should I make it easy for her?

Head and shoulders taller than her, I stare her down, my heart pounding like a hummingbird's wings against my ribs.

Blinking, she averts her gaze, eyes darting around, a mixture of suspicion and curiosity etched on her face. Maintaining a wary distance, she seems to hesitate, her angled body suggesting she isn't comfortable with my presence.

It's just as well, because I'm unsure of her motives too. I need to understand the nature of her relationship with Grandma to make sure she isn't exploiting my vulnerable grandmother financially or emotionally.

Yet, when she says, "Welcome," her voice, soft and resonant like a cello, washes over me.

For a moment, I forget to breathe. Forget to think. Forget to talk.

"Come inside," Grandma says, snapping me out of my temporary stupor.

What just happened? I shake my head and walk into the house.

This Seki woman is a riddle I need to solve if I hope to restore seamless order to my life.

5

Seki

The last time the house was this alive—with so much laughter and commotion—was months ago at Iye's birthday party. She had friends over from her days as head of nursing and midwifery at the Delta State University Teaching Hospital, where she worked for thirty-five years before retiring. There was family, as well. Her sister, nieces, and nephews. Even her former co-wives visited for the day to convey their well-wishes. I find it interesting how they all outlived their husband.

But today's palpable excitement far surpasses any previous experience. Ten days ago, Iye spoke to her grandson, Diaye, for the first time in months, perhaps years. And he is coming to Sapele.

Iye's energy seems boundless. She woke before dawn, even though she's typically up with the sun, and has not stayed still for more than a few minutes.

In preparation for Diaye's arrival, the house is filled with a whirlwind of activity and delightful chaos. I spend the morning cleaning and cooking. The gardener came yesterday and trimmed the hedges. Iye has a vegetable garden at the back of the house and potted flowering plants in the front-yard. Tending them has kept her occupied since her retirement. She is a life-giver, first as a mother, then as a midwife and nurse and now as a horticulturist. Everyone she touches flourishes just as she's been a blessing in my life in a short period.

This is the reason I don't understand why Diaye has stayed away from her for so long. He's a superstar millionaire footballer who can afford to fly out to visit her regularly. At least once a year.

Then again, who am I to judge him?

The only person qualified to judge him is Iye. And for her grandson, she is preparing a welcome fit for a king.

With all the commotion—the polished silverware, and the nervous flurry of activity—anyone would think the king himself was about to visit. Iye, despite her stepson being the Ovie, had never made such elaborate preparations for him.

The joyous occasion is unprecedented, as far as I know. Aside from the occasional birdsong and breeze rustling leaves, nothing much happens around here. Today is different.

We live in a quiet town with a port along the Ethiope River, which is a tributary of the Niger Delta. One of the largest employers is a flour mill. The other big employers are in the supply chain of crude oil and natural gas production. The area is residential, and our neighbours send their children to the most expensive private schools in the area.

By midday, the house is sparkling with decorations and fragrant with orange blossoms.

I'm finishing the meal preparation—seafood okra to go with the pounded yam swallow, and spicy beef stew served with steamed white rice and sauteed spinach. However, I also fried yam chips and attempted to cook battered fish for the first time in my life. It doesn't look like I succeeded because the fish is breaking up in the oil.

I'm thinking of scrapping it and starting afresh when I hear a car horn beeping outside.

Oh, no! That must be Diaye. He's arrived, and I'm out of time. The kitchen is a mess, and I don't have time to tidy up. I untie the apron around me quickly and toss it on the counter as I switch off the hobs.

"Iye," I call out in search of her and find her in the hallway arranging flowers in a handcrafted brown wooden vase.

"My dear, have you finished in the kitchen?" She places the vase where she wants it on the dark-wood side table.

"No. My attempt at making fish and chips didn't turn out well."

"Why? What happened to it?"

"I was following an online recipe, but the battered fish came out looking like scattered fish."

"Scattered fish." She hiccups as if she's trying to suppress laughter, but her eyes are bright, and she can't hide it.

"Iye, don't laugh." I can't help giggling because she is chuckling. "I was trying to offer Diaye something he eats in the UK, so he would have options. Now he's here, and I'm out of time."

"Diaye is home?"

"Yes, I think so. I heard a car outside."

"That's wonderful. Let's go and welcome him." She heads towards the front door.

Suddenly, the prospect of meeting Diaye for the first time is daunting. I know how much Iye loves her grandson.

And the man has lived in the UK his whole life. He's a superstar footballer with the world at his feet.

Meanwhile, I didn't even have time to apply any makeup, and I probably reek of grease and spice from all the cooking. After the way I spoke to him the first time on the phone, I'm not sure I'm ready to meet him.

"Iye, go and meet him. Let me go back to the kitchen and finish off." It's the only excuse I can think of to delay meeting Diaye.

"My dear, that can wait." Iye takes my hand as if she can sense my reluctance. "Did I ever tell you the story of the first time I cooked for my husband?"

"No," I reply, following her towards the front door. I can't refuse her anything.

Yet, my heart skips a beat at the mention of husband.

Does Iye think I cooked for Diaye because I want him to be my husband? I mean, that would be ridiculous. I don't know the man. From the little I know, I don't even like him. More to the point, I have a boyfriend.

Maybe she's just trying to distract me, so I don't feel self-conscious about meeting her grandson.

"The first time I cooked for my husband, we were newly-weds, and I had a housekeeper. But I wanted to cook for my man. I prepared the meal the way I was used to at home with lots of pepper and spice. Do you know this man took a bite of the food and started choking, right there? I'd never seen anything like it." She bursts into laughter as she reaches for the door handle.

"Are you serious?" I giggle as I open the door, and we step outside.

"Yes. The man was choking because of ordinary pepper. He couldn't handle the heat." She continues chuckling. "For years, we teased each other about that incident. It was a running joke between us."

I join her in laughing as I picture the scene and watch her. Her laughter is infectious.

"From that day, I realised cooking food wasn't my love language," she continues. "There were ways I expressed my love for him, but cooking wasn't one of them. In relationships, cooking food isn't everything. Some people say the best way to a man's heart is through his stomach. But trust me, there are other ways to reach a man's heart."

She winks at me, and I blush from my toes to my ears.

Tell me she's not saying what I think she's saying.

Before I can ask what she means, she starts singing and dancing and ululating.

I look up, and my breath hitches.

Three men are walking around the cloistered garden, across the paved courtyard, towards the veranda. At the back is Íruoghẹnẹ dragging two large suitcases and a backpack. The second man, I don't recognise, but he has a leather overnight travel bag slung across his shoulder. Leading them is the most beautiful man I've ever seen.

Diaye Zambo. Iye's grandson.

His long strides eat up the space between us and bring him closer within a few seconds as Iye continues her dancing and jubilation. He's wearing a burnt-orange short-sleeved linen tunic showing off broad shoulders and hard biceps. The matching trousers hug his sturdy thighs and long legs, ending in white leather sneakers. The gold chain around his neck catches the sunlight and glitters against his dark skin. His hair—mid-length brown-black locs—is neatly held together with a black band. His full lips stretch across flawless, natural teeth, and his eyes sparkle with humour as he stops in front of Iye and greets her.

Those photos of him in the house did not prepare me for meeting him in the flesh. I'm caught off-guard and can't stop staring at him. He's taller, wider, sturdier than I imagined. In his sharp two-piece attire, he cuts a figure of quiet devastation, a predator in tailored clothing. His presence, so powerful and compelling.

And seeing the way he returns Iye's warm-hearted embrace, something melts inside me, and I'm considering forgiving his past neglect of Iye as long as he maintains their renewed connection.

When they finally separate, he introduces his friend as Chinedu, who will stay with us for a few days. It's a good thing I prepared two rooms, as I wasn't sure if Diaye would visit with an entourage.

"Seki will prepare a room for him. Remember Seki? You spoke to her days ago." Iye echoes my thoughts as she introduces me.

"Yes, I remember her," Diaye says as his gaze sweeps from my face over my breasts down to my feet and back up.

No one has ever paid this much attention to me. It's not leering or lascivious.

My skin tingles under his assessing scrutiny. Does he approve of what he sees?

What am I thinking? I don't care if he approves. I'm not here to please him.

His gaze locks with mine, and my heart pounds in my chest, a frantic drumbeat against my ribs. A haunting wariness lurks in his dark, deep-set eyes, like shadows in a moonless night. As the silence stretches, punctuated only by the distant chirp of a bird, I realise he's waiting for me to speak, his gaze unwavering as I stand here, captivated.

Breaking the gaze, I swallow to clear my throat before saying, "Welcome," glad I didn't stammer because my body is behaving weirdly in his presence.

"Come inside," Iye gives me a knowing grin, as if she senses the effect her grandson has on me.

I move out of the way as Iye enters the house, followed by the men. They settle in the living room, and I hurry into the kitchen to find cold refreshments.

As I pour the chilled drinks into glasses, I replay the moment I met Diaye in my mind, chastising myself for the way my pulse raced under his gaze. It's just fatigue and the novelty of meeting someone new, I tell myself. Nothing more.

Balancing the tray of glasses, I walk back to the living room. Chinedu is speaking animatedly, his hands gesturing as he recounts a story, which has Iye chuckling softly. Diaye rests against the arm of the sofa, his expression less animated but his presence equally commanding.

As I step into the room, his eyes shift to me. The intensity is still there, though softened by a faint, almost imperceptible curve of his lips.

"Here," I say, setting the tray on the low table. "Lemonade or water?"

Chinedu reaches for a glass of lemonade with a grateful smile, while Diaye hesitates, his eyes lingering on me for a beat longer.

"Lemonade, thank you," he finally says, his voice low and steady.

I hand him the glass, careful not to let our fingers touch. The space between us feels charged, nonetheless. I retreat, sitting on the edge of a chair near Iye, who pats my knee with affection.

"You've outdone yourself, Seki," she says, taking a glass of water. "Always so thoughtful."

I smile at her, grateful for the reprieve her words offer. "It's nothing, Iye. Just some lemonade."

Chinedu starts another story, his voice buoyant and engaging, but I can feel Diaye's gaze flicker to me occasionally, as if he's reading something in my posture, my movements. My heart betrays me again, quickening against my will. What is it about him that unnerves me?

I focus on Iye's warmth beside me and Chinedu's laughter, trying to ignore the pull of Diaye's presence. Whatever this is, it's fleeting. It has to be.

"Excuse me," I say during a break in conversation.

Glad to leave them, I head back to the kitchen to clean up and bin the fish. Diaye will have to forgo the foreign food for tonight.

Afterwards, I dash upstairs to my room to freshen up before dinner. I wash up and change my top and spray some perfume. Then I return downstairs and set the dining table. Iye only uses the formal dining room when we have visitors. Otherwise, we eat meals at the kitchen table most days.

Everything ready, I walk back to the sitting room to find Iye and the men laughing at a story Chinedu was telling.

"Seki, my dear. Take a break. You've been working so hard all day." Iye beckons.

I go over to where she's sitting on the padded armchair and hug her from behind. "Iye, that's why I'm here. Dinner is ready. Please come to the dining room."

"It's true." She shuffles to the end of the sofa slowly. "Diaye and Chinedu must be hungry."

"I am," Chinedu laughs as he stands.

"I could eat." Diaye grins.

Knowing Iye sometimes struggles to stand, I place my hand on her back for reassurance and support as she rises.

A shiver runs down my spine as my skin prickles. I lift my head and meet Diaye's intense gaze. He watches us, a friendly smile crinkling the corners of his eyes, and I interpret it as definite approval. My heart stutters, and my chest warms. The unspoken acknowledgement from him feels strangely comforting, even if I wasn't looking for it.

Unrestrained, my lips curve into a smile as I walk beside Iye into the brightly lit dining room, the chatter of Diaye and Chinedu behind us.

6

Diaye

The next morning, I'm up at first light. I open my eyes and stare up at the white ceiling. The sound of an air-conditioner hums in the background, and the air is cold. At first, I think I'm in a hotel room, and it takes a few seconds to remember yesterday. The road trip from Lagos to Sapele. Seeing my grandmother for the first time in years. The home-coming and welcome were amazing.

Yet, there were moments of melancholy.

Being back in this house without my mother present is hard. It's the main reason I didn't visit for so long. Every time I've been in this house previously, my mother was always here with me.

Yesterday, I kept expecting her to join us in the lounge and sit on the sofa beside me as she used to. To ask me about football and my plans for the future.

Grandma tried asking, but I didn't talk in detail. Just mentioned the activities of the last two weeks. I left Chinedu to do the talking and tell his stories. They made Grandma and me laugh.

Then Seki invited us to dinner, and I witnessed the rapport she has with Iye. She was attentive to Iye's needs and seemed to anticipate them even before I could see them. Iye seems happy, and that's all that matters here.

My phone beeps, and I check the message. It's from Chinedu.

Are you ready for the morning run?

Give me five minutes.

I send the reply, get out of bed and pop into the ensuite to brush my teeth and change into the running gear.

Outside my room, Chinedu is already waiting in his sports attire and trainers. He's a former footballer who became a talent scout, and now he works for Mr O.

"Good morning," I say to him as I walk past and down the stairs.

"Morning." He follows me into the kitchen.

The refrigerator hums quietly as I grab bottles of water before we head outside.

"Oga Diaye, Oga Chinedu, good morning," Íruoghẹnẹ greets as he washes the car.

"Morning, Íruoghẹnẹ. Please open the side gate. We want to go for a jog. We'll be back soon." I do some quick stretches while I wait for him.

"Okay." He pulls the bunch of keys from his pocket and opens the heavy-duty padlock. Then, he pulls the gates apart and lets us out.

We jog around the neighbourhood. We took a walk last night after dinner, and we follow the same route this morning, doing a loop. My usual training schedule involves gym sessions in the mornings, followed by afternoon training on the pitch.

Since I'm on holiday, I don't need to follow the strict routine. However, I need to exercise daily to maintain my fitness for the upcoming season. To prove my fitness for the new team, I'll face gruelling physical tests, including intense running drills and strength assessments, before I can play in the first half of the season. I must trust Mr O's promise to return me to my prestigious premiership club by January.

Thinking about the changes sparks my anxiety, which makes me stumble.

"Are you okay?" Chinedu asks, jogging on the spot beside me.

"I'm okay." I shake it off and break into a sprint. I don't want to think about what's awaiting me when I depart from Nigeria in two weeks and need to immerse myself in the here and now.

By the time we get back, the sun has risen, and I'm sweating. I leave Chinedu outside chatting with Íruoghẹnẹ and enter the house through the side entrance. There are a few things I want to get done today.

Before I can head to the stairs to my left, I collide—*oompf*—with someone coming out of the laundry room to my right. *Seki.*

The basket in her hand takes a tumble as I grab her arms, pulling her towards me so she doesn't fall over. Soft curves land against me. Clothes spill all over the floor.

A bolt of awareness shoots through me. For a fleeting moment, I forget the messiness of my thoughts, the looming pressure of training, and the anxieties tied to my impending departure. Her presence grounds me in the present.

"Oh. I'm sorry," Seki cries out like I winded her. She's wearing a pink nightshirt and shorts set. There's a matching satin sleep bonnet on her head. "I didn't see you."

Her pulse thumps frantically against the dip between her collarbones. She looks up at me with the most compelling brown eyes I've ever seen. I noticed them yesterday. Yet, this morning, they seemed to be flecked with gold sparkles.

Will they change colour if toss her bonnet aside and I wrap my hand around the braids in her ponytail, tugging her head back? If I kiss her until her lips are swollen?

Not that I have any business kissing her. She's my grandmother's carer, and she's too sweet for my tastes. So why does my dick awaken with her softness pressing against me? Is it just that I need a woman? But I'm not interested in women. Not after Phoebe.

"It's okay," I say in a gruff voice and break contact, stepping back from her. Then I turn away and head up the stairs without giving her a second glance.

My skin prickles, just as my conscience nags because I didn't help her pick the fallen clothes. She must be watching me. Still, I ignore her and my conscience and stomp up the stairs. As selfish as it seems, self-preservation is more important than chivalry right now.

Some people think I'm selfish and despicable because of Phoebe.

Never mind if I was trying to protect my mental wellbeing after what she did.

With a huff, I open the bedroom door and walk straight to the ensuite bathroom. I turn on the shower, but not the heater. Then I strip off the shorts, trainers, and T-shirt.

Bracing myself for the sting, I step under the spray. The water is cold but not freezing. I stand there for a few seconds as the litres of water cascade onto my skin. It helps to clear my mind before I grab the shower gel and mesh loofah I put on the little corner shelf last night.

Ten minutes later, I'm clean and dry and in the bedroom, moisturising my skin and hair with the lotion from the bottle. I dress in a white tunic and trouser set matched with stylish white trainers.

Satisfied with my appearance in the full-length mirror, I grab my phone and message Chinedu, telling him I'm dressed. He already knows my plans for the morning and agreed to chauffeur me. His reply pings and reads: *I'll be down in 10.*

I go downstairs in search of Iye and find her sitting at the kitchen table. In front of her is a hot water flask, a filled teacup on a saucer, a plate with a buttered slice of bread. She's peeling a boiled egg.

"Good morning, Iye," I greet and approach her.

"Morning, my dear." She reaches out with her left arm and hugs me sideways. "How are you? How was your night?"

"It was good. I slept, probably the best I've slept in a while," I said, pulling out the chair opposite hers. "How about you?"

"Me. I slept like a baby." She chuckles, and I grin. "You look very nice. Are you going somewhere?"

"Yes, I want to go and see Mum. I haven't visited her since..." I trail off as my throat clogs with emotion.

Her smile diminishes as she reaches for my hand. "You are doing the right thing, and I'm glad." She pats my hand, and I nod, swallowing the lump in my throat. "Let me get you something to eat."

She shuffles as if she's trying to stand, and I place my hand on her shoulder.

"Iye, no. I'll sort myself out." Standing, I glance around the kitchen. The surfaces are clean, and everything seems to be in its place. "Where is Seki? Is she not helping you?"

"It's her day off, and she's gone out," she says before biting into the slice of bread.

My mouth drops open as I frown. I haven't considered what happens in their work-life relationship. "So, she'll be back tonight?"

"No. She'll be back tomorrow." She continues eating like it's no big deal.

"What? So, you'll be here on your own all day and night?"

"I'm not on my own. You're here."

"But if I wasn't here, you'd be on your own all day and night. Shouldn't someone else cover in her absence?"

"You're being dramatic. I'm not an invalid, you know."

"I'm not saying you are. Just concerned about you." I picture nightmare scenarios.

In the UK, there have been incidents of elderly people passing away in their homes and staying undiscovered for days and weeks. There was even a much-publicised incident of a well-known former Hollywood actor who tragically died recently.

"I know you are, but I have Íruoghẹnẹ in Seki's absence. So don't worry," she says.

But I worry. So many things I took for granted about her have changed since I last saw her. She was an active, sprite-ly lady when she was younger. Now, she has slowed down. I noticed she struggles to stand and sit, her movements stiff. Climbing up and down the stairs must be a struggle for her.

All it would take would be her tripping on something, and she could be undiscovered for hours if not checked regularly.

I must think of how to make her home safe for her to live in. Buying or building her a bungalow is out of the question because I know how much she loves this house.

"Are you okay?" she asks when I stand there contemplating the options.

"Not really. Would you be happy if I bought you another house? A single level house so you don't have to climb stairs."

"Is that what's worrying you?" She beams with a smile as she opens her arms. I step into her embrace, and she hugs me tight before pulling back. "You are a sweet boy. But no, you don't have to buy me a new house. This house has so many memories. When I stop living here, it should be to join my ancestors."

"Then let me convert the downstairs bedrooms to your quarters," I say. "Seki can have her room next to yours. I'll refurbish it and kit it out with whatever you need. You'll have the entire downstairs to yourself."

She tilts her head as if thinking about it. "That makes sense."

"Good." I beam a smile at how she agreed so readily. I expected her to decline. Grandma can be stubborn.

"I will agree only on one condition." She's grinning as if she knows something I don't.

I should have known she would have a comeback. "What is it?"

"Well, when I move downstairs, it means the whole of upstairs will be vacant. But that's good because you and your wife can have it." She's still grinning.

But my humour dies as I think of the implications of her word. "Grandma, I don't have a wife. I broke up with my fiancée, so I'm not getting married."

"Aghadiaye, listen to me. Whatever pain she caused you is temporary, only for a while. It will pass, and you will find your joy again. You will find true love and get married."

"Grandma, I don't know if that's going to happen." I shake my head.

"It will happen. You know you didn't tell me anything, but I sensed your despair and darkness. I prayed for you. I even called Mr O'Connell."

"You did?"

"Yes. I told him that a trip to Nigeria would help your frame of mind. It gave him the idea to arrange the PR events for you, I think."

Gasping, I stand there speechless, staring at my grandmother. I need a while to wrap my head around what she just revealed.

"See, it worked, because you're here," she continues. "That's how I know you will get over the heartache and true love will find you and embrace you. This house will be filled with your joy and your family's joy."

"Grandma, what are you saying? I don't live here," I say, confused by her words.

"I know you don't at the moment. But my condition for moving downstairs is that you and your wife and any children will live upstairs for a minimum of two weeks every year."

"Are you serious?"

"Yes."

"You mean I can have the whole of upstairs to myself?" I can picture spending two weeks every year in this house, and I would love it. I've always loved this house. And it sounds like my grandmother wants me to have it.

But I frown because even if I got back together with Phoebe, she would never want to spend two weeks here every summer. It's not an exclusive beachside resort.

"Yes, and while we're talking about it," Grandma says. "I want to let you know I made a will, and you are in it. You inherit what's left of my estate, including part of this house."

"Part of the house?" I'm back to being confused. "Why not all of it?"

"Well, I'm giving the other half of the house to Seki," she says nonchalantly, as if she hasn't just dropped a bomb.

"Seki, your carer? Is she related to you?" I'm so shocked, I ask without thinking.

"No, she's not. Not yet anyway. But she's like a granddaughter to me, and she cares for me like one."

Not yet anyway. What does it mean? Does Grandma intend to adopt Seki?

A weird sensation washes over me. I've always been Iye's only grandchild. Now it seems I'm competing for her affection with Seki, and I don't know how to feel about it.

Seki

"So, what is he like?" My younger sister, Imoni, is on the bed beside me, scrolling through social media on her phone.

"Who?" I reply, pretending I don't know who she's talking about as I try to concentrate on the paperback novel in my hand.

We're in my family's house in Warri, and I arrived early this morning on a bus from Sapele to see my family—my sisters and my father. Well, technically, my youngest sister and my father since they are the only ones who still live here. My oldest sister, Erhu, is married and lives with her husband on the other side of Warri. I'm the middle child.

"Your Iye's grandson. He arrived yesterday, didn't he?" Imoni says.

"Yes, he did. He's fine," I say dismissively because I don't want to confront what happened between Diaye and me this morning.

"Do you mean he's fine okay? Or that he's fine hot, as in tall, dark, and handsome," she presses.

Just like that, I remember my first glimpse of Diaye in the front yard of Iye's house yesterday. His swagger and beauty. Yet, it's the strength of his body and the way he held me this morning when I bumped into him accidentally which sends a pulse of desire through me. I press my thighs together and shift on the bed as my body heats.

"What's my business if he's fine or not?" I grumble and shuffle to the end of the bedroom I share with my sister. "You know I have a boyfriend, and I can't be looking at other men."

"Ha. You're allowed to look, now. It is touching other men that is not allowed." Imoni chuckles.

My cheeks heat. If only she knew have already touched Diaye. Well, he touched me when he saved me from tumbling over with the basket of laundry I was going to hang on the line. For those few seconds he held me, I forgot myself, forgot everything else.

Then, abruptly, he stepped away and hurried up the stairs without even looking at me while I stood there wondering what happened.

It's the reason I dressed in a hurry and left the house early this morning. The plan is to hang out here for a while today before returning to Sapele. I have work this afternoon at the same hotel where my boyfriend Mide works. Then, after work, we'll spend time together, and tomorrow, I will return to Iye's house.

"Since you don't want to tell me if he's hot or not, I will have to visit Iye to find out for myself," Imoni continues.

"No. You can't come to the house," I say and stand from the bed.

Maybe coming here was a bad idea. I don't want my sister finding out Diaye is a famous footballer. I didn't tell my family details about him. Just told them Iye has a grandson who lives abroad and would visit.

And my younger sister is the last person I want to find out about Diaye. She's a gossip and a flirt. If Imoni finds out his identity, she will not keep it a secret. Worst of all, she'll show up at the house with the plan to snag him for herself.

"Why not?" she challenges, sitting up in bed.

"Because Diaye is not for you," I blurt out without thinking.

Why the hell did I say that? How do I know that?

"Why not? Do you want him for yourself?" she accuses.

"Of course not. I have a boyfriend," I retort, although my face is flaming hot.

"Then why would you say such a thing to me? I'm your sister. Am I not good enough for him or something?"

"It's not that..."

I scrabble for what to say to douse this situation because I can see the way my sister is staring at me as if I've betrayed her or something.

"I think he has a fiancée in London," I blurt out, although I'm not sure if it's true or not. I was nosy enough to search him up on social media, and I saw something about his fiancée.

"If there is a fiancée in London, how does it affect the price of garri in the market? Sebi, Diaye is here and now without her. What makes you think if he sees me, he will not choose me over her," Imoni counters.

My mouth drops at my sister's audacity. "You know what? I don't even have anything else to say to you. I'm going back to Sapele. I have work this afternoon."

Stuffing the novel in my handbag, I slip my feet into my white tennis shoes.

"Are you not going to wait for Papa to return?" she asks.

"I already saw him before he went out. Just tell him I went back to Sapele. I'll see you people another time." I check my reflection in the mirror on the dressing table before heading for the door.

Imoni follows me to the front door. "So, when is a good time to visit Iye and her grandson?"

I turn to face her. "Are you serious about coming to the house?"

"Of course, I am. I want to collect my share of the gifts he brought from the UK, since you didn't bring anything for us."

Diaye didn't give me any gifts, but I don't correct my sister's assumption. I don't know if he even gave anything to his grandmother. He would have to be stingy to be a millionaire and not bring gifts for his grandmother after so long.

"You can come anytime you want," I say. She will have to find out for herself.

We say our goodbyes, and I walk down the road and catch a three-wheel motorised rickshaw to the bus park, where I take a minibus heading to Sapele. An hour later, I'm back in the town and at my second job working in a hotel bar restaurant.

I head for the staff changing room, dump my bag in my locker, and get changed into the uniform which is a black knee-length pencil skirt, a white shirt, and an Ankara print waistcoat over it.

Then I'm on the floor serving customers in the bar/restaurant. The lunch service is busy. I got this job to supplement what I was earning. The stipend from my nursing work placement covers transportation and basic lunch. It was Iye's influence as former head of nursing that ensured I got the work placement *and* the stipend.

My arrangement with Iye is that I get room and board. I don't pay any rent or bills or for food. Iye has capacity and mobility, so is still relatively active. From my assessment, she doesn't need a full-time carer. But she needs companionship and someone to take care of the house, which is where I come in. She is a pensioner, and I don't enjoy taking money from her, although she still insists on paying me. It's not a lot, but it pays for my expensive hobby—reading. I started working here so I could have an extra income and save money. I like it because Saturday and Sundays are the busiest days, and we get tips.

After the lunch hour rush, I take a break and sit in the staff room reading my book.

My phone beeps, and it's my boyfriend, Mide. He is the shift supervisor and works evenings and nights. It was his help that got me this job.

Hi, baby. Are you on break?

Yes. Where are you?

I'm on my way in. I should be there in an hour.

Good. I'll see you soon.

I can't wait to spend the night with you.

Me, too.

Cheeks heating, I look up to make sure no one is overlooking and reading the messages on my phone. No one is behind me.

Mide and I have been dating for six months. In the past few months, we have been spending Saturday nights in one of the hotel rooms. It's the most convenient way to spend time with him since he works night shifts. He arranges for us to use a room we don't give customers because it's stuck in a corner and overlooks a wall. Because of my work placement and Iye, I don't get to see him except on Saturday nights. When he has a break, he comes to the room and wakes me if I'm sleeping.

He talks about marriage and says when we get married, I won't work in the hotel. I tell him that before I get married, I want to go abroad and study for a master's degree in nursing. I tell him I want to be like Iye, become head of nursing and run the whole department. He says it's a big dream because going abroad is expensive. I know it is, but there's nothing wrong with having big dreams. I tell him he could also study and become the manager of a big hotel chain. We laugh about it.

My phone beeps, reminding me my break is over. I stuff it in my pocket and head back to the floor.

In the hallway, I meet another waiter I get on with. "Tori," I call out her name. "I didn't see you earlier."

"Seki, it's a long story. I was late. I'll gist you later," she says.

"Okay." We both enter the bar lounge. I get my pad and pen ready.

"Your section is looking busy," she says.

I look up, and the section I oversee is packed with guests. The low sofas facing each other and separated by a coffee table have four men sitting on them.

As I approach, I recognise one man facing in my direction—Iye's step-grandson, and the king's son, Harrison. He is a regular at this place, so I'm not surprised to see him. The person next to him is his friend, Stanley.

They are usually good tippers, although Harrison can get handsy. But anytime he tries any nonsense, I threaten to tell Iye, and he behaves himself. If nothing else, Iye commands respect, therefore no one disrespects me.

I plant a smile and head over there. However, I don't recognise the people on the opposite sofa who have their backs to me until I'm standing in the middle of the two sofas and come face to face with Diaye and Chinedu.

No. No. No. What the hell are they doing here?

"Good ... evening," I stammer as my whole body heats. I didn't want Diaye to know I worked here, but I still have a job to do. "I'll be your waiter tonight."

Diaye looks up, and I see the stunned expression flicker on his face. "Seki?"

Chinedu is smiling. "You work here?"

I swallow the frog in my throat. "Yes. On Saturdays."

"Didn't you know she works here?" Harrison says with a mischievous glint in his eyes.

This man is a troublemaker. I'm sure he brought them here so they could see me working.

"No," Diaye says, a frown marring his face. "Isn't this supposed to be your day off?"

Shit.

"Yes." I swallow again and continue. "From the house." I shift from one foot to the other, wanting to rescue the situation before I get into trouble at work. I need this job. "What drinks can I get you?"

"A bottle of Star," Chinedu says with an apologetic expression. It seems he can see I'm uncomfortable with the questions.

"Thank you," I mouth silently to him as the men shout their orders boisterously.

I breathe a sigh of relief, the tension leaving my shoulders as I head to the bar to get their drinks. The low hum of conversation and clinking glasses fill the air.

It's going to be a long night.

8

Diaye

After my chat with Grandma this morning, Chinedu drives me to the palace to pay my respects to the king and the royal family. Grandma said I should pay respect before doing anything else. It wouldn't look good if I was in town and didn't stop by.

The king is my late mother's half-brother. I want to see Harrison, the king's first son, who I used to hang out with when we were younger. The royal family seem pleased to see me, and they try to make a fuss. But I don't stay long. I tell them I need to get to the cemetery, which they understand.

On the way to the cemetery, I'm back to being solemn. Even the chatty Chinedu is silent. He stays in the car because I asked him to while I walk to my mother's grave. I recall the day she was buried, how heartbroken I was. My father told me I needed to be strong, so I bottled up my emotions and didn't shed any tears.

My therapist, Olivia, says that while I may have locked down my emotions by obsessing about control, I unlocked a new boss-level of emotion—anxiety. She thinks once in a while, all those bottled-up emotions protest their lockdown like a prison riot. Hence my anxiety.

Trust my emotions to behave like riotous prisoners. But I'm determined to let them stay locked down.

As I stand over the slab indicating where my mother is buried and read the engraved words, pain swells in my chest. It's like a constriction, and I can't breathe. My breathing becomes heavy and long. It's a worse feeling than I've ever felt. It's like being heartbroken all over again.

Bile rises in my throat as tears fill my eyes, making them blurry. Nausea washes over, and I hurry to the edge of the cemetery where there are bushes and throw up everything I ate today. I stay bent over as my body wracks silently and the tears continue to flow. I cry for everything I've lost—my mother, my relationship with Phoebe, my position at my old club.

"Aghadiaye, listen to me. Whatever pain she caused you is temporary, only for a while. It will pass, and you will find your joy again..."

Grandma's words from earlier fill my mind.

The pain in my chest eases a little, and I stop panting. Straightening up, I pull a handkerchief from my pocket and wipe my eyes and mouth.

Perhaps my grandmother is right.

I don't believe I can make myself vulnerable to another woman again, like I did with Phoebe. Phoebe came along after my mother died, and I threw myself into her. She became an integral part of my life. Aside from my father and siblings, I had two loves—Phoebe and my football club.

I spent five years with Phoebe and ten years at Bishampton United FC.

Now I have neither. Betrayed by one, discarded by the other.

Maybe with time, the pain of losing those two things will lessen.

But I will not open myself up to such betrayal again.

Perhaps I can find my joy in other ways. I can still love to play football in whatever club I end up in. Even though the idea of starting afresh makes me sick, and I heave. But nothing comes out of my empty stomach. I just spit bile and wipe my mouth.

Or I can still enjoy the company of women. I'm still a full-blooded human being. Temporary connections will work for me. Although this has never been my thing, I can learn. I know plenty of soccer players who play off the field. Many of them are in relationships and still playing away regularly.

Still, none of it matters now. I'm in Nigeria to spend time with my grandmother, which is what II intend to focus on.

Feeling a little better, I walk back to the graveside.

Grandma planted a rose plant next to the marble headstone. It's well-tended and blooming. She must be paying the cemetery attendant for the upkeep.

I spend the time talking to Mum, telling her about all the things I've done since her passing. She probably already knows these things. But it's cathartic to talk to her like I used to when she was alive. She was a good listener, and I feel she's still listening to me.

"I'm sorry, Mum," I say finally. "I haven't been a good son or grandson. But I intend to make it up to you and Grandma. I will visit more often. Once a year, at least. Grandma says I can have half the house. So, I have somewhere to stay when I come. Did you know she's giving half the house to her carer, Seki?"

I chuckle because I still haven't wrapped my head around that news yet. "I tell you, I didn't see that coming. But you know what? The house deserves to be lived in. And even if she gave it all to me, I can only be here a few weeks at a time every year. So perhaps she has a point to give it to someone who will live in it and take care of it."

But Seki will live in the house with her husband and children.

The thought whispers in my mind in my mother's voice.

I picture Seki living in it with her family, children playing football in the front yard like I used to, and the constriction returns in my chest. The idea of a different man living in the house raises a new emotion I don't recognise. All I know is I don't like it. I can tolerate the idea of Seki living in the house. But I don't want another man who is not her blood in the house for some weird reason.

"Mum, I have to go," I say, to shift my mind from the idea of another man in Grandma's house. "I'll come back and see you soon."

When I return to the car, Chinedu is standing outside it.

"Are you okay?" he asks.

"Yes. I think I will be," I reply.

We return to my grandmother's house. There's a lot I need to organise. The house needs refurbishment, and the car she uses is an old one my mum bought years ago. It's developing problems and costing her a lot of money in maintenance. I need to buy her another car, a low-maintenance newer model. I feel bad about how I haven't taken care of it years ago. But I plan to make up for it. I only have two weeks in Nigeria, so I want to get as much done as possible.

Harrison shows up in the evening with his friend Stanley, says he wants to take me out on the town, which is how we end up in this bar lounge.

"Harrison, I need your help," I say as I put the tumbler of beer on the low table and straighten before placing my right ankle on my left knee.

"Of course, you're my cousin. My blood. I'm always happy to help. What do you need?" Harrison asks, leaning forward from his perch on the opposite low sofa.

We're in the bar lounge attached to a four-star hotel with Chinedu and Stanley.

"I need a few things," I reply.

"Okay." He nods. "Let's hear them."

"First, I need an interior designer to manage the project of refurbishing Iye's house. I'm only here for a few weeks, so I need someone who is available and can get to work putting together a team straight away. Second, I need the contact of a car dealership. I want to buy Iye a new car."

"Well, that is no problem at all," Harrison says. "Stanley here can help with the second problem. He manages a car dealership for his father. In fact, they supply all the cars my family uses."

"That's true." Stanley shifts forward in his seat, beaming a smile. "I'm your man for the best automotive in this town. In fact, here is my card." He pulls out a black business card from his pocket, and I accept it.

"That's great. Can I visit the showroom on Monday to see what you have?"

"Of course. Just call me, and I'll make sure I'm there when you visit."

"That's wonderful and a relief," I say. "What about the interior designer?"

"I will get back to you on that—"

"Harri, darling!"

A stylish woman who arrives with a group of other similarly dressed women interrupts him. They are all made up impeccably, have long hair extensions or wigs, and dressed as if they are going clubbing in mini dresses or bodycon clothes.

"Rukky." Harrison stands and hugs the first woman before turning to the rest of us. "Diaye, this is my girlfriend, Rukky. I invited her to celebrate your arrival."

"It's nice to meet you." I stand and shake her hand.

"It's nice to meet you, too." She beams a sheepish smile. "I also brought my friends. They wanted to meet you. This is Ufuoma, Beverly, and Titi." She points them out.

"And this is Chinedu, and you already know Stanley," Harrison says.

Handshakes and hugs accompany the introductions, and we rearrange the seating arrangements. I end up sitting next to Beverly. Her eyes sparkle as if she has won a prize. I wonder if they drew straws to decide who will sit next to the famous footballer. She's pretty and dark-skinned and attractive. I have no complaints and can picture slaking my lust in her, if the evening goes in that direction.

"What can I get you?" a soft female voice asks.

I raise my head to find Seki standing there. She's not looking at me, almost as if she's avoiding my gaze. She's our waiter for the evening. There's a light pain in my chest because I'm shocked to find out she works here, and I still don't understand why, considering she works for Iye. But who am I to put down on someone's hustle? If she wants to work on her day off, it's her headache. As long as she's not doing anything illegal, which she's not.

"Can you bring a bottle of your finest champagne," Harrison says, and the women cheer. "And bring glasses for the ladies."

"Of course." Seki walks away without looking at me.

Does she feel uncomfortable about my presence? Yes, I asked a few questions earlier, but I didn't intend to make her feel bad. I know what it feels like for people to judge you incorrectly, and I don't want her to feel like I'm judging her. She's not doing anything to hurt me or my grandma.

In fact, from all indications, she is giving Iye excellent care, and I want this to continue. Maybe she's upset because I pulled her into my arms this morning and I had an erection. In which case, I need to apologise. I don't want her to feel awkward about taking care of my grandmother.

"Excuse me a moment," I say to Beverly, and stand. Then I walk to the counter where Seki is waiting for the bartender to deliver her order.

"Seki," I say when I pull up next to her.

"Oh. Diaye." She turns, rubbing her hand over her skirt. "Is everything okay?" She glances back at the table.

"Yes, everything is fine. I just wanted to talk to you briefly. I noticed you seemed a little tense earlier. You take care of Iye, and I appreciate it with my whole heart. If I did anything to make you feel uncomfortable, then I'm sorry. I know I'm a grumpy asshole, but I don't mean to upset you."

"No, you didn't do anything." She rubs her eyebrow with her index finger knuckle.

"Then relax, please." I place my hand on her arm as reassurance. "I'm just hanging out with my friends. Treat me like any customer, okay?"

"Okay." She swallows and nods with a small smile. "Thank you."

"No need to thank me. I just want to reward all the help you provide for Iye. When does your shift end? Chinedu and I can drop you off when you finish?"

She coughs, shifting from one foot to the other. "No. It's not necessary."

"Don't tell me you're working here all night?" My eyebrows draw together in concern as my muscles tighten. She's another person I have to take care of because she matters to Iye. It can't be good for her to work all these long hours.

"No. I'm not working all night. But ..."

"What is it?"

"I'm staying in the hotel for the night." She tugs at the collar of her shirt, avoiding my gaze.

"I don't understand. They give you a room here? You don't need it. As I said, I can take you home or back to Iye's house afterwards. You don't have to spend the night here."

I can understand if she's spending the night in the hotel because it's easier than trying to get transport home so late. But I'm willing to wait and drop her off.

"Is everything okay?" A man steps up to us and stands next to Seki, looking at her in a proprietary way. He has the manager's badge pinned to his waistcoat.

"Everything is fine," I say. "I was just talking to Seki."

"Okay. You must be Diaye Zambo. I was told you are visiting us today. Welcome to Crystal Palace Hotel. I'm the night manager, Mide." He extends his hand for a shake.

I take it, but his shake is limp, and I withdraw my hand. "Nice to meet you. I have to get back to my friends. Seki, think of what I said."

I leave them and head back to the group on the sofas, feeling someone's gaze burn into my back. Probably Seki.

9

Seki

I watch Diaye walk back to the group of eight in the corner, and somehow, I miss his presence. He's wearing a buttonless cream crochet polo shirt over bone-white chinos that show of his beautiful dark skin. On his feet are stylish dark tan leather bay sneakers with white soles. What perfume is he wearing? I bet it's very expensive because he smelled so delicious while he stood next to me at the bar.

I can't believe he apologised to me. He did nothing wrong. Yes, he was abrupt this morning, but I can understand it. I'm the one who was feeling awkward about serving him and his cousin and friends. I thought he would look down on me for working here. But he doesn't. Instead, he tried to reassure me and get me to relax. He even offered to drop me off after work.

"Seki, what is going on?" Mide asks, coming to stand in front of me.

Groaning inwardly, I turn to the counter to grab the champagne ice bucket the barman placed on it. I forgot Mide was even here while I was watching Diaye. What is wrong with me? I should know Mide by now. The man doesn't let me breathe when it comes to other men talking to me. He won't even let me be friendly with other male staff.

"Nothing," I say, picking up the tray with the champagne glasses.

"Come to my office," he says, as if I didn't know he won't let it go so readily.

"But I'm busy and still serving the guests." I need to provide a good service and collect the tips due to me when the group finally leaves. If nothing else, Harrison will tip well if I continue smiling and giving them what they want.

"Tori will cover for you. I need to talk right now." He stomps off.

Instead of waiting for Tori to take the tray to Diaye's group, I ignore his instructions. Mide will have to wait because I'm not about to lose my tips. I've worked hard for them.

"Bring the champagne, let's go. My clients are waiting for it," I say to the barman whose job it is to serve the champagne.

"Didn't Mide say you should leave it for Tori?" He indicates the tray in my hand.

"Leave it for who? Those are my guests, and they are more important. Oga manager will have to wait." I walk towards the table, and the barman follows me.

When we reach the guests, he puts the ice bucket on the table and pulls out the champagne bottle to show the group. I don't feel as awkward as I felt earlier, but I stay focused on the tray of glasses in my hands, so they don't topple. Management takes the costs of any breakages out of staff wages.

"Good. Open it," Harrison orders.

While the barman opens the bottle, I place the glasses on the table.

When I straighten, I glance in Diaye's direction, and he's smiling at me. My heart kicks in my chest, and before I know it, I'm smiling back. The man has an infectious smile, just like his grandmother. Everything else seems to fade, except his gorgeous face as his eyes lock on me. For an instant, I'm back in the corridor this morning, pressed up against him, a pile of laundry on the tiled floor around us. My blood burns hot. My pulse pounds as a shudder of pleasure passes through me.

The champagne pops, breaking the spell. I blink, and everyone else zooms into focus as they cheer.

The woman sitting next to Diaye whispers something in his ear, making him look away from me as he chuckles. Her hand is on his thigh, almost close to his crotch. She glares at me and then smiles at something he says in her ear, which I can't hear.

My mouth almost drops to the floor. Some people are bold sha.

If eyes could kill, I would be mortally injured. What did I do to her? Or is it because Diaye smiled at me? *Hian*, I scoff. She doesn't want him to smile at me.

I shake my head as I try to not laugh. She is cut from the same cloth as Mide.

This reminds me. I need to go and see him before he kicks up a big fuss. Leaving the barman to pour the drinks, I take the tray back to the bar counter and stop by Tori.

"Please cover my section. Oga manager wants to see me," I say to her.

"Okay. No problem."

She takes my pad, which has the duplicate copies of the orders placed by each table in my section. She will write new orders on the pad and give it back to me when I return.

The manager's office is at the back, stuck between the laundry room and the cleaning storage room. I walk down the staff-only corridor and knock on the door.

"Come in." Mide sounds angry from the other side of the closed door.

I turn the handle and push it open.

He is pacing the tiny space of the office and turns to face me as I enter. "You're late!"

"Late?" I shut the door so no one in the corridor will hear his outburst. "I was serving customers. Customers first is still the policy of this hotel, abi?"

"Don't play smart with me, you hear me so?" He slips into Pidgin, showing how angry he is.

I say nothing and clasp my hands in front of me in a demure pose, playing the meek employee. He's wielding a double-edged sword over me. He's my boyfriend, but he's also my boss. I must tread a fine line when it comes to relating to him on these premises.

I know where this is going, and on any other night, I might have welcomed it.

But the image of the woman clinging onto Diaye and glaring at me flashes in my mind. Then I flash back to Diaye standing by the bar, holding my hand and telling me to relax.

The one person who I thought was going to give me a hard time tonight was Diaye. Yet, he was trying to reassure me and relax me.

Instead, my boyfriend is shouting at me when I've done nothing wrong, and some random woman was glaring at me for smiling at Diaye. What a complicated life? I don't need this stress.

Mide walks towards me, his expression serious. "I told you to come to my office, and you disobeyed me. To top it off, you were letting that footballer come onto you."

"Come onto me?" I scoff, losing my temper. "Are you effing kidding me? We were just talking!"

"Talking? He was holding your hand. Do you let every man that talks to you to hold your hand?"

"No! But that was Diaye. He's Iye's grandson!"

"What?" Mide jerks back and tips his head to the side. "Diaye Zambo is Iye's grandson?"

"Yes. So, you see. Nothing was going on between us. He was just being nice because he found out I work here."

"Wait o. Wait o." Mide spins in a jerky, dramatic motion. "So, Dee-ah-ye Zambo—" he stresses the sounds and syllables of the name "—is your Iye's grandson and I never knew this until now. You kept it a secret from me."

Shit. I'm in big trouble o. Guilt washes over me because he is right. I kept Diaye's identity a secret from him and my family. To be honest, I don't tell anyone Iye's private affairs. But I can see how this will look weird to my boyfriend.

"You are keeping secrets from me." He stomps towards me.

I step back until my back hits the wall. "Mide, I'm not keeping secrets from you. You know Iye is like a client to me. I can't share her confidential information with other people.

It's part of the patient-nurse confidentiality charter." I don't know if that applies to Iye, but I hope he buys it.

"Me, your boyfriend. I'm now other people, abi?" He nods sarcastically.

"No. I don't mean it like that." I reach for his arm, but he pulls back. "Mide, come on. Don't be like this."

"Don't be like how? You're keeping secrets from me. I'm supposed to be your boyfriend, the man who will marry you. How do I know you're not having an affair with the Diaye guy?"

"Are you serious?" I chuckle and tamp it down when he glares at me. "I only met Diaye for the first time yesterday. *Yesterday*. How can I be having an affair with him already? You know I'm not that easy now. Moreover, you saw the girls at his table. He has his hands full already. Me, I'm just the person taking care of his grandmother. That's all he sees me as."

Even as I say it, bile rises in my throat. But, the words seem to have the desired effect.

Mide sucks in a deep breath and smiles. "You had me worried."

He steps close and places his hands around me, cupping my bum and pulling me until our bodies collide.

"You. You worry too much," I mutter as he leans down.

"You know me." He presses his lips to mine.

On any other day, I would have let him kiss me. But something feels wrong. He doesn't smell right, and I'm still conscious about Diaye being out there.

I push his hands down and step back. "We can't do this now. I have to get back to the customers."

"They can wait," he grouses with a frown.

"No, they can't." I reach for the door handle.

He slams his hand on the door, preventing me from opening it. "You know, if you go, I will punish you tonight."

My heart is pounding, and I know what he means, but I can't think of it right now.

"Mide, let me go," I say in a serious tone. He moves his hand, and I open the door and step out. "I'll see you later."

He doesn't reply as I walk down the corridor and out into the lounge. I collect my pad from Tori and thank her, glad to be back on the floor.

But I don't feel any relief when I glance in Diaye's direction and see him laughing and conversing with his friends. There are more guests standing around them. People taking selfies with him, and he seems happy to oblige them. The woman sitting beside him is still all over him, clinging onto his arm as if she is his date.

People from another table grab my attention, and I go to serve them. The lounge is fuller than usual. Sure, we get busy on Saturdays, but not like this. It seems word got out about famous footballer, Diaye Zambo, being in town. This means more people showed up here instead of going wherever they went on a Saturday night. I told you nothing much happens here. Gossip about Diaye's arrival must have spread like wildfire.

Although I'm busier than normal, I can't complain because the cash tips are coming in, and I should make more tonight than I've ever made here.

I return to Diaye's table with a tray full of small chops—nkwobi, suya, and pepper soup—and place them on the table.

"Seki," Diaye says.

"Yes," I reply, glancing at him.

"What time does your shift end?" He smiles.

"In fifteen minutes," I say, glancing at my watch.

"Good. You can come and join us after your shift."

"Are you sure?" I glance around. The woman next to him is still glaring at me. But I don't care about her. The other people are otherwise engaged.

"Of course. You can stay with us," he encourages.

I'm still not sure. Diaye is an international superstar football player who earns in millions of euros. Harrison is a prince of the land and influential. I am merely a student nurse from a working-class family who moonlights as a waiter in a hotel. These people are out of my league.

"Come on. We're celebrating my homecoming." He grins. "Or is there something else you will rather do?"

"No. Nothing," I say, even though I should go to Mide's office afterwards.

Knowing Mide is already angry, I know he will punish me. Last time, he made me wait in the staff room for so long, it was too late for me to go back to the house. I didn't want to go back there because I would have to explain to Iye why I came home in the middle of the night. So, I stayed in the staff room until Mide finally gave me the key to the room we use so I could sleep.

I suspect he is going to do the same thing tonight, and I can't put myself through such embarrassment again. "I'd love to stay after my shift ends and go back to Iye's house with you and Chinedu."

"Awesome! The more, the merrier." Diaye cheers, raising his glass which contains the Coke soda drink I brought for him earlier.

A part of me is glad he only had the one bottle of beer and switched to soft drinks afterwards. I don't think Iye would be happy if he went home drunk.

"Thank you," I say, and go back to my duties, serving other tables.

I return a few minutes later with the bill and put it on the table. Harrison grabs the leather envelope with the paper bill.

But Diaye stands up and indicates for me to come with him. I follow him to the bar, and he pulls out his wallet.

"I'm going to pay the bill for our table and everyone else in this lounge," he says.

"Really? Are you sure?" I'm gobsmacked at his generosity. But I know the people will love him for it. If anything, the hotel should pay for his drinks because he brought a huge crowd of paying customers tonight.

"I am. I know most of them came here tonight to see me. So put their bills on my tab." He hands me his credit card.

"Okay." I walk around the bar to process the transactions.

"And add a twenty percent tip for you and the other waiters working tonight," he says with a grin.

"Thank you so much." I'm grinning, too.

Diaye enters his code into the card-reader, and it's authorised.

But my smile diminishes as Mide joins us at the bar.

"Mr Zambo, I hope you're having a good time," he says as he stands in front of Diaye.

"I sure am. The people are great, and the service is wonderful." Diaye winks at me.

My heart soars at the praise. He seems to be in a very good mood.

Mide gives me the look that says he saw the wink and turns back to Diaye with a smile. "That's very good. You know, Seki didn't introduce us properly earlier. I didn't even know you are Iye's grandson, which means you're going to be my in-law."

Diaye frowns. "I don't understand. Are you getting married to a member of Iye's family?"

"Of course. Iye is like a grandmother to Seki." Mide waves at me. "Seki and I are dating, and we're going to get married soon. So, you will become my in-law by default."

Shit. I'm speechless as my heart thuds in my chest and my body flushes with heat. Why would Mide do this now? What the hell is wrong with him?

Diaye tilts his head and looks at me with a questioning expression.

"You and him are getting married? You know what? I don't care." He shakes his head. "It's none of my fucking business. Congratulations to both of you."

He snatches his card back from the counter and walks off.

10

Seki

My head feels like someone is playing a drum in it when I wake the next morning. The noise of the alarm on my phone isn't helping.

I roll over and grab it from the bedside table and tap the screen to shut it up. Then I groan and lay back on the bed with my eyes open.

The room is still dark with the minimal predawn grey light coming through the large window. It takes me a few moments to get my bearings. I'm lying on my bed in my room at Iye's house. I came home last night after work with Chinedu and Diaye.

Groaning again, I remember last night's stress with Mide.

Imagine him just introducing himself to Diaye like that at the bar without even giving me any kind of pre-warning. He just marched up to the man and told him they were going to become in-laws.

Who does this kind of nonsense?

Even if we were engaged, which we are not, was that the right way to announce it? We've talked about marriage, but Mide has never proposed to me. So, what is his deal?

Afterward, I told Mide I was going back to Iye's house after my shift. He was not happy. But I told him I didn't feel comfortable staying. I just wasn't willing to put myself through whatever shit he was planning to pull last night.

Diaye stayed with his friends for the rest of the night.

When my shift ended, I went to the staff room and changed into my normal clothes—a pair of wide leg jeans trousers and a white crop top and a jeans jacket over it.

I returned to Diaye's table and told him my shift was over. He was standing with a group of two other men. He looked at me with a blank expression. "Wait for us in the reception area. We'll tell you when we're ready to go."

He went back to chatting with his friends.

I stood there, shocked for a few seconds. I guess he revoked my invitation to join his homecoming party because of the way Mide behaved.

It annoyed me, but I couldn't argue with him. He had the right to change his mind about asking me to join his party.

I sat in the reception area and read my book while I waited for him and Chinedu.

Mide came to the reception area and asked me what I was doing there. I told him I was waiting for my lift home, and he left me alone. He couldn't do anything because guests and staff were around there. He sent me text messages, but I ignored them.

Diaye and Chinedu finally came out an hour later. I followed them to Chinedu's car and sat in the back while they sat in front. Diaye didn't say anything to me. A part of me was glad he didn't bring that woman home with him. Chinedu chatted for most of the drive, mentioning he would leave the next day.

This reminds me...

I roll out of bed and perform my morning routine, then I go downstairs to prepare a meal so Chinedu can have something to eat before he leaves. I hear the men get up and go for a jog, like they did yesterday.

Iye is dressed and comes to the kitchen, and we eat breakfast. The men come down and eat in the dining room. Diaye thanks me for the meal, just like Chinedu does, and says nothing else. Chinedu heads off not long after breakfast.

Afterwards, Íruoghẹnẹ drives me, Iye, and Diaye to church. Iye likes to go to the early one-hour service. Today, she's happy to show off her visiting grandson to her friends and congregation.

After church, we return to the house with some of Iye's friends, and they sit in the sitting room chatting with food and drinks.

I'm in the kitchen tidying up when Diaye walks in.

"I have a guest in my room. Can you bring some food and drinks up, please?"

I turn around to ask what specifically they wanted, but he's gone.

I didn't know he had a guest, but I suppose Harrison or one of the other friends from last night could visit.

Plate of food prepared, I put it on a tray with a clean glass and a bottle of soft drink from the fridge and a linen napkin. Then I carry the tray upstairs and knock on his door.

"Come in," he calls out.

Although I prepared the room for him, I haven't been in it since his arrival. I push open the door and walk in. Working in a hotel has taught me how to balance a laden tray and open doors.

There's no one in the bedroom, but the door to the balcony is open. The sun is warm, but it's an east-facing balcony so is shaded in here in the afternoons.

My heart drops when I see the person sitting on the padded chairs with Diaye. It's the woman from last night. He must have invited her over. It's like a gut punch, and I don't understand why. I just don't like her. Maybe because of the way she looked at me last night.

Silently, I place the tray on the table between them. When I straighten, the woman is smirking at me.

"Beverly, do you need anything else?" Diaye asks.

So that's her name.

"No. This will be fine. Thank you," she says.

"That will be all," he says, dismissing me as if I was a waiter back in the hotel.

My annoyance spikes, but I grit my teeth and walk out instead of saying something nasty.

I return to the kitchen and send Mide a message.

Can we talk when you wake up?

I know he's usually sleeping the day away when he's done a night shift, so I don't expect him to respond immediately.

• • • •

THE NEXT FEW DAYS GO in a kind of blur. I'm back on work placement at the hospital on Monday. I leave the house early and don't come back until late afternoon.

Mide doesn't message me, although I've sent him several messages. I'm getting worried about him.

I come home on Monday night to find a new SUV in the carport. Diaye bought a new car for his grandmother. Íruoghẹnẹ is so happy because he will get to drive Iye in a spanking new car. In the meantime, Diaye drives it. It turns out he used to drive around town when he was a teenager.

I arrive home on Tuesday, and there is a man in the house taking measurements. Diaye introduces him as the builder who will project-manage the house renovations. Also at the house are new security personnel sent by the palace because of Diaye.

On Wednesday, I buy myself a new phone. I've been saving for it since my old one got damaged. With the extra tips I got last Saturday, I can afford a reasonably priced one, so I don't keep using Iye's phone.

On Thursday, I walk through the gates into the front courtyard, and Íruoghẹnẹ tells me Mide visited the house and saw Iye and Diaye. I can't believe he came to this house when he's not even returning my messages.

Instead of entering the house via the side door, I go over to the padded bench under the pergola at the southwestern corner of the garden. I dump my bag on the waterproof cushion, retrieve my new phone from the pocket, and call Mide again.

The phone rings once before his hushed voice comes through. "Seki, I can't talk right now."

Any relief I feel at hearing from him after five days disappears because of his hurried tone. "Mide, what's going on? You came to my house."

"Yes, I went to apologise to Diaye. It seems he wasn't happy last Saturday, so I wanted to explain the situation."

Why is he whispering? Isn't he at home?

"Explain the situation. What situation?"

"Baby, I can't talk right now. I'll see you on Saturday, and we'll talk about it, I promise. I have to go."

The line cuts off, and I growl in frustration. I can't take this anymore.

If Mide won't talk, then I'll get the information from Diaye. The car is parked up front, so he must be home. I grab my bag and walk to the side door. Before I can reach for the handle, it swings inward and Diaye's frame occupies the space. He's in a cream polo shirt, a pair of chinos two shades darker and matching sneakers, phone and car keys in his hands.

My pulse accelerates as our eyes lock. Any warmth his ever held disappears like the sun behind a cloud. He's barely spoken to me since last weekend—it feels more like the sun vanishing at dusk. His displeasure is so potent, it radiates through the air and into my body like a deadly poison.

He approaches the threshold, his powerful, muscled frame moving with single-minded surety.

Tingles of alarm cascade down my spine and every self-preservation instinct screams for me to move out of the way. Yet I stand my ground. I need to speak to him.

"Good afternoon," I say.

Why do I sound out of breath?

He steps outside, right in front of me, close enough for me to inhale his decadent cologne as I suck in a sharp breath. My heart crashes in my chest and I think he's going to collide with me. For a second, he's all I can see, my view, my world.

Then, he side-steps and walks past me without saying a word.

I blink rapidly as my brain freezes. What just happened?

His thudding footsteps on the paving get me moving. The heat of frustration rising in my chest, I hurry after him. "Diaye, hold on. Can I talk to you?"

"What is it?" He doesn't stop, and his tone drips with contempt.

What is his problem? Is this still about last Saturday, or did something else happen with my boyfriend's visit? More reasons to ask him.

"I heard Mide came here, and you spoke to him." My voice is strained but calm. I don't want to raise my voice when Iye can be in the sitting room, overlooking the front yard.

"Yes. And?" He presses the fob, and the lights flash on the new car.

"And I want to know what you talked about." My tone sharpens, and I step closer, determined not to let him brush me off.

He opens the car door and climbs in. Then he starts the engine and finally turns to face me, his expression unreadable, though annoyance flickers in his eyes. "I suggest you go and ask him."

"No! I asked him already!" I shout, losing my shit, and clinging onto the car door so he can't shut it. "He's been avoiding me for days, and you're doing the same thing. What is your problem? Why do you have to be such an asshole?"

Diaye kills the engine, gets out of the car and towers over me, his voice low and calm in contrast. "You mean an asshole like your fiancé? What do you even see in him if he's making you so angry?"

I open my mouth to retort, but nothing comes out. He isn't wrong? I *am* angry at my boyfriend. Why am I with Mide when he keeps being passive aggressive? He knows I hate being ignored. Yet, he does it all the time to punish me.

"You know I'm right." Diaye takes advantage of my silence and raises his hand. His thumb brushes my bottom lip.

My breathing shallows and I freeze.

What is he doing? Why am I not stepping away?

Instead, I look up at his lips, curved into a lazy smile. They are full and lush and tempting.

"Come over to the dark side. I promise it will be more fun." He takes his time exploring the curve of my mouth, sending tingles down my spine.

My body heats at his double entendre, but the mockery in his tone smacks me out of the momentary haze. Of course, he doesn't want to have anything to do with me. Nor do I want anything to do with him.

"I would rather poke needles in my eye," I retort, my anger swelling again. "You know what? Fine. I'll figure it out myself."

Without waiting for his reply, I turn on my heel and march away, my footsteps heavy with fury. The car door slamming shut behind me feels like the punctuation to our conversation.

On Friday, I take Diaye's advice and go to Mide's house after I finish at my work placement. Mide doesn't work on Friday nights, so he should be home. I don't tell him I'm coming, so he doesn't try to avoid me. I want to resolve this issue between us because his silence is stressing me out. I can handle him shouting at me. But I can't deal with him ignoring me.

I already told Iye I won't be home tonight. So, she knows not to expect me. I asked her about Mide's visit to the house. She says he spoke to Diaye in private. So, I'm still none-the-wiser about the content of their conversation.

He lives two hours away from Iye's house, with Crystal Palace Hotel being an hour between the two points.

By the time I get to his house, it is dark, and there is a drizzle of rain. Thankfully, I have an umbrella. He lives in a BQ annex, and the gateman lets me in after I knock. I've been here before and know my way around. I walk down the side of the main house to the BQ. The light is on through the window of the living room. I knock on the door.

Someone says, "Hold on."

It sounds female. I know his sister visits him sometimes from Ibadan. Maybe she is here this week, and that's why he couldn't talk yesterday.

The door is pulled inwards, and a woman stands there. "Hi, who are you?"

"I'm Seki. Is Mide home? You must be his sister?"

She frowns. "His sister? I'm Tinu, his wife."

"His wife?" I stumble back as blood drains from my head.

"Yes, I arrived yesterday from Ibadan."

She stares at me through narrowed eyes, and I feel sick, bile rising in my throat.

"Of course," I say, trying to cover my tracks. "We're colleagues at work. He mentioned you were coming. Has he left for work already?"

"No. He went out. He'll be back soon. Do you want to come in?"

"No. I need to get to work. I was hoping to get a lift with him."

"He's not going to work tonight."

"Isn't he? I must have got the days mixed up. I'm sorry to disturb you. I have to go now. You have a good night."

I turn around and stumble towards the gates, blinded by the pouring rain and my tears. Thankfully, the rain masks my tears as the gateman lets me out. It feels like my world bottomed out, and my body aches.

This has to be a big misunderstanding. How did I not know? How did I miss the signs?

I trudge through the mud and rain, the recriminations battering my mind. It's dark and flooding in places. I look out for transportation, but there's no tuktuk or bike in sight. I'm so distressed, I don't know what to do. I'm stranded with nowhere to go. The only people who can come and pick me are Íruoghẹnẹ or Diaye. But I need to speak to Iye first.

I dial her number.

"Hello, Seki?"

As soon as I hear her voice, I break down in tears.

"My dear, what's the matter?" she asks, sounding worried.

"He is married," I bawl.

"Who is married?"

"Mide. Mide is married."

"Oh."

"I met his wife tonight. I went to see him at his house, and his wife is there," I ramble.

"Send me your location pin right now. I'm coming to get you."

I'm shocked to hear Diaye's sharp tone instead of Iye's soft voice, but I acquiesce. "Okay."

Beggars can't be choosers.

I send him my location and huddle in the corner of a brick wall, using the umbrella to shelter from the rain. My body is numb, chilled to the bone, and soaked to the skin. The downpour stops, but I'm shivering as I watch the flash of headlights which slows and stops beside me.

My heart hammers against my ribs, a frantic drumbeat in my ears. I peer at the large car, which looks similar to the one Diaye bought for Iye, unsure who is inside.

A tall figure emerges from behind the beam of head-lamps and walks towards me with deliberate movements. "Seki!"

Recognition dawns.

"Diaye," I acknowledge as I stand stiffly and hobble towards the car.

He holds the door open and orders, "Get in!"

I climb into the front passenger seat, and he slams the door before walking around to the driver's side. He starts the engine, turns the car around, and heads back in the direction he came. Thankfully, the heating on my side is blasting, and the air warms my chilled skin.

He doesn't say anything to me. I feel awkward and ashamed, and the silence is killing me.

"Thank you for coming to pick me up," I say.

He doesn't reply, and the silence stretches as the car eats up the kilometres.

Sullen and brooding, he cuts a rigid silhouette in the shadowed interior of the speeding car, the only sound the hum of the engine and the blur of the unlit highway outside.

The silent treatment feels like a lead weight in my chest, suffocating and isolating. It drives me nuts. It was bad enough with Mide. I don't think I can tolerate any more of it today.

"You can stop being a grumpy asshole and be nice to me. I've been stuck out in the rain for hours," I snap.

"I didn't tell you to get involved with a married man," he says and doesn't even look at me.

His words, sharp and cold, slice through me like a knife twisting in my gut. Pain and anger swirl. I know I should be directing my anger at Mide. But I won't suffer in silence.

The arrogant man sitting next to me right now looks like a suitable target for my rage. And since he wants to be an ass, he shouldn't complain because I'm about to kick it.

I turn in my seat, facing him, chin tilted in defiance, my tongue sharpened to cut deep.

"You think say because your money miss road. Say you fit talk to anybody anyhow?" I launch into Pidgin because I'm in kick-ass mode. "Use that your money go buy better attitude. Nobody likes an asshole, millionaire or not."

He slams his foot on the brakes. The car lurches violently, throwing us forward against our seatbelts. A sharp, metallic screech pierces the air. The interior light comes on as he turns to face me. His glare burns my skin and threatens to melt the vehicle.

"I go dash you money so you can buy some sense," he says, and I'm almost impressed by his Pidgin because it's the first time I've heard the local lingo from him.

However, his insinuation that I'm clueless sends my skin from hot to cold.

He drags his gaze over me, his expression of mocking cruelty, and continues. "Unlike some people, I don't derive my self-worth from pleasing other people."

Oh, hell, no! He's definitely throwing shade at me and hitting the mark. The most painful insults are the ones that, while cruel, hold a sliver of uncomfortable truth.

Well, I might be a people-pleaser, but I can dish out uncomfortable truths, too.

"I read online that your fiancée left you. I saw photos of her living her best life at a party on a yacht in St Tropez. I don't blame her for leaving you. If I was engaged to you, I would probably leave you, too."

His body stiffens, and he averts his gaze. His grip around the steering wheel is so tight, I fear it will crumble beneath his death grip.

It's a hit. The scores are 3-2 to me so far.

My heart is in my throat as I await his response. Surely, he'll comeback with more taunts. I can do snarky, even cruel banter.

When he turns back in my direction, I expect anger. But his expression is devoid of any emotion, his eyes hauntingly cold. He flicks off the interior lights, restarts the car and continues driving.

We're back to silence.

I exhale a heavy breath as the adrenaline drains from my body.

I may have won the battle, but the war still rages.

11

Diaye

The next day, I get up before the sun and pull on my running gear and leave the house for my morning run. One of the security men Harrison assigned to me follows. This has become a daily habit since my arrival in Sapele. I'm a creature of habit. Patterns and repetitions help me maintain order in my life. Helps me to calm my mind when I'm surrounded by chaos.

The energy in this house has felt chaotic for the past week. Of course, it can be attributed to the builders who have been transforming the guest quarters downstairs into Grandma's new residence. They're replacing the bathroom with a new set and installing a shower bench, so Grandma can sit instead of standing in the shower cubicle. It's safer for her.

They are repainting the bedrooms, and I've ordered a new height-adjustable bed, which means she can get in and out of bed easier as her mobility deteriorates. It also has a riser-recliner which raises the upper body so she can sit up in bed, and the foot can also be raised to help her avoid oedema. Seki and Grandma selected the suitable bed from the website, and I paid for fast delivery. It should be here in a few days.

Talking about Seki...

I stop my sprinting and do some lunges instead.

If I'm honest, it's been a long chaotic week because of Seki.

From the fateful night a week ago when I found out she was dating that Mide guy, the hotel night manager. I didn't like the man from the moment I set eyes on him, even before I knew he was dating Seki. Then a chat with Harrison on the same evening confirmed my suspicions. The man was no good for her.

And Seki couldn't seem to see it.

Women are all the same!

Adrenaline surges through me and my heart palpitates. The strangling feeling starts in my chest, and I bend over panting, trying to catch my breath. I pull my phone from the side pocket of my shorts.

I need to get out of here. Time to speak to Mr O.

But he's on holiday in Antigua, and it's the middle of the night over there. So, I record a voice note for him instead.

Good morning, Mr O. It's Diaye. Sorry to disturb your holiday. I need to get out of Nigeria earlier than planned. You remember the early summer training camp Milan offered? Is it too late to participate in it? Can you find out, please? I don't want to go back to the UK and stare at the walls of my flat. Or have Dad turning up to harass me about Phoebe. Hopefully, he's in the south of France for the summer. Thank you.

I stop the recording to catch my breath. Then I start another one.

ᴵᴵᴵᴵᴵᴵ *Sorry. I should have asked how you and Mrs O are doing in Antigua. I hope you're having a good time. Give my love to the family.*

Then I stash the phone into my pocket and sprint back to the house. Íruoghẹnẹ lets me in, and I toss the empty bottle into the recycling bin at the corner before entering the house through the side door. The house is silent. It's Seki's day off. She might still be in bed or has gone out like she did last week.

I head straight to my bedroom to shower and change. Then I go downstairs to find something to eat. Grandma is in the kitchen when I walk in.

"Good morning, Grandma," I greet on my way to the fridge.

"Morning, my dear." She is cutting a lemon into small pieces on the chopping board.

The kettle is on, and the flask she normally uses for her tea is on the counter.

"Can I help with anything?" I ask, taking out a carton of mango juice from the fridge.

"Yes, make an omelette," she replies.

"An omelette?" I ask, a little confused.

Grandma likes her eggs boiled.

"Yes, an omelette," she repeats, putting the pieces of lemon into the flask before pouring the hot water in.

Another anomaly because she normally drinks black tea with milk. Not lemon tea. But she can have whatever she wants.

"Okay." I shrug and grab a mixing bowl. I take eggs from the crate and crack them into the bowl. "What would you like in the omelette?"

"Just a tomato and green pepper," she replies as she goes to sit at the small table. She takes a sip from a drink in a mug, her breakfast already on the table.

I take the vegetables from the fridge and wash them in the sink. Then I cut them into tiny pieces on the chopping board.

"Grandma, I didn't know you eat omelette," I say as I mix some seasoning with the eggs and whisk it with the fork.

"I eat omelette sometimes. But that's not for me. I want you to take it to Seki when you finish."

My spine stiffens at the mention of the name. "Seki? Where is she? Can't she make her own food?"

"She can't. She's heartbroken," Iye says.

Heat flashes through me, and I scoff to shake off the niggle of guilt. "You make it sound like she's sick. She'll get over it."

"You mean like you got over your heartbreak?"

My entire body freezes, and I look at Grandma. Her eyebrows are arched. Is she taunting me?

"Grandma, are you comparing her situation with mine? I wasn't having an affair with a married woman. Phoebe was my fiancée. I was going to marry her. Meanwhile, she was having an affair. And I ended it when I found out. I ended it!"

"Did it lessen your heartache that you broke it off? Hmmm?"

Sharp pain pierces through my chest. I can't believe my grandmother is talking to me like this. What did I do wrong?

"Grandma, why are you talking to me like this?"

She lets out a sigh as if I'm being difficult.

That weird sensation returns. The one I felt when she told me she would give half the house to Seki. If I don't know better, I'd think she loves Seki more than she loves me.

Maybe I don't know better. Maybe she loves her more.

I drop the fork on the counter and step away from it, shaking my head.

Enough of this. I didn't come here to compete for affection. I already have to deal with it with my father and half-siblings. It's not happening here, in my grandmother's house, as her only fucking grandchild!

"I came here because I thought this was a safe space for me. But I can see it's not because you're mocking me."

"Aghadiaye, I'm not mocking you. This is a safe place for you and will always be a safe space for you. I was simply trying to hold up a mirror so you could see yourself. You were talking like your father, and I responded to you the way I respond to him."

I throw my hands up in the air. "What has my father got to do with this?"

"Everything. Your father has everything to do with it. Without your mother, you've been under his influence for too long. He has the emotional intelligence of an infant, and you have learned terrible habits from him."

My breath hitches. Grandma is not mincing her words, and I wonder what has brought this on.

"You show little sympathy for a girl whose only mistake was falling in love with the wrong man. Yet, do you show the same contempt for your father who sleeps with women indiscriminately?? How many women have children for him?"

Wow. I didn't know she kept track of Dad's affairs. Did she always hate my father?

William Zambo was a serial cheater. It was the reason my mother divorced him. I have four siblings from three different women.

I'm not a fan of my father's affairs.

"My father's relationships are none of my business," I say.

"And have you ever condemned him for them?" she asks.

"My father is a grown man, and what he does is none of my business," I retort.

"Seki is a grown woman, and what she does is none of your business. Yet, you stood there judging her because she made the mistake of dating a married man. Or is it because she's a woman? Men can misbehave and be forgiven. But a woman has to be pure and holy, otherwise she's a witch and a prostitute."

My jaw stiffens as I gasp. Now, I'm offended, and I narrow my eyes.

"Grandma, that's not what I meant!"

"Isn't it? If it was one of your friends who found out his girlfriend was already married, would you be so hard on him?"

My frown deepens. She has a point. "Maybe not."

"Of course not."

"But Grandma, she should have known he was bad for her a long time ago. As soon as I saw the Mide guy, I knew there was something wrong with him."

"That's because you're a cynic. You see the worst in everyone. She sees the best in everyone. She wants the best for everyone."

"Then she's naïve, and the world will eat her up and spit her out."

"Perhaps. But I have hopes you will be there to take care of her."

My heart jolts in my chest. "Grandma, what are you talking about?"

"Just make the omelette and take it up to Seki along with the flask of tea I made for her." She smiles at me.

I don't know what she's up to, and I'm not sure I like it. But I love her, and I can't refuse her anything.

So I say, "Okay," and make the omelette while Grandma eats breakfast.

Our conversation plays on my mind. Does she really think I'm becoming like my father?

I would hate to be like my father, especially with the way he treats women. But perhaps my father became the man he is because a woman cheated on him at some point the way Phoebe cheated on me. I'm not trying to make excuses for my father. But doesn't every villain have an origin story?

Then again, would I want to spend the rest of my life cheating on other women because Phoebe cheated on me? The answer to that is a resounding NO!

I have control over my libido and would rather stay celibate.

"I'm coming," Grandma says as she stands from the chair and leaves the kitchen.

I finish making the omelette and transfer it to a plate. Then I arrange it on a tray with the flask and some cutlery. I don't know if Seki wants bread, as well. But I put two slices on a plate and add it to the tray.

Grandma returns with yellow and white flowers in a slim vase and places it on the tray.

"What are the flowers for?" I ask, my eyes narrowing in suspicion.

"They will cheer her up."

"But they look romantic, like I'm giving her flowers, which I'm not. It's bad enough I made the food for her and I'm taking it up to her," I grumble.

"You know that's your father talking again." She gives me the disapproving look once more. "But that aside, Seki has been cooking and serving you since your arrived. Was she being romantic?"

"No. She is paid to cook. It's not the same thing," I refute.

"Aha," she says. "I don't pay her to cook for you."

"What?"

"It's true. She's not supposed to cook for you. But she does it out of the goodness of her heart. She likes to take care of people."

I'm stunned by the revelation and have nothing to say.

"Diaye, sometimes being selfish is necessary," she continues. "This is not one of those times. Seki needs you."

"Needs me? As what?" My heart rate spikes. I really don't like where this is heading.

"As a human, a friend, a shoulder to cry on."

Oh, I definitely know where she's going with this, and it's all kinds of wrong.

"But Grandma, you said it yourself. I'm not good at any of those things."

"Then it's time you started learning. Go on, take the tray. The food is getting cold."

My heart hammers a frantic drumbeat against my ribs as I lift the laden tray. I stride to the door and make a flippant comment. "Grandma, don't blame me if this all goes wrong."

"Aghadiaye, let me warn you. If you plan on treating that girl the way your father treated your mother, I will castrate you myself."

She's smiling as she says it, but a chill travels down my spine.

She is deadly serious.

Seki

The room is dimly lit, casting soft shadows on the walls where memories once danced with joy. The sun is up, but the curtains are closed, blocking out the bright rays.

It's a good thing today is my day off and I don't have to do anything. I showered and dressed, intending to make breakfast for Iye. But she already came to the room, saw how miserable I was, and gave instructions for me to stay in bed and rest.

Now, I sit on the edge of the bed, my slender fingers clutching my phone. On the screen is a photograph of the two of us—Mide and me—months ago when we started dating. It was taken at the cinema complex because there was a movie I wanted to see. Our smiles are frozen in time. Yet, now it's a cruel reminder of what once was. In the image, my eyes are vibrant with love and laughter. Right now, they brim with an ocean of tears threatening to spill at any moment.

My breaths are shallow, each one a painful reminder of the betrayal which shattered my world. The air feels thick, almost suffocating, as I replay my conversation with Mide's wife in my mind.

I'm Tinu, his wife.

I couldn't sleep last night because all kinds of questions were running through my mind. How did I not know he was married? When did he get married? Has he been married all along? Or did he get married recently? Does it effing matter? He is married!

I have undeniable proof. I did some investigating, too late. But I did it. I scoured through his social media accounts and found no images or mentions of a wife or children. However, I searched for his wife online and found his pictures on Tinu's page. He is married with two children. The youngest is only a baby.

The weight of the truth presses down on my chest, making it hard to breathe, as if a thousand tiny needles are pricking my heart.

I stand, my legs unsteady, and walk to the window, but I don't open it. I closed the windows last night because I was shivering with cold. The sun is high, its bright glow drying out the left-over puddles from last night's rain on the empty street below.

I wrap my arms around my body, trying to ward off the chill seeping into my very soul. The world outside is silent, indifferent to my pain, and a profound sense of loneliness like I've never felt before envelops me. I can't bring myself to call my sisters. How do I explain this to my father? He was expecting Mide to come with his people and discuss wedding plans soon. It's never going to happen because I have no intentions of being wife number two or breaking up anyone's home.

The memories of our time together play like a cruel movie in my mind—the laughter we shared, the promises whispered under the stars, the dreams of a future now in ruins. I can still hear Mide's voice, smooth and convincing, telling lies I believed with all my heart. The betrayal cuts deep, leaving a wound that bleeds sorrow and anger in equal measure.

As I stand here, the tears spill over, cascading down my cheeks in a torrent of despair. I press my forehead against the cool glass, the sobs wracking my body as I give in to the overwhelming grief. My phone slips from my grasp, crashing to the floor, and I crumple with it, my spirit broken.

Hours seem to pass in a blur of heartache and tears.

A knock at my bedroom door has me sitting up. It could be Iye coming to check on me.

"Hold on," I say in a croaky voice, wiping my eyes with the heels of my palms.

Feeling hollow and drained, I drag myself off the floor and trudge to the door, unlocking it before pulling the handle.

Diaye fills my view, and he's holding a tray in his hands.

My muscles tense, and my pulse speeds up.

What is he doing outside my door with a tray? Maybe he brought food for his grandmother. This only annoys me more because he should know Iye's room by now.

"You've been here long enough to know Iye's room. It's at the end of the corridor." Hissing, I step back and slam the door in his face.

Before I can move away and give in to my wail of misery, there's another tap on the door. I yank it open and yell, "What?"

"This is for you." He holds up the tray.

"Fine. Give it to me," I snap.

"No. Move out of the way." He turns the tray to the side.

I'll have to leave the safety and comfort of this room to get it, and it's not going to happen.

"You're not coming into my room," I retort, and release the door handle so I can take the tray with both hands.

It gives him an opening. With a grunt, he pushes the door wider, steps around me, and strides into my room. I gasp, whirling around as he walks to my dresser, the sound of his footsteps echoing in the quiet room. He pushes my toiletries aside to set the tray down. His cologne, a familiar and comforting scent of sandalwood and amber, permeates the space.

"Fine. Thank you for bringing the food. You can go now," I say in a sharp tone.

He ignores me and goes to the window. "This room is hot and stuffy. You need some fresh air."

"It's none of your business," I grumble, my voice tight with irritation.

"Grandma sent me. So, it is my business." He pulls back the heavy velvet curtains, letting in the bright morning light.

"Grandma sent you to do what, exactly?" My voice is sharp as suspicion spikes through my senses.

He pauses, hand to his jaw, a thoughtful frown furrowing his brow. "She wants me to fuck you."

"What?" A sudden spasm seizes my throat. I choke as a racking cough tears from my lungs.

A forceful thump on my back between my shoulder blades startles me. Thankfully, he's familiar with the steps involved in dislodging an object from someone's airway. Does he know how to perform the Heimlich manoeuvre as well?

I picture him holding me from behind, his hard muscles pressed against my back, the memory of his warmth and strength still vivid from our accidental collision last weekend.

What am I thinking? A wave of heat floods my cheeks, my skin tingling with a delicious awareness. It feels like a thousand tiny sparks dancing beneath my skin.

The coughing fades to a final rattling gasp, and I straighten, stepping away from him. "What did you say?"

"I said that Grandma wants me to fuck you." His expression is a blank slate, devoid of any emotion.

The heat of desire tingles on my skin, and my mouth waters at the thought of being entwined with him.

But he can't be serious. Surely, Iye wouldn't say that to him.

"What exactly did she say when she sent you up here?" I query with a frown.

He walks to the ornate door, its brass handle gleaming, and turns the key with a soft click. "She said, 'Seki needs you ... be a friend and a shoulder to cry on.'"

"That makes more sense," I say, nodding slowly as some pieces to the puzzle of his presence in my room click into place.

"You see?" He opens the balcony door, letting in the bright morning sun and a gentle, warm breeze, which carries the scent of blooming jasmine from the back garden.

"I don't see anything. There is no correlation between the two. She told you to be my friend, and you took it to mean that you should fuck me."

"Friend—" he lifts his left hand "—fuck—" he lifts his right hand. "Same difference."

"Really? Do you fuck all your female friends?" I shake my head in disbelief, the words catching in my throat.

"Actually..." he muses aloud, tilting his head as if considering something deeply. Then a warm smile illuminates his features. "Yes, I do."

"Oh, wow." My mouth drops open, a silent gasp escaping my lips as I stare at him, speechless.

Returning to the bedroom, he carefully lifts the clear vase filled with white and yellow flowers from the tray, their delicate fragrance filling the air. The vibrant colours and delicate petals of the flowers fill me with such joy, melting my heart.

Did he pick them for me? I shake my head, the ridiculous notion fading as quickly as it came. It's more likely Iye selected them.

He carries the tray of food, the clatter of dishes a counterpoint to the morning sounds, and sets it down on the white plastic table I sometimes use for studying.

"Come and sit down, and eat this food I freshly made," he commands, his voice firm yet inviting.

I stand by the door, hands akimbo. "Do you boss your friends around, too?"

"Absolutely. I wouldn't be the best defender in the world if I wasn't bossy." He sinks into the chair across the table, the wood creaking softly beneath his weight.

Groaning, I cover my face with my hands. "Dear Lord, what kind of arrogant, grumpy human being, reeking of expensive cologne and radiating disdain, did you send my way?"

"The kind that cooks breakfast for his friend to cheer her up, even when she doesn't want his fucking. Or does she?" There's a dryness to his tone, an unexpected, subtle wit.

"No, she doesn't." The joke startles me, but the humour is infectious. So, I laugh, taking my hands away from my face, warmth spreading through me.

He grins the most gorgeous grin I've ever seen on a man. Maybe it's the bright sunshine, but his straightish teeth are a crescent of dazzling white against the brown plumpness of his lips. I imagine his perfect lips trailing against my inner thighs and kissing me intimately. My pussy clenches, and I wish for the fucking he mentioned.

"Then sit down and eat." He waves at the chair.

With a cautious step forward, I sit gingerly, the silence amplifying the creak of the aged chair. I lift the silver cover off the plate, showing a golden-brown, folded omelette. The food looks appetising, and a tantalising aroma fills the air. "Did you really cook this?"

"Of course I did. Go ahead. Take a bite." He watches me, his gaze lingering, heavy and intense.

I pick up the gleaming fork, cut a tender morsel, and place it on my tongue, savouring the initial texture. Then the buttery softness and crunch of the bell peppers explode on my palate, a symphony of sweet and savoury flavours dancing together.

"This is really good." I can't hide my shock.

"You sound like you didn't think I can cook." He opens the flask and pours amber liquid into the mug.

"It's a pleasant surprise to know you can cook." I take another bite of omelette. "At least you won't starve."

"That's the thing about being an only child. You learn survival skills."

"I thought your father had other children," I say without thinking.

He looks away, his frown returning.

"I'm sorry. I didn't mean to upset you." It's so nice to have him talking and smiling for a change, instead of being so grouchy.

"No. Don't apologise. I have half-siblings. But I lived alone with my mother until she passed. She taught me the skills to take care of myself because she knew I would be away from home at a young age because of football."

"That makes sense." I put the cutlery down and pick up the mug of lemon tea.

He takes a slice of bread from the plate and picks up the fork I was using.

"What are you doing?" I ask, blowing into the tea before sipping.

"Having some breakfast." He scoops omelette onto the slice of bread, rolls it into a wrap, and takes a bite.

"That's my food you're eating," I protest jokingly.

"Actually, it's my food since I cooked it." He carries on chewing.

"You made it for me."

"No. I said, Grandma said I should give it to you."

"Same difference."

"Right." He chuckles. "Since we're friends, we can share it."

"Okay." I smile. "Only because I'm a nice person."

"Thank you," he says.

"You're welcome," I reply.

We sit there and eat the rest of the omelette in relative silence. He even drinks the lemon tea. I realise we shared the same plate and mug, and warmth fills my chest.

Spending time with Diaye makes me forget Mide and the heartache. It might be a temporary solution, but I'm grateful Diaye is here. His presence gives me confidence.

At least, it helps me resolve to pick up the pieces of my life and move on with each passing moment we are together. I know healing will be a long and arduous journey, but I deserve better. I deserved honesty, loyalty, and true love.

First, I need to prepare myself for facing Mide at work today.

"You're quiet. You're never quiet. What's on your mind?"

Diaye's deep voice cuts into my thoughts.

I raise a brow. "I could say the same thing about you suddenly being so chatty. You are usually grumpy and quiet."

"I'm trying to be a good friend."

I heave out a sigh. He is doing a good job of being a friend. I can't fault him.

"I was thinking about working this evening and facing Mide," I say.

"Do you want to go to work today?" he asks, looking serious.

"No. I don't want to, but I have to. Plus, it will look like I'm afraid of him or avoiding him if I don't show up."

"To hell with him and what he thinks. If you don't want to go to work, don't."

"But that's selfish."

"Yes, and? I'm selfish many times, and I do well. You need to be selfish for once in your life. Think about yourself and your wellbeing."

"You're right. I need to take care of myself. Alright, I'll call work and let them know."

"Good," he says and picks up the tray. "I'll leave you to it."

I hear my bedroom door shut as he leaves.

With a deep breath, I walk back into my room and grab my phone from the floor where it fell earlier, ready to face the painful process of moving on. The road ahead is uncertain, and the scars of betrayal will take time to heal.

But I feel a glimmer of strength within me, a flicker of hope which refuses to be extinguished. I will rise from the ashes of my shattered trust, stronger and wiser, and one day, I will find the love I deserve.

13

Diaye

As I step out of Seki's room, a sense of fulfilment washes over me. I can still hear her laughter echoing in the hallway, a stark contrast to the depressed state I found her in when I first saw her this morning. Seeing her smile again, even if just for a moment, lifts a weight off my shoulders.

With a sigh of relief, I carry the empty tray downstairs, the guilt over my role in her situation fading with each step. The kitchen, earlier bustling with Grandma's activity, is now silent and empty. I take the time to scrub the used pans and plates, removing remnants of our meal, and then wipe down the counters, leaving them sparkling. My obsessive need for order and control prevents me from leaving even a single dirty dish in the sink. The sight of them will drive me mad.

A sharp buzz vibrates against my thigh, and I reach into my shorts' pocket, pulling out my phone. The name Harrison flashes on the caller ID.

"D Strongman," he uses my nickname. "Are you coming to the gym?"

"Of course. I'm on my way."

It's part of my daily routine, and I don't skip it.

Grandma is weeding her vibrant flowerbeds when I go outside to tell her my plans. The morning sun warms my face. I drive out to the gym with the bodyguard. Harrison makes a great gym partner, and we get to discuss other matters. He will be my eyes and ears in Sapele when I leave. He will oversee any problems requiring action for Iye and Seki and feedback progress to me. Also, as Harrison part-owns Crystal Palace Hotel, he's handling Mide on my behalf.

Last week, after Mide announced he was engaged to Seki, I was infuriated, and I asked Harrison about him. The revelation that he was already married and his family lived in Ibadan wasn't surprising. He is a narcissistic player. I could see it in his demeanour as soon as I met him. He reminded me of my father. I knew I had to do something about him.

However, I feel guilty because my actions precipitated Seki finding out about Mide's wife the way she did. I didn't think she would go to his house so late at night and get stranded. I didn't think she would be so heartbroken about his marital status.

Hence my irritation this morning when Iye was defending her. But Iye was right in scolding me. I should be more sympathetic towards Seki. I didn't realise she was so upset about the Mide guy until I saw the mournful sorrow in her eyes. I'm glad I made breakfast for her and will do whatever I need to do for her to be happy again and forget Mide.

Returning to Iye's house, I find her devising a plan to distract Seki from her evident sadness. With a list of groceries and other essential items in hand, she wants to go to the shopping centre with Seki.

Anticipating the sights, sounds, and smells of a busy marketplace, I volunteer to drive the car instead of Íruoghẹnẹ. At the mall, I pay for the mountain of goodies Seki chooses—groceries, toiletries, and clothes—the ringing

POS machines a small price for her joyful squeals. The late afternoon sun casts long shadows as I drive back to the house while Seki and Iye are engaged in playful conversations, the earlier distress forgotten.

Back in the house, we sit at the dining table, the aroma of the takeout filling the air as we eat our meal. The connection between Grandma and Seki is apparent. Despite the generations separating them, they share a strong bond. Honoured and privileged, I feel the comforting weight of their acceptance, as though I have always been an intrinsic part of their lives.

I'm reminded of the good old days with Mum and Grandma in this house. The laughter and joy with the two most important people in my life.

It feels almost the same now. Iye has adopted Seki as one of hers, and as such, she is now part of my family. I doubt I can separate the two. I don't want to separate them. They love each other. I can see it.

Like an epiphany, I realise these are my people—Grandma and Seki—my family. They will have my back always. Grandma, certainly. Seki, too, if I let her. She will be a good friend. She doesn't have an evil bone in her body. Although her tongue is sharper than a sword.

"...I don't blame her for leaving you. If I was engaged to you, I would probably leave you, too."

I haven't forgotten her cutting words to me last night. Painful, but at least she's honest.

I can use honest friends.

Silently, I swear I will take care of Grandma and Seki. I will provide whatever they need.

After dinner, I leave them in the sitting room and head upstairs to shower and change for the evening. I promised I would meet Harrison tonight.

I pause for a second, leaning against the doorframe and taking a deep breath. The air feels lighter, the atmosphere less tense. It's amazing how a simple shopping trip and a few shared moments can transform the mood. Knowing I could help Seki, even in the smallest way, fills me with a quiet joy.

I make my way into the shower, the memory of our afternoon adventure playing in my mind. Her eyes lit up at the sight of the new clothes and groceries, and her laughter was infectious. It reminds me of the strength that lies within her, even in the face of sorrow.

My phone buzzes as I come out of the bathroom. It's Mr O getting back to me about the message I left this morning. He says the summer pre-season training camp in Italy starts in two weeks and I have a place there. So I can stay in Nigeria like my original schedule and then return to the UK to pack what I need before moving to Italy.

He also mentions how another team, Viva City FC, is interested in signing me to start with them in January next year. Viva City Panthers are a newly promoted club to the EPL. It could be a great opportunity for me to return to playing topflight football in the UK. However, several issues trouble me.

First, Viva City club manager wants to add a marriage clause to the contract offer. Because they are concerned about how my personal life will affect my professional performance.

I complain about the club's new status in the Premiership and the strong chance of their relegation back to the Championship. I dread the idea of a season in the lower league. Their influence isn't strong enough to make such a bold demand of a veteran player like me.

I'm not willing to sign for Viva City FC. But Mr O tells me to think about it. The offer will be open for several months because I'm their top choice. They are the only EPL club showing an interest in signing me.

I tell him I'll think about it, but I want to focus on the Italian club where I'll be playing football for the next five months at least.

He confirms the management team arranged a return flight for me in a week. Chinedu will be back for the road trip to Lagos. I'm excited about playing the sports I love so much, at a topflight club in Europe. It took me a while to get used to the idea. But the PR events helped me re-establish my love for football. And being in Sapele has reminded me of my love for life. It's a boost I've needed for so long, and I can't wait to get started.

As I head downstairs, the sound of the television reaches my ears, mingling with the distant chatter of Grandma and Seki. The thought of sharing my good news with them brings an uncontrollable smile to my face, a warmth spreading through my chest. The future, once a blurry and daunting landscape, now feels bright and full of promise.

I enter the sitting room with a light heart, eager to see the expressions on their faces when I tell them about the training camp in Italy. But for now, I bask in the simple joy of knowing how, today, I've made a difference to Seki's day.

"My regards to your family," Iye says on her phone before placing it on the sofa next to her.

"Grandma, I have news," I say, crossing the room towards them.

"What it is?" She looks up with bright eyes and a warm smile.

"I spoke to Mr O. I have an offer to play for a football team in Italy for the first part of next season."

"That's wonderful," Iye says and opens her arms, giving me a hug.

"Congratulations," Seki says, beaming a smile.

"Thank you," I reply, settling on the sofa opposite them. "It's great because one of my biggest frustrations last season was not playing. And it looks like I will be on the new team roster this season."

"I'm so proud of you," Grandma says.

"So am I," Seki adds.

"I appreciate both of you and all the support you've provided since I arrived in Nigeria. It's been really important to get myself into the right headspace."

"You're welcome." Grandma glances at Seki with a curious expression.

"The club has a pre-season training camp I need to attend so I can do all the preliminary training to prepare for the new season. Also, I will need to undergo a crash course in learning the Italian language since I will live there for a few months. It will also help me acclimatise to the environment."

"It's good." Seki's face crumples into a frown. "But when you leave, will we see you anytime soon?"

"I'm not sure when I will be back. Once the football season starts, I may not be able to travel except in the case of an emergency. We will get a break around December-January for the World Cup friendlies and pre-qualifier matches. I will have to see which national team will call me up since I was dropped from the English team."

"What does that mean?" Seki asks.

It's nice to see her showing an interest in my football career. I need the support.

"It means I could be called to play for Cameroon or Nigeria, since I qualify to play for both."

"You should play for Nigeria." She cheers.

"We'll see." I chuckle. "My dad thinks Cameroon will call me up. He has connections to the Cameroon Football Association."

"So you think you might be in Cameroon in December to play football?"

"Yes, it's highly probable."

"Then you must invite Iye and me to come and watch you once it's confirmed."

"Really? You would come to watch me?"

"Of course we would. Won't we, Iye?"

"Of course. It would be my chance to get on a plane after so long. I miss my trips abroad when your mother was still alive. Haven't been on a plane since. So, of course, I'll visit Cameroon if you invite us," Grandma says.

"Then it's settled. You're coming to watch me play if I make the Cameroonian team," I say.

"It's not a matter of if, it's when."

I love Seki's confidence in my abilities. I just hope I can live up to them.

"Thank you." Their reassurances are a boost I didn't realise I needed until I came here. I hope to make them proud. "I'm going to pop out to see Harrison. I shouldn't be too long out."

"Before you go, I want to talk to you privately. Seki, excuse us," Grandma says.

"Okay." Seki gets up and walks out of the sitting room.

14

Diaye

"Come here." With a warm smile, Grandma pats the soft cushion beside her on the floral sofa.

Concerned, I walk around the smooth, dark wood coffee table and lower myself to the seat next to her, the cushion sighing beneath my weight. "What is it?"

The warmth of her hands cups mine, sending a comforting feeling through me. "I was just speaking to Mr O before you came downstairs."

"Oh?" I question, raising an eyebrow in curiosity.

"He mentioned that you have been offered a contract with a new club in London," she replies in a calm tone.

My spine stiffens. "Yes. But I told him I don't want to sign with them."

"Why don't you want to sign with them?"

I shrug. "The club has only just been promoted to the Premier League for the first time in their history of playing football. I don't think they will survive their first season in the premiership. I think they will be relegated back to the championship."

"I see." She nods sagely, a knowing smile playing on her lips. "You only want to play for a big club, the prestige, the money. It's all that matters to you."

"Yes. I deserve to play for a big club. I want the huge stadiums, the roaring fans, the fame and fortune. What's wrong with that? I've been playing for one of the elite clubs on the planet for the past ten years. Why should I step down?"

"But this new club can also become big with your help."

"Perhaps. There is no guarantee."

"There's nothing wrong with building something from scratch. I know your father worked to get you into a big club, and that's all you know. You've had everything packaged for you and given to you that way. But you see, it didn't work out so well for you. The moment there was a little trouble, that same big club dumped you."

The forgotten pain flares, a burning reminder of my past ordeal, and my breath catches in my chest.

"I'm not saying this to upset you or belittle you," Grandma continues, still holding my hand. "I just want you to reexamine your reason for rejecting the offer from the new club. Sometimes, all that glitters is not gold. The real gem lies in the dirt, and you will have to clean it up for it to shine."

"But Grandma," I protest. "Viva City wants to include a marriage clause in my contract."

"Marriage clause? What does that mean?"

"It means they want me to be married or have a stable family life because they are worried my unsettled private life will impact my performance on the football field."

"They are not wrong."

"But that's not my fault. I'm not taking Phoebe back. And Dad just stresses me out with his demands."

"You don't need Phoebe. She came to you already packaged and glittering. But she wasn't gold. Just gold-plated. The true gem is closer to home."

"The true gem. Who is that?"

"Seki," she states matter-of-fact.

"Seki?" I burst out laughing, shaking my head. "Grandma, are you saying I should marry Seki?"

"Yes. She is one hundred percent better than that Phoebe girl. And she will provide a buffer between you and your father. Your father will calm down and leave you alone when you show him you're a grown man."

I stand, shaking my head. "But I'm not in love with Seki."

"Do you hate her?"

"No."

"Do you like her?"

"Well, yes. She's a nice person."

"Nice enough to marry?"

"I don't know. I haven't thought about her like that."

This morning, I was thinking about fucking Seki. Only because I wanted her to forget about Mide. Not because I wanted to date her. I don't want to date anyone, let alone get married.

"Better start thinking about it. What if another man came here tomorrow and said he wants to marry her? Would you let her marry him?" Grandma gives me a curious stare.

This gives me pause. I just got used to the idea of Seki dating Mide and then finding out he was married. If she has any sense, she will take a break from dating anyone for a very long time.

But as usual, I deflect the question because I'm not sure I'm ready for the answer.

"Grandma, what about Seki? How does she feel about what you're suggesting?"

"Call her and let's find out."

"Fine." I step out, glad for the breather.

Seki is in the hallway, pacing, and she looks agitated. Was she eavesdropping?

"Seki, Grandma wants to talk to you," I say.

"Yes, I heard." She avoids my gaze.

"You were listening," I say.

She doesn't reply and walks around me into the sitting room.

"Iye, you wanted to see me." Seki stands in the middle of the room, fidgeting with her dress.

"Yes, I was talking to Aghadiaye." Grandma points at me. "He needs a wife, and I suggested he marry you."

Seki puffs out a heavy breath. "Iye, I heard your discussion with Diaye. But he already said he is not in love with me."

She folds her arms across her midriff as if I hurt her feelings.

Guilt pelts at me. "Why are you saying it like that, as if it's all on me? Are you in love with me?"

"No, I'm not," she mutters, and it feels like a stab in my heart.

Why do I want her to be in love with me?

"Iye," she continues. "You can see that we're not in love with each other. So, marriage between us won't work."

"Hmmm." Grandma sighs as if she's dealing with a bunch of toddlers. "What is love? I mean, what is romantic love? Can any of you tell me?"

Seki looks at me, and I shrug in a 'don't look at me' way because I don't know the answer.

"Love is a powerful attraction and emotional attachment to another person," Seki says hesitantly.

"Good. Now let's break it down. The first part is the attraction. So let me ask you. Are you attracted to each other?"

I glance at Seki and shout 'hell, yes!' in my mind. I've been attracted to her since the first day I saw her. Today, she is wearing the two-tone classy midi shirtdress that showcases her curves. It's the most stylish outfit I've seen her wear all week.

But neither of us responds to Grandma's question.

"So, none of you want to answer me, abi?" Grandma scolds.

"Diaye is good-looking. Of course he's attractive," Seki mumbles.

My head and other parts swell with pride. Feeling happy she finds me attractive, I speak without thinking. "Seki is sexy." Seki gasps and covers her mouth as she meets my gaze, and I correct myself. "I mean, she's attractive."

"I see. You're both attracted to each other. So, one part of the equation is accounted for." Grandma gives a sly smile.

"The other part, which is the emotional attachment, comes with time. It is expressed through showing and sharing respect, patience, kindness, forgiveness, selflessness, humility, truth, joy, hope, and trust. These are not things that happen in one day. When you show each other these things over time, that's how you develop the powerful emotional attachment to each other. That's when you fall in love and stay in love."

Her words are profound, and I don't know what to say in response. Seki says nothing.

Seki and I took the tentative steps into friendship this morning. A friend with benefits at most. But am I ready for the marriage thing? No.

"Look…" Grandma's voice softens. "I know you may not understand what I'm saying now. But with time, you will see that I was trying to do the best for both of you. Diaye, you are my only grandchild, my blood. Although Seki is not my blood, I have adopted her as a granddaughter. Not legally, of course. But in here." She taps her chest. "I love both of you and want the best for you. Seki has been with me for over two years. She might be too trusting, but she has a heart of gold. Diaye, you are too proud and could learn some humility. But you are very protective of the ones you love. Together, you will be great for each other."

We contemplate her words in stunned silence for a few minutes before I speak. "Grandma, you really want me to marry Seki?"

"Of course," she replies. "Why do you think I'm giving both of you this house in my will?"

"What?" Seki's gaze darts from me to Grandma. "Iye, I'm in your will?"

"Of course you are, my dear. You deserve half this house as much as he does. So, the two of you will inherit it."

"Oh," Seki says, pacing the living room. "And when did you decide to add me to your will?"

"Months ago. Before Diaye called and came home."

"Wow. You wanted me to marry Seki even before I met her." I'm still trying to wrap my mind around her determination to get us together.

"Yes. And you met each other and like each other. See, I'm not so senile, after all."

"I still think this is a crazy idea."

"So do I," Seki says.

"I'm going to lie down. It's been a long day. The two of you can discuss it and decide for yourselves." Grandma shifts, and Seki supports her to stand.

"Do you need me to help you with anything?" Seki asks.

"No." Iye waves her off as she walks to the door. "I'll be fine. Stay and talk to your future husband."

We stand still and listen to her walk up the concrete stairs with slow, steady steps.

I hear the creak and click of her bedroom door as it opens and shuts.

"Can I say something?" Seki asks.

"Sure."

"I don't want to get married to you. I have things to do with my life," she says.

This stings a little, and I retort without thinking. "But you wanted to marry Mide."

"Exactly the reason I don't want to get married. Do you think I want to go from a man who promised me marriage when he was already married to a man who has sex with every woman who is his friend?"

I open my mouth to tell her I've only ever had one woman I class as my friend and I was engaged to her. But I bite my tongue. It might be better for me if she thinks I jump in and out of bed with women.

"As I said before, the whole thing is a bad idea anyway," I say instead. "You don't want to get married. I don't want to get married. So, let's forget about it."

"But Iye wants us to get married, and she's giving us this house. I don't want to disappoint her."

"So, what are you saying?"

"I'm saying can we not work something out that will make Iye happy?"

"You mean like a fake marriage?"

"Maybe. You need to get married to secure your spot on the new London team, right?"

"Yes."

"And if we get married, you get your contract and restart your football career. Iye gets her wish of us getting married. But what do I get?"

It's another kick in the gut. Seki doesn't think I'm much of a catch as a husband. Never mind that I have millions in the bank and many women want to snag me, including Beverly, whom I met only days ago.

Well, she's entitled to her opinion.

"I don't know. What do you want?" I grumble.

"I want my education and career," she states confidently. "I want a life beyond being someone's girlfriend or wife. I want qualifications and a career in nursing. I want degrees from prestigious universities in the UK. But I can't afford to pay for all that."

"Okay." Her words and passion give me an idea. "How about we make a deal?"

"I'm listening," she says.

"Marry me and stay married to me for the duration of my playing career. I will pay the tuition fees for any degrees or qualifications you gain while we're married. At the end of our marriage, I will pay you half a million euros for every year we're together up to a maximum of three million euros."

"Seriously? You want to pay me to marry you?"

"Yes, that way, you get something out of marrying me, and I get the contract I need to restart my playing career. Then Grandma will get her wish of us getting married."

"The money would change my life and my family's life. It would be a dream come true to go to the UK to study."

"So, do we have a deal?"

"Yes, we do."

I narrow my eyes at her. "Grandma is right. You are too trusting. Are you not going to negotiate? Don't you haggle when you go to the market?"

"But this is different. You are going to pay for me to go to the UK. You will cover all my bills, tuition, rent, right?"

"Yes. But you can still negotiate."

"Why? I'm not greedy. You will pay me for each year I'm married to you. Five hundred thousand euros is more than any employer will pay me as a nurse per annum. And I will still have a career once I get my qualifications and get a job."

As I listen to her, it becomes clearer why Grandma wants me to take care of Seki. Her pure heart, while a beautiful thing, leaves her vulnerable to exploitation. It explains why Mide took advantage of her.

"Seki, I'm sure you know I am one of the highest paid footballers on the planet. Take advantage of it. Ask for more."

"Fine! If you're limiting the amount you're paying to three million euros, then we're only staying married for three years."

A smile curls my lips. "Are you negotiating?"

She smiles back. "You bet I'm negotiating."

"Good. I'll pay you one million euros for each year we are married, up to a maximum of five million after we break up. Do we have a deal?"

"Wait. We're just pretending to be married, right?"

"Mostly," I say. "We still must do the formalities like have a wedding ceremony and get a marriage certificate for all the legal paperwork. You will come to Europe, and we'll live together because it's expected."

"In which case, you will come and perform the traditional wedding rites. My father will expect it. I can't tell him I'm pretending to get married," she says with a frown.

It seems like a lot of hassle for a fake marriage. But for some reason, I want to please her, so I say, "Okay. We'll do the traditional wedding if that's what you want."

"Yes, I want it."

Yet, the frown remains on her face.

"Why are you frowning, then?"

"I—" she fidgets again, glances at me, and looks away. "If this is a fake marriage, then we're not having sex, right?"

"If you don't want it," I say, a little annoyed at her reticence.

"Okay." She nods twice. "Not that I care, but are you going to sleep with other women when we get married? Because if you are, tell me right now so I know beforehand."

I tilt my head and study her. She is getting agitated by the second and pacing as she waits for my response.

"You say you don't care but you do," I prod.

"Fine." She tosses her hands in the air. "I care if my fake husband will be faithful to me. I don't think any amount of money in the world will make up for a cheating husband."

Interesting. She's reluctant to take my money, yet quick to demand fidelity from me. Not that I have any plans of cheating during my marriage, fake or not.

"You know what?" she continues, still pacing. "If you're going to sleep with other people, then so will I."

Her words are a trigger and conjure up Phoebe's betrayal. Before I know what I'm doing, I block Seki's path, looming over her.

"Seki, get this fucking straight. From the moment we make this agreement, you are exclusively mine."

Her eyes widen. "What?"

"You heard me," I assert. "There will be no fooling around with other people or fucking other people. If you betray me, I will end the agreement and marriage, and you will not get a naira from me. Do you understand me?"

"Yes." She nods. "Cheating by either of us is a deal-breaker."

"Absolutely. I'm glad we understand each other. So let's shake to confirm our agreement." I extend my hand.

"Agreed."

Her hand finds mine, the unexpected intimacy sending a shiver of pleasure through me, a connection I felt since our first meeting.

Staring into her beautiful brown eyes, the rich, warm depths of their colour captivating me, I suddenly have the urge to kiss her.

Her gaze is fixed on my lips, a flicker of recognition in her eyes, as if she feels the same pull.

Leaning closer, I breathe in her sweet scent—jasmine, orange blossoms, and musk, an incredibly sweet and heady perfume. The muscles in her throat ripple as she swallows, the action making me blink, breaking the fog of lust.

What am I doing? We already established we don't want to fuck each other. And a few minutes ago, we didn't want to get married to each other.

I release her hand. "I will speak to my lawyer to draw up a prenuptial agreement for us."

"Wait." She jerks back. "We need a prenup? You think I will ask for half of your income when we get divorced? You don't trust me?"

She sounds outraged, and I grin. For someone who was adamant she didn't want to marry me, she is behaving as if this setup is real.

"Wifey," I say as I reach out and stroke the soft skin on her cheek. Her nose flares in response to me calling her Wifey. It's going to become my new favourite word. "You should know this about me. I don't trust anyone. Not any-more. I trusted Phoebe, and I knew her for five years. Yet, she betrayed me. I've only known you for one week and a day.

Do you really think I'm going to trust you with my hard-earned money?"

Seki

"OMG! You're getting married," my sister Imoni squeals as we stand in the kitchen while I prepare lunch. It's Sunday afternoon, and she was at Iye's house when we arrived home from church. "This means I'm going to be the chief bridesmaid."

I laugh as I loop my arm around her shoulders. "You didn't even let me land, and you're claiming chief bridesmaid."

"There is no wasting time here because you have landed on your feet," Imoni says. "I was worried about you when you messaged me about Mide being married. It was Dad who even sent me today to see you to make sure you're okay. That man Mide is a bastard for what he did to you. But you know it is a blessing in disguise that you found out when you did because now you are free to marry Diaye."

"But are you not worried that it is all a little rushed or wrong?" I ask, a niggle of guilt poking me. I didn't explain the full situation to my sister. Imoni is the last person I can tell this secret to, because it won't be a secret for long. "Last week, I was dating Mide. This week, I'm engaged to Iye's grandson."

"There's nothing wrong or rushed about it. You were both single when he asked you to marry him, right?"

"Yes."

"And as for being rushed, there's something called love at first sight. I saw online the other day, a couple who met on Valentine's Day got married less than two months later. When you know who you're meant to be with, you know. It's not like you guys have to save up for a wedding. The guy is a millionaire."

"Money isn't everything," I say, feeling guilty about how much Diaye is willing to pay me to become his pretend-wife. I couldn't believe it when he offered me half a million euros a year last night. I would have settled for that amount. But he even insisted I negotiate it upwards. In the end, he will pay me up to five million euros. I've never even had one million naira in my account.

"But the man wants to marry you. Or is there something I'm missing?" She eyes me suspiciously.

I stiffen. "Of course not."

"This ring is beautiful." My sister raises my left hand, admiring the sparkling diamond ring on the third finger.

"It's his mother's engagement ring," I say.

The reality of the agreement I made with Diaye to marry him is sinking in. This morning before church, a very jubilant Iye presented the ring to Diaye, who, in turn, slipped it onto my finger. Our engagement was even announced in church. So, it's official. The train is moving along a lot faster than I envisaged.

"Eyah. That's so romantic. Like in the movies."

The low purr of a powerful engine fills the air.

"That must be him. I have to take a look." My sister's smile broadens as she heads for the door.

I follow her because, for some reason, I don't want to leave Imoni alone with Diaye. He had to drop off one of Iye's friends who followed us home from church today.

Imoni is outgoing, charming, smart, and a bad bitch. Today, she is in a shiny auburn wig with tresses down to her hips and a dress hugging bountiful curves. She is my younger sister, but she has bigger breasts and bum than me. Whenever we are out together, she attracts more attention than me.

So, I guess I'm feeling a little insecure about how I look compared to her. Especially since I'm wearing a modest high neck maxi dress which is cinched at the empire line and flows to my feet.

We walk out the side door, and the car is pulling up to the carport. Diaye steps out, his poise unmatched, an arresting sight that defies description, and a vision of impossible grace in the two-piece embroidered tunic, aviators, and monogrammed loafers. The bling around his neck and wrists complements the gold embroidery around his collar and hems.

He takes off his sunglasses, his eyes cool and unreadable, taking in our little driveway welcome party, the sound of bird chirps faint in the background.

"OMG, he is hot." Imoni nudges me in the ribs.

I scowl in protest. Diaye might be hot, but he is arrogant and impossible, too.

"Welcome home," I say.

"Thank you." He flashes his pearly white teeth as he approaches.

Hand extended, Imoni steps in front of him. "I'm Seki's sister, Imoni."

I frown at my sister's audacity. She should wait for me to introduce them.

"Nice to meet you." He shakes her hand. "I'm Diaye."

But his gaze never leaves my face, and I can't read his expression. He shakes her hand briefly before stepping past her and walking to the front door. He unlocks it and enters the house.

"Congratulations on your engagement." My sister follows him instead of coming around to the side entrance to the kitchen.

This means I have to follow them.

"Are we going out to celebrate?" she continues.

"Going out?" Diaye glances at my sister as if she's a pesky fly bothering him.

"Yes, now. You just got engaged. We have to celebrate," Imoni replies as Diaye enters the sitting room.

"Imoni, stop," I say in a harsh whisper as she goes to follow him.

"What?" She shrugs me off.

"You're back," Iye says to Diaye as he walks to the sofa where she's sitting and kisses her on the cheek.

"Yes, everything went well," he says and sits beside her.

"Iye," my sister starts, walking around the sofas. "I was saying to Seki and Diaye that we should go out and celebrate their engagement."

"It's not necessary," I say sharply, eyeing my sister.

"It is necessary," Iye says with a smile. "The two of you must spend as much time as possible before he goes back abroad. When he leaves, you will miss each other."

I want to scoff that I won't miss Diaye. That I barely know him enough to miss him. That we are only fake engaged. But the little voice inside my head tells me: *you will miss him.*

"Yes," Imoni cheers. "We should go to Crystal Palace restaurant, and you can show off your engagement ring."

"No. That's not a good idea," I reiterate.

"I think it is a good idea," Diaye says and pulls out his phone. "I'll call Harrison to meet us there. The more, the merrier." He stands and leaves the sitting room.

"Yes." Imoni claps, looking excited. "Seki, you need to change your outfit."

"What's wrong with what I'm wearing?" I frown.

"It is your engagement party. You can't be looking like Church Girl. You need to look like the woman who is engaged to superstar Diaye Zambo. Do you get me? Abi, am I lying, Grandma?"

Iye chuckles and looks me over. "Imoni is right. You should change into something more party-like."

"But I don't have any party dresses. I don't go to parties," I protest.

"Didn't he buy you some new clothes yesterday? Try one of them," Iye says.

"That's a good idea." I hadn't thought about that. In fact, I hadn't had time to try on the new clothes because things accelerated yesterday. At the start of the day, I was grieving the loss of Mide, and by the end, I was engaged to Diaye.

"Good. Come on. Let's get you changed." My sister tugs my hand.

"Iye, I'm coming," I say and follow her to my bedroom.

Thirty minutes later, I come downstairs dressed in a fitted, halter-neck, A-line, red-green-white Ankara dress which skims my curves and reaches my ankles. On my feet are matching mid-heeled strappy sandals. My face is made up, and my natural hair is styled in a chignon, thanks to my sister. I don't have any jewellery except the engagement ring and the wristwatch with sparkling crystals Iye gave me for my birthday. Still, I feel like a celebrity or one of those big social media influencers.

"Dum, dum, dum." My sister makes the sound as if beating a drum as I enter the sitting room. "What do you think?"

Diaye is sitting on a sofa with his back to me. He twists in the chair and looks over. Something flickers in his gaze—I don't recognise it—and he stands, his mouth dropping open.

A frantic rhythm hammers in my chest. Does he like it or not?

"You look beautiful," Iye speaks first.

"You think?" I ask, feeling unsure since Diaye hasn't said anything. Maybe I overdressed for a simple trip to a venue I work in.

"Of course. You always look beautiful," Iye says. "Isn't that so, Diaye?"

"Absolutely." He breaks into a smile. "You look stunning."

Warmth fills my chest, and I let out the breath I was holding. I wanted him to like the outfit. He'd bought it, after all.

"Thank you," I say, smiling like a loony in a psychiatric hospital, his praise making me feel floaty. "I'm ready to go when you are."

"Right." He grabs his phone and car keys from the side table.

"Have fun," Iye says as I hug her briefly.

"We will," my sister announces, and I chuckle as we leave the house.

This time, one of the security personnel drives the car with my sister in the front passenger seat. I sit in the back seat with Diaye. There are more security men in a second car behind us.

There's enough space in here, and we don't touch. Yet, my skin prickles with awareness of him. I want to touch him. My heart beats fast because of his nearness. Each breath I take fills me with his comforting cologne of sandalwood.

My sister chats nonstop, and I respond to the conversation. Diaye doesn't say much, which is normal for him. He's not talkative. I talk when I'm excited, but my sister is much more verbal than me.

An hour after leaving the house, we're at the hotel, and it seems they were waiting for our arrival. The hotel manager greets us at the entrance. He ushers us into the bar lounge, which has been cordoned off and reserved for us. The place is decorated with balloons and flowers, and there's a banner which reads 'Congratulations!'

"This is beautiful," my sister says.

"It is. I'm pleasantly surprised." I turn to Diaye. "Thank you for organising this."

"You're welcome," he says as he directs me to a sofa.

I sink into the leather sofa, and my sister sits next to me. Not long after, Harrison arrives with his entourage, and the party is in full swing. I can't believe all the fuss is for me. Usually, I'm the one serving guests in this very spot. Now, I'm the celebrant, and my colleagues are serving me. Tori is on duty, and she's serving our section. She seems shocked at my engagement to Diaye. I tell her we'll catch up later.

Harrison's fiancée, Rukevwe AKA Rukky, arrives with her entourage, which includes Beverly. As soon as I see her, my body stiffens, and my sister notices.

"What is it?" Imoni asks.

"Remember I told you about the woman who was all over Diaye last time I was working here?"

"Yeah?"

"That's her. She even came to the house twice to see him."

"Really?"

"Congratulations, Seki," Rukky says as she comes over.

I stand and hug her briefly. "Thank you. This is my sister, Imoni."

"Nice to meet you." They shake hands.

She introduces the other women—Ufuoma, Titi, and Beverly. They all mutter congrats, but none of them hug me. I don't mind. Rukky probably only hugged me because she is engaged to Diaye's cousin. She feels obligated. The women sit beside us on the sofas but chat amongst themselves. The men stand mostly, chatting in groups. Diaye is in a group with Harrison. There's music and food and drinks.

I'm glad my sister is here because it means I don't feel left out. I didn't have enough notice to invite my friends who are colleagues at the hotel or fellow students at the nursing school.

When Tori gets a break, she joins us on the sofa and gists us about what has been going on.

"Do you know Mide has been suspended?" she says.

"What?" My heart jolts.

"Yes o. The gist is several women have been complaining about him to management that he was sexually harassing them."

My stomach drops, and I feel sick. "Are you serious?"

"I am totally serious. Yesterday, he came to work, and he was marched out of here by security. He is not allowed on the premises until the investigations into the allegations are completed."

"Ewo!" Imoni exclaims. "That man is something else. Did you know he was married?"

"Married ke?" Tori says. "Since when."

"He has a wife and two children in Ibadan. Seki only found out two days ago."

"Hey. No wonder. That man is the devil himself."

All the information is making me feel awful. I can't believe I trusted Mide. That I was even considering marrying him. Meanwhile, he was harassing other members of the staff. How could I have been so gullible? Nausea washes over me.

"Excuse me. I need the ladies." I stand and rush to the bathroom. Luckily, by the time I get there, the feeling subsides, and I fight back tears. I use the loo and wash my hands, trying not to think of Mide or my heartache.

I'm supposed to be happy because it's my engagement party. Even if it's fake, the people don't know it's fake. I plaster a smile and return to the lounge.

My body freezes to the spot at the sight in front of me.

Standing at the bar is Diaye. Next to him is Beverly, who has her hand on his upper arm. She is saying something to him, and he is smiling at her words.

My hands clench at my sides, and I'm sure I'm glowering at them.

Diaye must sense my glare because he turns in my direction. He must see something in my expression because he walks over to me. "What is it?"

"What are you doing with her?" I grit out, tilting my chin in Beverly's direction.

"Oh, Beverly. You've met her, right? She's just a friend."

"A friend like all the ones you fuck, right?"

"Come on. You can't use that against me every time." He chuckles.

It only makes me angrier. "You know what? The deal is—"

Before I can finish speaking, he wraps his hand around the front of my throat and tips my head back as he lowers his lips to mine, shutting me up.

It's like nothing I've experienced before. I forget I'm standing in the middle of our engagement party and sink into the feeling. His lips are full and soft.

As he strokes my skin, all the nerve endings in my body awaken as if they've been asleep all my life and all they needed was his touch. I arch my neck, my body into him, to feel more of him.

His tongue traces across my lips before sinking into my mouth like I wish the erection prodding my belly will sink into me, too. His other hand moves down my back, feeling me through my clothes. I haven't been touched like this in forever.

Why did I insist on having no sex with him? If this is how he will make me feel each time we make contact, I want everything he has to offer.

I open my mouth for him, welcoming him into my depth, tongues twisting together, his hand to my lower back, my hand gripping his shirt, my nipples aching for touch.

A soft moan escapes my lips as he pushes me against the bar, breaking the kiss. The sheer size of the hardness between his legs is unmistakable as it presses against my belly. His hips press against mine as he leans in for another kiss.

I long for him with a hunger consuming me. A white-hot ball of searing heat blossoms between my legs, radiating outwards in waves. Our embrace grows more intense as we continue to kiss and grind against each other. I pinch his nipple through his shirt, causing him to gasp and bite my lip.

My clothes are suddenly scratchy and uncomfortable. Every piece of fabric that stands between me and his penis fills me with frustration. I long to feel the warmth of his sweaty skin pressed against mine, his hard and hot erection throbbing with desire, his hands caressing my breasts. I long for the solid, dry thrusts to become actual slick, gliding sensations as he moves inside me.

He looks down at me, and the intensity of the lust in his eyes is nearly intimidating.

"Wifey," he says in a husky voice. "I promised no fooling around with other people, and I keep my promises."

My throat ripples as I swallow. "Okay."

"Good. Now smile so we can go back to our party. Unless you want to cause a scandal in sleepy Sapele by simulating sex in front of your guests."

My cheeks heat at his outrageous words and our actions in public. I can't believe we were dry humping each other at our party. But his grin is infectious, as if he doesn't care.

A giggle escapes my lips. "You are a bad boy."

"Oh, you don't know the half of it, Wifey." He steps back, as if reluctant to break contact.

Why do I feel so floaty when he calls me Wifey? It's all for show, right?

The place explodes in whooping and cheering and clapping.

I giggle some more as my sister runs up to me and hugs me.

"That was so hot. God, give me this kind of man, abeg."

I glance at Diaye, and he winks at me.

I'm in so much trouble.

Diaye

Once my engagement to Seki is officially announced, my worry about my career recedes. I make peace with signing a contract with Viva City FC. Playing football trumps everything else. Including my reluctance to get married.

For the most part, I think pretending to be married to Seki won't be bad as long as she keeps to the bargain we made and stays out of my way.

Unless there are other people around, and we have to act like a couple. Which is almost all the time in Iye's house. Grandma insists we must spend time together and go on dates. It's easier to oblige my grandmother than to argue. So Seki and I go on a couple of outings together. To be fair, she is good company when we're not quarrelling.

Spending time with Seki creates an additional problem. A new personal hell for me.

Every time I see her, I'm fighting my arousal for her. She doesn't want to have sex, and I don't want to push it. Hence, I avoid her. Then she calls me a grumpy asshole—I think it's her nickname for me. We argue. Her feistiness arouses me. I fight the urge to hike up her clothes and bury myself inside her against the nearest flat surface. I walk away. The cycle repeats.

So, I'm no closer to liking the idea of marriage than the first time it was mentioned in this house. Yet, I'll go through with it because I have no other choice.

Hence the reason I'm sitting under the pergola with Seki this afternoon as we browse the list of universities offering nursing degrees near Viva City on my tablet. I don't have a residence in London, but I know the area I want to live in when I relocate there.

She is in a white bodycon T-shirt and sky-blue cotton cargo trousers. Her nails are manicured with white tips and embedded with tiny sparkling gems. The long braids at the end of the cornrow are loose around her shoulders.

It's a cool, secluded corner of the back garden. We're in the shade of the pergola roof, surrounded by trellises and shrubs. The sun is still high and behind us. Iye is inside, napping.

Sitting so close to Seki, her perfume invades my nostrils and stirs my craving for her. Our bodies touch as we sit side by side. This bench is a padded loveseat for two. There's no distancing myself. No room for escape.

Seki's eyes gleam as she scrolls through the different websites and she speed-talks through the offerings. Her excitement is palpable. She's like a child in a toy shop.

For a moment, the throbbing in my dick fades as I concentrate on fulfilling her desire to study in the UK. The sounds of her contentment washes over my discomfort. We narrow the search down to three universities within commuting distance from Viva City and she emails them, requesting prospectuses.

"Oga Diaye." Íruoghẹnẹ hurries down the garden path towards us. He's in a T-shirt and jeans, which is his regular attire. Since I hired the extra security, he's undergone some training to improve his personal protection skills.

"What is it?" I lean into the back slats of the wooden bench.

He glances along the side of the house towards the driveway. "Seki has a visitor."

"Me?" She raises her head and glances up from the screen in her hand. "Where?"

"Outside the gates." He tugs his shirt down, clearly uneasy.

"Let them—" she starts.

But I interrupt before she can finish, sitting up. "Who is it?"

Íruoghẹnẹ's throat ripples as he swallows. "It's Mide."

No wonder he is restless. I warned him not to allow Seki's ex into this residence ever again after the man came to see me last week. I was pissed off he dared to come here, and I threatened Íruoghẹnẹ and Mide. It seems the gateman learned his lesson, but Seki's ex hasn't. My anger simmers, but I keep a lid on it as I watch for Seki's response. Does she want to see her ex?

"He's here?" Seki stands, her grip tight on the device in her hands. She seems agitated and I don't like it one bit.

"Yes. Outside the gates," the gateman repeats.

"Seki, go inside the house." I straighten from the bench.

"What?" She blinks up at me, and her brows furrow.

"Do you want to talk to your ex?" I stress the last word, so she remembers his status in her life. My pulse thumps and a headache brews.

"No—"

"Right answer," I cut in. Otherwise, I might have to burn shit down.

"What?" She jerks back.

"You heard me. You are not talking to your ex. Go into the house."

"You can't tell me what to do!"

My pulse thumps. I won't entertain this. Not today. Not ever.

"Oh, I can." My tone hardens. "You are my fiancée, and I say you are never talking to that Mide guy again. Try it and this engagement, the marriage, is over!"

Her breath hitches, her eyes going wide before she scoffs. "You're not serious."

"Deadly. Try me." I nod towards the front entrance where her ex is located, challenging her to take a step in that direction. "And your dream of studying in the UK disappears."

I need the marriage to secure the playing contract. But I have boundaries lined with fucking explosives, which will cause devastation if she crosses them.

Seki talking to her ex is a definite deal-breaker.

She glares at me as the muscles in her jaw tighten. "You are so horrible!"

She chucks the digital tablet on the loveseat and storms off down the garden path, hips swaying, enters the house, and slams the side door.

"Let's go," I say to Íruoghẹnẹ, who just witnessed our public fight post-engagement. He's seen us argue before, about a week ago. The last time Mide came here, who seems to be a common denominator, a trigger for our arguments.

Now, Íruoghẹnẹ avoids eye contact and hurries down the side passage to the paved driveway. I grab the discarded tablet and head in the same direction. The two beefy security men kitted out in black outfits with visible, holstered weapons stand at the security post looking menacing.

I notice the man standing outside the shut metal gates, through the slats in the high barrier. Mide.

Adrenaline surges through my body. Blood flows to my extremities.

The fucker dared to show up here again!

Vibrating with violent rage, I've never felt so fucking territorial. I stare at the handgun strapped to the bodyguard's hip. Shooting someone will bury my career with certainty, and I would never stoop to murder. But I'm tempted to cross the line.

Because I won't tolerate the disrespect from Seki's ex. Fake or not, she is engaged to me now. My fiancée, damn it!

The last time he came here, he dared to ask me for money. Claiming he needed it for his marriage plans to Seki. Did he think I was a mumu, easily tricked like Seki? The way I laughed in his face and sent him away with his tail between his legs. Today, I feel no humour.

What the fuck does he want with her?

He's pacing the length of the pavement and is in a white shirt and black trousers and holding a manila folder as if he's just been to work. He had a disciplinary meeting at the hotel today. I know because I instigated it after the last time he came here.

I told Harrison to do whatever it takes to ensure Mide is no longer working at the hotel. They could sack him outright, but it would attract undue attention to the business. So they are going the legal route and following all the formal processes.

And taking too fucking long because I want this man not just out of Crystal Palace Hotel, but out of Sapele. He can go back to Ibadan for all I care. I want him nowhere he can accidentally bump into Seki.

I walk to a quiet corner away from the gates, pull out my phone, and call Harrison.

"What's up?" he says when he answers.

"That Mide guy is outside Iye's house, causing a nuisance," I say without preamble.

"Seriously?"

"Yes. I want him arrested immediately."

"He's outside Iye's house? He get mind o. Anyway, the bodyguards are there and will stop him from entering the compound."

"Don't you get it?" I lose my composure. "He was harassing Seki on the phone, and she blocked him. Now he shows up here. He's stalking my fiancée and has to be stopped."

Harrison sighs. "You're right. It could escalate. I'll call our regional liaison officer at the police station. They will be there soon."

"Good. Thank you. Talk later." I end the call. One privilege of being wealthy and having royal blood, when you make a request, it's fulfilled.

I intend to keep Mide here until the police arrive. So, I return to the security checkpoint. "Íruoghẹnẹ, open the gate."

"Okay." He rushes over and unlocks the heavy padlock and pulls the squeaking bolt back before tugging both ends of the metal barriers open.

Mide moves towards the gateway, as if they were opened for him. The fool doesn't understand he's walking into a trap.

"Hey, you. What are you doing here?" I demand, chin tilted up, hands clasped in front of me holding the tablet, projecting calm and composure I don't feel.

His heavy-lidded eyes fix on me with a baleful glare. "I came to see Seki."

"Not happening." My jaw hardens. I don't move from my spot in the driveway. Any forward movement will be violent. I'm not about to get physical with him. It's why the body-guards are here.

They take the cue and move in on both sides of Mide as he crosses the threshold, standing behind him.

"But I have to. I need to speak to her. She's my girl-friend." He shrugs, oblivious to the storm brewing under my calm exterior.

"Íruoghẹnẹ, close the gates!" I order, the sound echoing in the courtyard.

The gateman obeys, the heavy iron gates clanging shut with a resounding snap, like a sprung trap.

Mide glances around, noticing the armed men at his rear. He swallows, and sweat beads his forehead. He gives me a strange expression. "Look, I'm not here for trouble."

At least he understands he found trouble. Grim satisfaction passes through me.

"But you came anyway, after I warned you never to return to this house," I say.

His throat bobs as he swallows hard, and he shifts from one foot to the other. "I only came to talk to Seki. I don't know what's going on. She's not replying my messages or returning my calls."

I bark out a laugh, but there's no humour in it. "Of course you don't know what's going on. How could you? You're as innocent as a newborn. It's not like you have a wife and kids and were lying and cheating on them while fucking your way through the female employees at Crystal Palace Hotel."

Iye is right. I'm influenced by my father. It's the reason I could spot Mide's narcissism from the moment I met him. I lived with my father long enough to recognise the signs. Especially the inability to take responsibility for his actions. He would blame everyone else but himself for any problems and never acknowledge the part he plays in his troubles.

Just like Mide is doing.

His hands ball into fists. "How do you know—"

"That's not the right fucking question." My composure shatters as I cut him off, my pent-up rage erupting. "The question you should ask is how you are going to get out of here alive because you picked on the wrong woman!"

I've never threatened anyone like this, certainly not in public. I'm putting a lot on the line, all because of Seki.

"Look at this one." He glances around and sneers. "Is it because you're Diaye Zambo and I was trying to chill with you? Let me tell you. I'm not afraid of you. If you touch me, I will sue you and your generations."

He breaks into a string of another language I can't understand, which I presume is Yoruba.

The bodyguard on his left, Tyson, replies to him rapid-fire in the same language and kicks out in a sweeping motion which sends Mide sprawling onto the paving on his knees. The papers from his manila folder spill and flutter out. He shrinks back as Tyson looms over him, holding the hilt of his shining hunting knife, and says a few more words before turning to me.

"Sir, he was cursing you in Yoruba, and I put him in his place. He will be more compliant," he says. "I told him I will gut him like a fish if he opens his dirty mouth again."

I believe him. These men are retired special forces. They've seen and done things beyond my imagination. They are well-trained, professional, and morally flexible enough to handle Mide on my behalf.

"Thank you, Tyson." I turn back to the subdued Mide. "You know, I thought you were a smart guy when you came here the last time. I warned you not to come back here."

He appears ashy and sweaty as he kneels in front of me. "I'm just stressed out because so many things are going wrong and it's all because of Seki. I told her not to go to my house because I'm not always there. But she went there and met Tinu. Things were not going well between me and Tinu, and I would have divorced her and married Seki. But now Seki is telling stories at work, and they have suspended me and I could lose my job. I just came here to understand why she would tell lies about me."

"You mean like you told her lies?" I seethe.

"It's not the same thing. I didn't tell her I was married. Doesn't mean I lied. And what I did doesn't jeopardise her job. In fact, I got the job for her. Now she wants to make me lose mine. How is that fair?" Mide speaks fast, like he's afraid the bodyguards will attack him for talking.

This man is unbelievable. Listening to him talk, you'll think he's a reasonable human being. But it's all a façade. He still hasn't admitted any wrongdoing. But I'm about to shut him down.

"Seki is not the reason you're going to lose your job. I am." A vein throbs in my temple.

"What? How?" His eyes go wide, darting all over the place.

"Technically, you are the architect of your own doom because you did all the things you're being accused of. However, I am the judge and executioner to ensure you pay for your actions."

"Is this about me dating Seki while married to Tinu?" Mide raises his hands and waves them in a wait-let-me-explain gesture. "You don't understand. I love Seki—"

A terrible calm descends on me along with its darkness. Any iota of human empathy I have vanishes. "You love her, yet you've been fucking every woman who would open their legs for you in Sapele and beyond."

"That's not true." His throat ripples repeatedly as he swallows, and he's sweating profusely.

His similarities in behaviour to my father are stark, and I despise him. For being an unrepentant cheat. For hurting Seki.

"You wouldn't know the truth if it bit you in the arse," I snarl, and he flinches. I take a deep breath and wait for the explosive rage to pass before I step back, slowly and deliberately, so I don't reach down and strangle him. "Do you know how I know about your affairs?"

He opens his mouth, closes it, and shakes his head.

"From the first day I met you, I've had people following you and monitoring your movements. I have photos of you with different women—" I tap the device in my hand, and his eyes widen in shock. A thin smile touches my lips. "—including one Karo Francis who I have been reliably informed is the wife of the head of the local mafia."

"Mogbe!" He rubs a hand over his face. "Diaye, I—"

"Don't fucking say my name. Here's what's going to happen." I pin him with a hard stare. "You will sever all ties with Seki immediately. I don't give a fuck if you think she's the love of your life in that warped mind of yours. She no longer exists to you. You will not see, talk, message, or communicate with her in any way. If you do, I will send the photos of you and Karo Francis to her husband, and he will kill you and hang your head from a lamppost to deter other people from touching his wife."

"Please!" Mide explodes in agitation. "You can't—"

"Interrupt me again, and I will send him those photos right now," I say icily.

He falls silent, his hands fidgeting, his expression panicky.

"The police will arrive any minute now, and they will arrest you. You will spend a few days in the cells, but will eventually make bail. When you get out, you will pack everything and leave Sapele within a week. In fact, you are not permitted to live anywhere in the south-south or southeast regions. Do you understand me?"

After a long silence, he presses his lips into a thin line and jerks out a quick nod.

"I don't hear you!" The continuous sight of him is making me murderous.

"Yes, I understand," he mutters.

"Now, get out of my sight!"

He must sense the impending danger because he gets up in a hurry and picks his papers scattered around the driveway. Meanwhile, a marked police van arrives at the gates, and I indicate for Íruoghẹnẹ to let them in. He goes to open it.

"And Mide?" I say, and he glances at me. "Contact Seki, or violate my rules, and you'll wish you were never born. Consider this your final warning."

• • • •

A WEEK LATER, I GAZE out of the small window of the airplane, watching the sprawling landscape of Lagos lights fade beneath me. The two weeks I spent in Nigeria with Seki and Iye have been nothing short of transformative. As the plane soars higher, a sense of nostalgia washes over me, mingled with the anticipation of returning to my life of playing football.

One thing I was never confused about was my dream of becoming a professional football player.

It was my favourite sport since the very first time I kicked a ball. It was the only thing I ever talked about, and the only thing I want to do, all day, every day.

At the age of six, I was already out there on the local pitches, battling for the ball and battling to be the best.

I was far from the only youngster with those superstar dreams, however. Football is the most popular sport in the United Kingdom where I grew up, and also across the whole, wide world. So, the road to the top was a long and winding one, especially for a boy from Leeds.

Leeds is a city in the northern English county of Yorkshire, famous for its rich industrial heritage. These days, it's famous for its vibrant cultural scene and links to the arts and entertainment.

Our footballing claim to fame comes in the local team, Leeds United FC. It had its heydays back in the 1960s and 70s when it won quite a few major trophies.

Football was an inescapable part of my childhood. There were many kids showing off their skills in the local fields. Also, I had many footballing heroes as a child. Most notable was my father, William Zambo, who had a successful career as a midfielder. He'd been spotted by a scout back in Cameroon and had played for clubs across Europe before ending his playing career in the UK where he settled.

My mother came to the UK from Nigeria as a student and was studying medicine. According to the story she told me, she met my father on a night out with friends. It wasn't exactly love at first sight. She thought my father was arrogant and too sleek. But he was persistent and persuasive. A year after they met, they were married, and she was pregnant with me.

Grandma was there at my birth. She took a sabbatical from her job to spend time with us so Mum could finish her studies and qualify as a medical doctor. This is one more reason I have huge respect for Grandma. She's always been a part of my life.

So although I'm confused about her insistence for me to marry Seki, I indulge her.

Mum used to say, *"You'll never figure it all out."*

Maybe this is one of those things I'll never figure out.

Having parents from different countries was a little weird for me in those days. There was a lot of competitive banter about football in my house.

"Some of the most talented football players in the world are from Nigeria. You've heard about Okocha, Kanu, Taribo West," my mother would tease.

"Yet, you married a Cameroonian footballer. What does that say?" my dad would reply with a smile.

"Nigerians have power, pace, flair and skills. We've won AFCON and even won the Olympic championship in football," my mum said, laughing.

"Cameroon has won the AFCON cup four times. More than Nigeria. We are the only African country to beat Brazil," my father countered.

However, the banter fostered my love for the sport, and I was determined to bring together the best of Nigeria and Cameroon in my playing abilities.

When I arrived at my first training session with the local youth team in Leeds, the coaches asked me the usual question. "What position do you like to play?"

"Striker," I replied without even thinking.

For a seven-year-old, the celebratory high-five after scoring was much more satisfying than the mundane act of preventing goals. A powerful impact, the ball meeting the boot with a satisfying thwack, sending vibrations up the leg. The awesome sight of it flying past the keeper, a blur of motion, and into the net. Best of all was the thunderous roar of the crowd, a symphony of cheers and applause celebrating your incredible achievement.

Is there anything more satisfying?

Shooting, with its explosive power and sudden impact, or tackling, the raw physicality of a brutal collision. Was that even a question worth asking?

Not to young me. I knew which one I preferred.

However, my coaches noticed something about me. My confidence and my size.

I towered over the other boys on the team. My height and strength were undeniable once the game started. I kicked off the first match as a striker, but I didn't remain in the position for long.

I darted and weaved, constantly pursuing opportunities to acquire the ball, my eyes scanning for openings instead of waiting for a pass. With a calm and collected demeanour, I seized control of the game, making calculated moves that threw our opponents off-balance. Overpowering my opponent with my size and strength, I regained possession of the ball, then used my dribbling skills to drive forward, making precise passes to set up my teammates for a score.

My coaches said I looked so comfortable on the ball, and I wasn't shy for a new kid on the team. I was organising everything, telling my teammates where to go and what to do. Already, at the age of seven, they said I was clearly a leader. And I was a defender or midfielder, not an attacker.

The youth team coaches were delighted with their new young signing, and so were the players. Suddenly, the goalkeeper had hardly any saves to make, and the other defenders didn't need to panic anymore. Because, if our opponents got through, I was always there to save the day.

No one got past me. No one.

What I lacked in speed, I made up in strategy. I was superb at reading the game and working out what the striker would do next.

I loved every minute of every match, and I was happy about not being the striker. It meant I got to be more involved in the action—the passing, the tackling, the battling for the ball.

I wore my team jersey with passion and pride. I was playing for a proper team now, with my own special shirt number on the back, just like my heroes. It felt like the first step on my journey to the top.

The academy had links with the professional football club, Bishampton United FC, and then after that? Who knew! Well, I had a plan, of course.

One day, I would play in a Champions League final, and I'd be the captain of the Three Lions, too!

I went ahead and achieved those goals. Bishampton United FC won the Champions League twice while I was with them, and I have captained my national team.

Somehow on this flight back to the UK, I feel like that seven-year-old, excited about the opportunities to restart my professional career.

For once, I have no clue what the future holds for me.

My dream to continue as a professional football player is unwavering. The path to the dream will be challenging, but I'm ready for the next phase of my life.

The time spent in Nigeria gave me a renewed sense of purpose and a deeper understanding of who I am. I feel prepared to face whatever comes my way.

17

Seki

The soft glow of the evening sun fills the room, casting long shadows across the walls. I walk slowly, my fingers trailing along the edge of the dresser, my mind lost in thoughts of Diaye.

He left for Lagos with Chinedu a week ago and subsequently caught his flight from Murtala Muhammed Airport, which landed at London Heathrow. Then he caught a connecting flight to Bishampton where he lives. Or lived. Today, he flew out to Milan where he will play football for the next five months. His former English club, Bishampton United FC, loaned him to the Italian club for five months of the season.

I know all these things because, at Iye's insistence, Diaye sent me his itinerary via email before he left Sapele.

Her exact words were, "Your fiancée needs to know your schedule. Do you know how ridiculous it would be if someone asks Seki about you and she can't speak knowledgeably about your wellbeing or whereabouts? It's not done. So, you must keep in touch. You can't disappear and show up at your convenience. No more."

He gave me the contact details for Mr O, his agent, and for his management team. So, I can reach out to them if I can't reach him. I have the address of his residence in

Bishampton. However, since he'll be living in Italy for the foreseeable future, he will send me his new address when he has it. In the meantime, he will stay in a hotel.

He didn't give me the details for his father or siblings because he's not on good terms with them at the moment. I don't know what that's about. But I'm hoping he will repair his relationship with his paternal family.

I can't imagine not talking to my siblings or my father. We've always been supportive of each other regardless of any disagreements.

This reminds me. The last weekend before his departure, Diaye visited my father to introduce himself as my fiancé. Another action instigated by Iye. She advised us to visit my father together, since Diaye will be away for months, and there's no guarantee he will return to Nigeria before I travel out to live with him.

My sisters were excited about the visit, and if I'm honest, so was I. Everyone was making a fuss. It was the confirmation I was going to marry Diaye Zambo.

Little me from Sapele via Warri will marry superstar footballer, Diaye Zambo. Even though it's a fake marriage and pre-arranged to end at a certain date, it's still beyond my wildest dream. To top it off, I'll travel and get to fulfil my dream of studying abroad. It's an extra topping for an already delicious cake.

My father was a little concerned, considering I'd only recently broken off with Mide. But, he conceded, Diaye seemed to be a much better prospect as my suitor.

To be fair, Diaye was like a different person in his second week in Sapele.

Week one, he was grumpy, reserved, and arrogant. A total pain in the backside.

Week two, he was calm, observant, reserved, still with a large side of cockiness. But he loosened up a bit and laughed more.

Iye insisted I take him out and show him some sights. So, we took a boat trip on the River Ethiope and attended an Isoko festival. I even got him to dance. The memory makes me chuckle now.

Experiencing Diaye's gentler side was a welcome change from his sometimes overbearing presence. He showed me he could also be thoughtful.

Showing up late at night to pick me up from a location he'd never been to before was considerate, although I berated him for not being nicer that night. The breakfast he made for me the next morning was thoughtful. Although Iye instigated it, Diaye could have refused to make it. Taking me out on a shopping trip to cheer me up was another sign that beneath the cool exterior was a beating heart.

And I felt more than his thumping heart when we shared a kiss during our engagement party. A kiss so hot, I've started having wet dreams for the first time in my life, waking up in the throes of orgasm, imagining Diaye inside me. Even now, my skin is tingling with the memories.

I step onto the balcony, and a fresh breeze cools my skin.

Then I remember Diaye sitting in the chair, persuading me to take a bite of the omelette he made for me. Even eating the food with me.

A smile curls my lips again.

His memory haunts every corner of this house, a testament to his absence. The place feels emptier, quieter without him.

I lower my body onto the chair and scroll through the gallery on my phone. There are photos of us—Diaye and me—taken during our various trips around Sapele and surrounding areas.

My fingers freeze on one photo. I have the phone in my outstretched hand, taking a selfie with Diaye next to me. We're surrounded by festival goers. Ours smiles are bright and eyes sparkling. Yet, as I stare into the camera, Diaye is gazing at me. It's like in that moment, surrounded by the sights and sounds of the festival, all he can see is me.

My heart thuds in my chest, and I scroll through the other photographs, trying to find others where he is looking at me. But there aren't any.

I return to the photo and stare at it again. There's a dark vulnerability in Diaye's haunting gaze. It's something I've never seen in him. He is always so composed, so closed-up. The only other time I've seen him burn with passion was when he kissed me at Crystal Palace Hotel. Even then, there wasn't this rawness I captured in my phone camera. Or at least I don't think there was.

I trace Diaye's face with my fingertips, a surge of longing washing over me.

Is there a possibility he feels more for me? I know he likes me enough to want to have sex with me. But...

Why am I even going there? I already decided I'm not getting involved with another man. Mide's betrayal is all the heartache I can take in one lifetime. I'm not willing to subject myself to all of that again.

Talking about Mide.

He's been blowing up my phone, complaining it's my fault he got suspended. I won't let him gaslight me. So, I blocked his number. Then the foolish man had the temerity to show up at Iye's house.

I was sitting under the pergola with Diaye when Mide showed up at the gates. Íruoghẹnẹ didn't let him in. You should have seen the drama. I got agitated, and Diaye ordered me to go inside the house. That I was never talking to Mide. I have no intentions of talking to Mide, but the command from Diaye pissed me off. In the end, I went into the house and stayed with Iye.

I don't even know who Diaye called. Next thing, Police showed up and bundled Mide away in a van. Diaye suggested I should press charges for harassment. He even retained a lawyer for me to file a restraining order against Mide.

I agreed. Mide needed to be stopped. Ignoring him was ineffective. I needed to do something else. So Diaye drove me to the police station, and I made a formal complaint about Mide's harassment and showed evidence of the messages he'd sent to me on my phone.

Then last Saturday, I was called into a meeting with the HR manager when I arrived at work at the hotel. She said they were investigating allegations of sexual harassment against Mide and interviewing all his subordinates. You bet I told her what happened between me and Mide, including the fact I'd filed for stalking and harassment against him with the police. The HR manager documented my statement and told me they would be in touch. Things are not looking good for Mide. He will lose his job.

And he deserves it for what he did to me and other women he was supervising.

Diaye was concerned that when the police releases Mide on bail, he will carry on stalking me, regardless. So, he's retained the security men around Iye and me. Can you imagine I now have a bodyguard who goes everywhere with me? I can use Iye's car when Iye doesn't have any prior appointments. For the past week, I've been going to my work placement in a chauffeured vehicle and with a bodyguard.

Listen. I can't lie. I'm enjoying the perks that come with being engaged to Diaye.

It's made me Miss Popular at the hospital. Someone even questioned why I was still coming to work when I was engaged to a millionaire and going abroad in a few months.

But staying with Iye has taught me to strive for a career. I can't even imagine not working. Not being independent. And my experience with Mide had taught me to be financially independent. You never know when a man will pull the rug from under you, and you'll be left with nothing.

So as long as I'm able to work, I will keep doing so.

Moreover, I love what I do. Going out, interacting with other people, helping others, and saving lives since I'll be graduating as a nurse in a matter of weeks. Why deprive the world of my compassion and skills?

Ah, Diaye's arrogance is rubbing off on me.

I chuckle at the thought.

"Seki."

At the sound of Iye's voice calling my name, I look over the balcony guard rail. Iye is standing on the patio outside her new bedroom on the ground floor.

The builders completed the renovations of the downstairs rooms previously used as guest accommodation. They were converted to bedrooms with ensuite bathrooms and mini walk-in closets for the clothes. They also installed the new furniture Diaye ordered.

Iye wanted to have direct access to the garden. She loves her plants and doesn't want to be locked out from them if her mobility declines. They put a hole in the outside wall and installed a glass patio door, which means she gets a direct view of the garden from her room. Also, they built a raised concrete platform outside the door, which created a sitting area she can use.

She lowers her body into the padded outdoor black metal armchair, a round, intricately designed, cast aluminium table with a parasol next to her. The table seats four. In the corner sits a large square container with a Canna lily which has bright orange blooms and dramatic orange, burgundy, and green foliage. Gold hibiscus sits in another container on the other side with richly-hued flowers that pop against the deep green of the glossy foliage. The outdoor space is so beautiful, I want to keep potted plants on my balcony.

"Iye, I'm up here," I say, attracting her attention with a wave.

She tilts to the side to look up at me. "Come here. I want to talk to you."

"I'm coming." Leaving my room, I hurry downstairs and head for the side door to go outside.

The original idea was for me to move downstairs and stay in the room next to hers. The upstairs would be converted into an apartment for Diaye.

However, once the downstairs refurbishments were completed, Iye informed us she was inviting her relative, Auntie Ebimo, a widow, to come live with her. Auntie Ebimo is sixty years old and retired as a primary school teacher. Instead of moving back to the village, Iye wants her to stay in Sapele as her companion when I travel abroad.

Iye said since I'm getting married to Diaye, the whole of the upstairs is for both of us to stay whenever we visit Sapele.

I'm still flabbergasted she will give me this house. Not that I want her to pass any time soon. I have vague memories of my maternal grandmother. I never met my paternal grandmother. So, living with Iye is a gift I deeply cherish. I can't even describe the attachment I have to her.

So will or no will, I fear losing her. I want her to live forever. I value her wisdom and advice. Although I still don't buy this idea of marrying Diaye, I can see she's doing it from a place of love. I feel honoured she thinks I'm good enough for her only grandchild. That I'm good enough to be her grandchild.

So, I want to make her happy, and marry Diaye, I will.

As long as he doesn't change his mind.

My heart jolts at the idea as I round the corner into the back garden. Although my belly is in knots at being dumped by Diaye after all the announcements, I plaster a smile on my face when Iye turns in my direction.

"There you are." She smiles as I approach. "Come, sit down."

I pull out the chair next to her and settle down. The bowl of pawpaw I placed on the table earlier is empty and so is the mug.

"Did you want more tea?" I ask.

"No. I wanted to find out if you've spoken to Diaye today?"

The mention of Diaye's name always sends my heart tripping. I swallow before I speak. "Not today. You know he called us when he returned to Bishampton."

"And since then, have you spoken?" She stares at me with reproach.

"No. We've been chatting via text messages."

"Every day?"

My cheeks heat. "No. Not every day. He's busy, and so am I. We can't be chatting every day, as if we don't have anything else to do."

Iye side-eyes me. "Is he not your fiancé again?"

"He is, but..." I avert my gaze, frowning as I trail off.

"My dear." She reaches out and covers her hand with mine. "See, eh. Let me tell you something about Diaye. You shouldn't ignore him. If you ignore him, he will ignore you. Trust me, you won't see that boy for another five years."

"What?" My body jerks as I turn to her.

"I'm telling you. You see, he is an only child. He is used to catering for himself. His parents divorced when he was about eight years old. So he spent most of his time with his mother when he wasn't at the football academy. She was the closest person to him. When she died, his world turned upside down. I was devastated. Esosa was my only child. Aghadiaye was here for the funeral. But when he left, he never returned for five years until two weeks ago."

"But why? He should have come to see you." I feel awful for Iye, who must have felt as if she lost both her daughter and grandson when he didn't show up for so long.

"He should have. But you see, he is the definition of the saying 'out of sight is out of mind.' He has a form of ADHD which means he has two gears, hyper-focus or apathy. It's why he's so great at football, because when he's on the pitch, that's all that's in his mind. Esosa was his anchor. When she died, I tried to become his anchor. But the distance didn't work in my favour. Then his father introduced him to Phoebe, and she became his fixation. And after that, he stopped getting in touch with me. If I didn't call him, he wouldn't call me. Mr O kept me up to date about his life. When I found out he was having problems with Phoebe, I spoke to Mr O'Connell about finding a way to send Diaye to Nigeria. That's how he came home when he did."

"Wow." I'm too shocked to form proper words.

"When you came to live with me, I suspected you could be a good match for Diaye. I want a woman who will care about him. Not just one interested in fame and fortune. Seki, you have the right qualities to be his life partner. Don't be intimidated by his wealth or status. Those things mean nothing as long as he is loving you correctly. And he will, if you let him."

This makes me shift in the chair. "You think Diaye could love me?"

"Absolutely. I could see it already in the way he looks at you. You people think I don't notice things. I see it all. You're already in love with each other. You're just too afraid to allow your hearts to direct you because of your past hurts."

18

Seki

Five months later

The bustling energy of Heathrow Airport is a welcome contrast to the long flight from Lagos. As I step onto the glossy tiles of the terminal, I inhale deeply, the air colder and lighter than the tropical familiarity of Nigeria. It's January, and winter over here. Everything around me feels foreign—the swift pace of travellers, the clipped British accents announcing arrivals and departures, and the muted colour palette of the walls and ceilings.

A myriad of emotions swirl within me. Apprehension, excitement, and a quiet hope I can't name. I'm in London for the first time, and Diaye is picking me up. I haven't seen him since the brief trip to Yaoundé to watch him play in an international friendly game between Nigeria and Cameroon. As a Nigerian, I was happy we won the match but concerned for Diaye. He was still waiting to find out if the deal his agent was brokering for him would come to fruition. Thankfully, the January transfer window opened yesterday. So, I'm hopeful Diaye will get to carry on playing the sports he loves.

Clutching the small carry-on bag, I scan the arrivals hall. My gaze darts across strangers' faces, searching for him. Then I see him.

Diaye is leaning casually against a chrome barrier, his tall frame draped in effortless confidence. He is dressed in a tailored charcoal jacket which seems to mirror the verdant hue of his eyes, paired with dark jeans and polished boots. A smile breaks across his face like sunlight piercing through London's cloudy skies. It steadies my wavering heart and melts my away my initial unease.

"Seki," he calls out, his voice rich and low, cutting through the hum of the airport.

I approach him cautiously, my steps measured, as though crossing a threshold into an unknown chapter. When we met in Yaoundé, there was a tension around him which I attributed to the uncertainties in his life. He appeared withdrawn, and everything else going on meant we spent little time together.

"Welcome to London, Wifey," he says warmly, his gaze lingering on my face as if memorising every feature.

I swear, something happens to me when he calls me 'Wifey.' Perhaps because he hasn't used the endearment since he was in Nigeria. The tension eases from my shoulders.

"Thank you," I reply, barely recognising my soft voice as some shyness washes over me. He is my husband, after all. The traditional rites were completed in December.

"Your jacket." He indicates the cream leather coat I'm wearing over the woollen pullover and jeans trousers. "It looks familiar. Where did you get it?"

I brush my hand over the smooth leather. "Iye gave it to me because I didn't have a suitable warm jacket for the UK winter. She said it belonged to your mother. Do you mind?"

Something flickers in his gaze and is gone before I can name it.

"No." He shakes his head. "I don't mind. It looks good on you."

He takes the large luggage from me, the gesture feeling intimate in its simplicity. "The car is this way."

Following him through the terminal towards the car park, I marvel at how different everything feels. The air is crisp, the architecture streamlined, and the cars in the distance all seem tidy and organised compared to the vibrant chaos of Lagos traffic.

Diaye leads me to his car, a sleek black Mercedes gleaming under the overhead lights. The vehicle exudes sophistication, mirroring its owner's impeccable style. He opens the passenger door for me, his movements fluid and precise, before placing my bag in the boot. Once I'm seated, he steps into the driver's seat with a practiced ease.

The car purrs to life as he navigates through the serpentine lanes of the airport's exit and merges onto the main road. London unfolds before me in fragments—lumbering red buses, cyclists weaving through traffic, and rows of terraced houses standing like sentinels of history. I gaze out the window, fascinated as my eyes drink in the unfamiliar cityscape.

"This place is amazing," I say, breaking the comfortable silence.

"London takes some getting used to," Diaye replies. His voice is steady, but there is a softness in his tone, as though he is anchoring me in this new world.

"It's...different," I admit, my words layered with curiosity and wonder.

As we drive further north, the city begins to shift. The streets become narrower, lined with trees swaying in the morning breeze. The houses grow larger, their façades more ornate, hinting at affluence. I notice how the world outside seems to slow down, the urban energy giving way to a quieter elegance.

Diaye glances at me, catching the awe in my expression. "You're going to love it here. It might seem overwhelming at first, but London has a way of growing on you, they say. I'm not a Londoner, but I've lived in big cities. If there's anything you're unsure of, just ask. Okay?"

He's being kind. I meet his gaze and feel a strange comfort in his words, as though he is offering me more than just reassurance about the city. He is offering me a space in his world.

I remember Iye's cautionary words. *"Don't ignore him."*

Against my own misgivings, I took her advice and kept in touch with Diaye regularly. As well as the intermittent text messages, I sent him voice notes once a week, giving him an update on what was happening with me and Iye and asking him about him. He sent no voice notes back. But he would reply with a text message. Once, we did a video chat, but not for long. The connection kept breaking up.

Witnessing his warmth towards me now, it seems my persistence in keeping in touch with him is paying off.

"Okay." I swallow. "Thank you."

"You're welcome," he replies, his eyes on the road.

We arrive at a grand gated Georgian-style house tucked into a leafy street in North London. The car rolls into the driveway, its tyres crunching against gravel. The house stands proud, its white façade glowing under the morning light. It's imposing yet welcoming, its large windows spilling warm, golden light onto the manicured lawn.

Diaye parks and turns off the engine, turning to me. "We're here."

"Is this your house?" I ask, glancing around the place with widened eyes.

"You mean, is this our house?" He grins at me. "Or are you not my Wifey again?"

A smile blossoms on my face. "Are you serious? This is our house? Did you buy it?"

"No. My team found it, and we're renting it. But we could make the owner an offer if you love it so much," he says.

I swallow and nod, my fingers gripping the strap of my purse. This is my first step into the life I always glimpsed only from afar. He takes the luggage out of the boot before coming over to my side. As he opens my door and helps me out, I look up at the towering house, its presence both intimidating and enchanting.

"Come on," he says with a small smile, leading me towards the entrance and dragging my heavy suitcase.

I hesitate, feet frozen to the gravelly driveway. This is it, the start of a new chapter alluded to when I took that first telephone call from Diaye, a stranger wanting to speak to Iye. Six months on, and today, I'm about to walk into a house where I will live with him as husband and wife. Our fates are intertwining, inescapably, and I need to make the most of the opportunities presented to me.

He reaches the large front door and inserts the key into the lock before turning to look at me. "Are you okay?"

"Yes, I'm okay. Just taking it all in." I move my feet and head in his direction.

He opens the door and waves me in. "Welcome home."

The warmth of the interior envelops us as soon as Diaye pushes the door open. It contrasts with the brisk North London chill outside, and I step hesitantly into the vast foyer. My eyes dart from the gleaming oak floorboards to the intricate crown moulding adorning the high ceiling, which seems to stretch towards infinity. The walls are painted in soft taupe, lit by a chandelier resembling a cascade of tiny golden stars. The space is elegant yet inviting, a balance of sophistication and comfort.

Diaye places the suitcase by the staircase and gestures for me to follow him.

"This way," he says, his voice calm, yet filled with a hint of pride. He leads me down a hallway that opens into a large living room.

My breath catches as I take it in. Windows as tall as the room itself reveal a manicured garden outside, its flowers a riot of colour even in this early season. A plush cream sofa sits by the fireplace, its mantel adorned with minimalist art and a single photo frame—its emptiness beckoning for our stories to fill it.

"The fireplace works," Diaye points out casually, lighting up the room with his smile as he brushes his hand across the polished marble. "Perfect for those chilly nights. It's been a lifesaver lately."

From there, we pass the dining room, where a rustic wooden table stands under a pendant light, its surface begging for a hearty dinner or a lazy Sunday breakfast. Then into the kitchen—a modern marvel with glossy black countertops and state-of-the-art appliances. I run my fingers along the cool surface of the island, its texture grounding me in the overwhelming reality unfolding around me.

"Come upstairs," he says, one hand resting on the banister and the other lifting my suitcase. Then he ascends the wide staircase.

I follow, my heart pounding against my chest as each step brings me closer to whatever awaits.

On the landing, he points out the doors. "This one's the guest room, that one's for storage, and this—" He swings open a door at the eastern end of the hallway.

The room is flooded with light spilling in from tall sash windows. The walls are painted a muted sage, calming and serene. A spacious bed dressed in crisp white linens occupies the centre, its headboard an elegant curve of dark wood. Shelves line one side of the room, empty yet promising to hold books, memories, and trinkets. A soft, plush rug sits underfoot, and the faint floral aroma of fresh-cut lilies fills the air.

"This is your bedroom," Diaye says, propping the suitcase against the wall and stepping aside to let me enter. "I hope you like it. There's space for anything you'd want to add."

I stand there, speechless, my fingers grazing the edge of the doorway. My bedroom. In this house. In this new chapter. The possibilities stretch out before me as vast as the London skyline outside the window.

"It's beautiful," I whisper, the words barely audible as I take cautious steps into the room.

Diaye leans against the doorframe, smiling as he watches me absorb the space.

"It's your home now," he says simply.

This single sentence sends waves of emotion rippling through me, grounding me in the reality of what's ahead.

I have to give him kudos. He is keeping to the bargain we made months ago when I said I would not share a bed with him in our pretend marriage.

Yet now, as I stand in this beautiful room, some sadness washes over me as he keeps to his words.

He didn't show me his quarters while he was doing the tour of the house.

"Where is your bedroom?" I ask before I can think better of it, turning to face him.

He points over his shoulder. "At the other end of the hallway."

"So far away," I whisper, feeling as if there is an enormous chasm between us with his room at the other end of the long corridor.

"Any closer, and I might accidentally stumble into your room and fuck you. We can't have that, remember?"

My heart pounds, an erratic drum against my ribs. I'm at a loss for words; I don't know what to say to him. The thought of having sex with him and then losing him terrifies me. It would devastate me. I can't give my body to him without giving my heart to him.

Yet, I'm afraid I will lose him because I'm not having sex with him.

It's a Catch 22 nightmare I don't know how to wake from.

"I'll leave you to settle in. If you need me, I'll be downstairs." He swivels and walks away, his footsteps clipped.

I slump on the edge of the bed, clutching my midriff.

19

Diaye

The kitchen is quiet, its air heavy with the scent of brewed coffee. The low winter sun breaks through the cloudy skies beaming in through the window. I lean against the counter, my hands resting on its cool surface as my thoughts swirl like the steam rising from the forgotten mug in front of me. The faint hum of the refrigerator is the only sound, a muted rhythm which matches the turmoil in my mind.

Seki's presence has already transformed the house in ways I didn't anticipate. It's as if her energy, subtle and captivating, fills every corner of the space she hasn't even explored yet. Her laughter, hesitant and tender, from the car ride home plays on repeat in my memory, mingling with her soft expressions, which seemed to speak volumes about the stories she carried.

I was up before sunrise so I could drive out to the airport and be there when the flight landed. As I waited for her to walk out through Arrivals, I was filled with the same anticipation I felt before stepping onto the pitch for an important match—a blend of nerves and excitement I couldn't quite shake.

Now, she is upstairs, settling into her bedroom, her presence impossible to ignore even from a floor away. It isn't just the reunion. It's the weight of her being here, a reminder of how much I'm beginning to value her, perhaps more than I'm ready to admit.

I remember the way she looked at me when we first locked eyes at Arrivals, the brief flicker of surprise in her expression, followed by a smile that seemed to warm even the frosty January air.

As she approached me, the sight of her took my breath away. She was dressed simply in denim trousers, a mustard-yellow woollen jumper, and stylish trainers. Yet, the cream leather coat seemed to envelop her in an air of quiet elegance.

I recognised the jacket. It belonged to my late mother, a woman whose presence still lingers in my memories in ways both comforting and bittersweet. Seeing Seki in it was like watching a page from my past turn into something new, something alive.

The coat fit her perfectly, as if it was always meant for her, even though I'd never imagined anyone else wearing it. There was a strange, almost surreal beauty in the moment, a blending of past and present that caused my chest to tighten. Seki carried it with a grace reminding me of my mother's poise, but intertwined with her own charm, as though she were breathing new life into the garment while honouring its history.

Thinking about it, an unexpected wave of emotion rises within me—a mixture of pride, vulnerability, and a sense of connection I didn't anticipate. It's as if my mother's coat is a bridge between two parts of my life, stitching together threads of family, loss, and the growing importance of Seki's presence in my world. She looked radiant, yet the coat's significance made the moment feel intimate, almost sacred—like an unspoken promise I couldn't put into words.

My gaze drifts towards the window, where the sunbeam outside presses against the glass. January is finally here—the transfer window. The words from my football club manager echoes in my mind, sharp and unrelenting, like the sting of a ball hitting bare skin on a crisp winter morning.

The crux of it, they want to get rid of me. For the first part of the season, they loaned me to another club. My stint in Italy was stressful. Off the pitch, I had to deal with headlines and stories like:

"Zambo has joined Internazionale on loan until the mid-season transfer window following a bust-up with Bishampton manager. It remains to be seen if he wants to go back to Bishampton where club bosses are keen to offload him in January."

However, on the pitch, I tried to block out everything else and prove I was still one of the best defenders who ever played the beautiful game. Thankfully, once my presence in the Italian team started making an impact, I got headlines like:

"The Bishampton centre back has impressed since joining Internazionale on loan."

"Zambo plays a crucial role in Internazionale ten-match no loss streak."

There were headlines about the possibility of me staying on at the Italian club.

But my heart wasn't there. In any case, I'd made plans—we'd made plans—for Seki to move to England to study. The idea is for us to fulfil my grandmother's wish for us to live together as husband and wife. It won't work if we're living in two different countries, a thousand kilometres apart.

Hence the reason I got my team to find this house for us. I didn't want to move back to Bishampton or Leeds. Too much toxic energy in both locations from my old club and family.

Technically, Bishampton is still my employer. But since I'm not on the team sheet, I don't have to play for them. I requested some personal time for Internazionale to release me early.

My old club wants to sell me. I'm no stranger to the politics of football, the way players are treated as commodities, their value measured in goals scored and contracts signed. Yet, this feels different. This isn't just about moving to another club—it's about leaving behind the familiarity of teammates who have become family, the roar of fans who have chanted my name with fervour, the city that became my second home.

Despite everything, I feel torn. On one hand, there is the allure of new opportunities, the chance to prove my worth in a different club, perhaps even on a grander stage. But on the other hand, there's loyalty—a deep-rooted connection to everything that has shaped me as a player and as a person. The club's decision to sell me feels like a betrayal, yet I also understood the logic behind it. I'm caught in the crossfire of ambition and sentiment, a battle which leaves me confused.

"Learn to embrace confusion."

Iye's words play on my mind, making me smile. I pick up the mug of coffee, the warmth seeping into my palms as I hold it close to my chest. Seki's presence and the transfer drama seem to intertwine in my thoughts, pulling at me in different directions. She is a reminder of life outside football, of relationships that matter beyond the confines of a contract. Somehow, her arrival forces me to confront not just my career choices but also my identity—who I am when I'm not wearing a jersey, who I am to her?

Taking a sip, I lean against the counter once more, my focus shifting to the faint sound of footsteps upstairs. It's Seki, moving around, perhaps adjusting to the unfamiliarity of the bedroom.

I feel a pang of guilt for not staying with her longer after the airport, for retreating into my own thoughts. But I need this moment—to think, to process. Tomorrow will bring more clarity, maybe even answers to the questions weighing on me today. For now, I let the warmth of the coffee and the complexity of my emotions settle around me like a blanket while the world outside remains shrouded in January's icy grip.

The soft creak of the stairs pulls me from my reverie. I turn towards the sound, watching Seki appear at the doorway. She's taken the coat off. Covering her braided hair is a grey knitted beanie hat. An oversized beige cardigan is draped over her like a shield against the lingering chill of morning. On her feet are pink socks. The only skin visible is her face.

Damn, she looks cute in a chaotic way. I've never seen anything like it. The muscles on my face twitch as I suppress the laughter threatening to burst out. I don't want her to feel awkward or like I'm laughing at her.

But she is chaos personified right now, and I hate chaos.

Yet, warmth spreads in my chest. She looks kind of cute and endearing.

Lifting the coffee mug cradled in my hands to cover the smile creeping onto my face, I ask in a warm, tentative tone, "Are you okay?"

Seki's lips purse, her eyes scanning the room before settling on me. "No. Not really. I'm cold."

She stands at the threshold and tucks her hands into her sleeves, wrapping it around herself as if she is uncertain and uncomfortable.

My skin itches with unease. I should have realised she would be cold and increased the temperature.

"I'm sorry. That's my fault." I set the mug on the counter. "Come, let me show you how to adjust the thermostat so you can have the temperature how you want it."

"Okay." She comes closer.

I point at the small digital device mounted on the wall and show her how to adjust the temperature by pressing the buttons on the touchscreen. I get her to try it out and set it to the level she wants. She seems to get the hang of it.

Gesturing towards the stove, I ask, "Hungry? I can make you an omelette."

Her smile lingers, a spark of amusement lighting her features. "Is it the only thing you know how to cook?"

"At this time of the morning, yes," I tease, moving towards the refrigerator. "But I can cook a mean jollof. Better than your Naija jollof."

"Blasphemy!" Seki chuckles softly, stepping fully into the kitchen and pulling out a stool at the centre island.

The rhythmic clink of plates and the soft sound of eggs cracking fills the space as I begin my task.

"So," I say in a calm voice, my curiosity getting the better of me. "Iye. How is she?"

I pause and turn my head towards her as an image of Grandma fills my mind.

Seki's expression softens. "I just spoke to her briefly. She is happy I arrived well. She and Auntie Ebimo are well."

"Good. I'm glad they are doing well." I grin and shake my head. "You know my grandma is an amazing woman. The things that woman has done."

"I know, right?? She is ... I don't even know the right adjectives. She is ... Iye. Strong, stubborn, full of wisdom you didn't ask for but desperately need. She's been so excited about me coming here, about our marriage. It's like she's running out of patience with us."

I laugh. "Tell me about it. She was on Mr O's neck to make sure the paperwork was sorted out with your university admission and visa, so you could be here as soon as possible."

Seki giggles. "Anyone would think she was the one going abroad."

"Or getting married," I chime in. Then, after a pause, I add. "I remember the way she stared at me one day while I was in Sapele and said, 'Aghadiaye, this one will keep you on your toes.' How did she know so much about us?"

I turn back to the stove, the edges of the omelette curling into a perfect golden hue.

"Iye has always known everything," Seki says. "She's got this way of reading people, of knowing what they need even before they say it. She told me once that life is like a river—it twists and turns, but it never stops flowing."

I nod, flipping the omelette onto a plate before turning to place it in front of Seki. My gaze wanders as memories surface.

"Life in Sapele had its own rhythm, didn't it? The mornings with her on the veranda, the afternoons with the kids playing soccer in the dusty fields... It felt simple yet full."

Seki picks up her fork, her movements slow as if savouring not just the food but the moment itself. "The place stays with you. Even here, in this house, I feel like I'm carrying pieces of Sapele with me—the smell of the rain on red earth, the sound of Iye's voice comforting or cautioning me."

"Maybe that's why I'm so torn about everything—the clubs, the transfers. I'm trying to figure out where I truly belong." I lean against the counter, watching her take a bite and nod with approval at my culinary efforts.

"Oh," she says. "Don't you want to sign for the London club? What is it called? Viva City?"

"It's not that I don't want to sign for them. It's just that I have a niggle of uncertainty. Well, I had until you arrived this morning. Suddenly, your presence gives me clarity. I know we arranged to be married for five years, and you're only here because you want to study. I don't want to change that for you. But I know this—whatever comes next in terms of my footballing career, I want you to be part of it. I realise why I was uncertain, and it's because I lost the feeling of being grounded. Of being settled. But, Seki, seeing you here, in this house, I know you could be the one who settles me, the anchor grounding me when the world around me is turbulent."

Her eyes soften, a quiet understanding passing between us. "Are you sure about this?"

"Yes—"

The buzzing phone on the counter interrupts me. I glance at the screen, and my mood changes, my body freezing. Angry, I turn away from it.

"Aren't you going to answer it?" Seki asks.

"It's my dad," I say ominously, as if that answers the question in her eyes.

"Your dad? Then answer it," she pushes, and my anger spikes.

She has no idea what she's asking. This will open the viper's nest into our faces.

"You answer it!" I snap, walking away from the kitchen down the corridor into the living room. I turn on the TV and scroll mindlessly through the channels, trying to find something to distract me from thinking about my father.

Footsteps announce Seki's arrival in the living room.

"I spoke to your dad. He's coming over," she says tentatively.

"What the fuck have you done?" I turn and glare at her.

I push past her, pacing the room like a caged animal. "You don't get it. You've just invited chaos into my life. Into your life. Into everything."

Her eyes widen, but she doesn't back down. "Maybe it's time to face him. Whatever's between you two, running will not fix it. You know that just as well as I do."

I stop mid-stride, my jaw tightening as her words sink in. "You think this is some storybook reconciliation waiting to happen? It's not. People like him don't change. They don't even try."

Seki crosses her arms, her gaze steady and unwavering. "People can surprise you. Maybe he's trying now."

I laugh without humour, shaking my head. "Trying? Please. The only thing he's ever tried is tearing me apart."

She's lived a sheltered life and will never understand. Maybe having her here is not such a good idea, after all.

20

Seki

I'm shocked at Diaye's outburst.

One minute, we're having a meaningful conversation about Iye. The chat was easy and seemed to get us over the initial awkwardness of being alone with each other.

Then he mentioned something about needing me as an anchor to ground him. Iye mentioned the same thing months ago when we spoke about not ignoring Diaye.

I wanted to ask him if he was sure I was the right person. It felt good that he would consider me as someone to help him settle.

But I'm not sure if I can be this person. Actually, the idea scares me when all I want to do is face my studies and maybe have a little fun along the way.

The past few months, I've been reassessing what I want at this stage of my life. Do I want to be tied to anyone at twenty-five?

So, I was glad when the phone rang. It was the distraction I needed from all the seriousness.

Of course, Diaye not wanting to talk to his father only spiked my curiosity.

I want to understand the dynamic within his family before getting myself deeply involved with him.

When he tells me to answer the phone, I reach for the device on the central island counter as he storms out of the kitchen.

"Hello," I say.

"Who is this? Put Diaye on the phone," a deep voice speaks in a French-English accent. Noise in the background suggests someone is talking to him and he tells the person, "There's a girl on his phone. She sounds African."

Something about the way he says 'African' makes my spine stiffen. Maybe I'm reading too much into it.

"This is Seki. I'm Diaye's wife."

"You, what!" He laughs into the phone. "I'm Diaye's father. Stop messing around. I would know if my son got wedded."

"We're not messing around. Diaye and I are married. He's not here right now, but I can tell him you called."

"What game is this boy playing?" the man mutters. "Tell Diaye I'm in London and on the way to see him."

He ends the call.

Looking at Diaye now pacing the living room, I can understand partly why he doesn't want to talk to his father. The man is condescending.

Diaye looks agitated.

"Calm down," I say. "He's your father. He can't be that bad."

"You have no bloody clue what he's like," he bites out. "He'll come here, and you'll see for yourself. I have the bloody mind to go out and leave you here with him, so you'll learn the hard way."

That sounds sinister, and a chill travels down my spine. My eyes widen as my heart skips a beat. I panic. "What do you mean? Are you going to leave me here alone with him?"

"Of course not. As much as I'm angry with you, I will never degrade you like that. But I'm telling you now, this is the last time you will meddle in my affairs. In fact, for the foreseeable future, keep out of my way, because I obviously can't trust you to mind your business."

This pisses me off.

"Mind my business? You are my husband!"

"Your husband. Ha. You're having a laugh. You only married me, so you can come to England. If you are my wife, why are you in a different bed—"

The sound of a buzzer cuts him off. He stomps into the hallway. Angry, I follow him.

"Who is it?" he says into the speaker on the wall.

"It's your dad. Open the gates."

He presses a button on the wall.

"Shit," I mutter. "I'm going upstairs."

"No, you don't. You don't invite the devil to my house and leave me alone to handle him." He stalks to the front door.

"Okay," I speak hesitantly. Nervous energy courses through me, and my body is trembling. I'm hot all over and sweating.

Diaye opens the front door, letting in cold air, which makes me shiver. He stands by the threshold, waiting. I hear the rumble of tyres against gravel.

This is not how I want to meet my father-in-law. Not on my first day in the country when I haven't got the lay of the land.

How do I even look? I dressed for functionality to keep warm. But now the heating is up, I'm hot. Pulling off the oversized cardigan, I roll it up and walk back into the kitchen, placing it on the stool. My half-eaten omelette is still on the plate on the counter. I pull the beanie hat off and tidy up my hair.

The sound of conversation filters into the house, and I walk back into the hallway, bracing myself against the cold draught coming in from the open door.

Diaye walks into the house as a shadowy figure looms in the threshold.

"What is this I hear about you having a wife?"

A silver-haired black man who I assume is Mr Zambo Senior steps inside with an air of authority, his imposing frame filling the narrow hallway. He is well-dressed in light-blue button-down shirt and cashmere vest and navy woollen blazer over tan chinos and polished brown loafers. He is good-looking for a middle-aged man and still physically fit from the way his body fills out his clothes.

"Dad, this is Seki, my wife." Diaye side-waves with his hand.

I approach them and curtsey. "Good morning, Dad."

"Morning," he grunts. His sharp, calculating eyes sweep the space, as if seeking flaws, judgments already forming behind his furrowed brow. The faint scent of cologne and cigars clings to him, mingling with an aura of disdain which seems to darken the room. "You're the one I spoke to on the phone."

"Yes, I am. It's good to meet you, sir," I babble, filled with nerves. The man is almost as tall as his son, yet twice as imposing.

Mr Zambo nods and walks past me. "This looks like a nice house."

"Is this her?"

Someone else steps into the house. He is biracial, younger than Diaye and dressed in brown chinos, a check shirt, and leather jacket with leather boots.

Diaye shuts the door. "Seki, this is my brother, Liam."

Brother? They don't look alike.

"Nice to meet you, Liam," I say with a smile.

Grinning, he just stares at me as if I'm a curious object in a museum.

"In here." Diaye points at the living room.

Mr Zambo leads the way, followed by Liam.

I glance at Diaye, who walks stiffly past me into the living room, but he doesn't look at me. His body is tense, and I can't blame him. These people brought destructive energy, and I can feel it.

Sighing, I follow them inside the living room.

"The house is nice, but it needs a proper lady's touch," Mr Zambo says casually as he settles into a cream leather sofa.

My back stiffens. Was Diaye's father implying I'm not a proper lady? Sure, the place was a little too minimalistic for my liking and needed some colour. But Diaye has only been in here a few days, and I only arrived today. Maybe Mr Zambo meant nothing by what he said.

I keep the smile on my face and offer, "Can I get drinks for you?" like I was raised to be courteous.

"Freshly brewed black coffee would be nice," Mr Zambo says.

"Oh." I shift uncomfortably. I saw a complicated coffee machine in the kitchen. "I don't know how to use the coffee machine yet."

Liam laughs, covering his face.

Diaye glares at his brother, and Liam covers his mouth with his hand, looking away as he sits down.

My cheeks heat, and I want to hide away somewhere. What kind of wahala just walked through the door?

"Dad, I'll get you the coffee," Diaye comes to the rescue.

"No. Don't worry about the coffee. Just get me a glass of water," Mr Zambo says.

"Okay," I reply. "Liam, do you want a drink?"

He shakes his head and fiddles with his phone.

I walk out of the living room but pause in the hallway when I hear Mr Zambo speak.

"Where on earth did you find this girl? Some village in Nigeria?"

"Dad, this girl is my wife," Diaye says in a harsh whisper, as if he doesn't want me to hear it. "And no, I didn't find her in a village. She lived in Sapele with Grandma."

My heart warms that he is defending me, even though he's still angry at me for answering his father's phone call.

I don't hear Mr Zambo's response as I hurry into the kitchen. But somehow, I trust Diaye to stand up for me. I find a tall clear glass from the cupboard and fill it with cold water from the tap. In Sapele, we have to boil, or filter tap water.

When I return to the living room, the men aren't talking, as if they fell silent because of my presence. I place the glass of water on top of the glass coffee table.

"Thank you." Mr Zambo picks it up and takes a sip and then his brows furrow. "Is this tap water?"

"Yes. Is there a problem?" I glance at Diaye, feeling confused. Doesn't the man drink tap water like everyone else?

"I don't drink tap water." He places the glass on the table.

"As in, never?" I retort at the ridiculousness, unable to help myself.

Diaye smiles and meets my gaze for the first time since his father arrived. We share a moment which makes my heart skip a beat and a smile curl my lips.

"Watch your mouth, girl." His father's sharp voice breaks the spell.

"I'm sorry, Dad." I shouldn't have retorted the way I did.

"I'm not your dad," his voice rings with disapproval.

"Dad, she's trying to be nice," Diaye says.

"If she wants to be nice, she can go to the kitchen and cook something." He waves his hand in the air. "Fufu, jollof—"

"Stop it!" Diaye snaps. "Seki is not my cook. She is my wife."

"Your mother used to cook when we had guests," his father replies.

Diaye's entire body freezes.

"Seki is not my mother." His voice is cold. "And I'm not you."

"You're telling me? Your mother was a looker, smart as hell, too."

"If you came here to insult Seki..." Diaye stands.

"No. I have better things to do." His father raises his palms in an 'it's your funeral' gesture. "Actually, we're in London because Duke's Park Rangers signed your brother to play for them in the January transfer."

Diaye swallows and nods. "Liam, congratulations."

"Thanks, bro," Liam says, grinning.

"It must feel good to be finally playing in a senior team."

"It is. Dad said there is a strong chance Duke's Park Rangers will be promoted to the Premier League in the new season."

"Yes. I'm very proud of him. I worked hard to secure this deal for him. Junior listened to me, and it all worked out," their dad chimes in.

"That's great." Diaye rubs his palm over his face.

"If you had listened to me, you would have had a great contract," his father taunts. "There was a time you listened to me. You can still turn things around, instead of wasting your talent and life. Are you planning to return to Bishampton soon?"

The man sounds domineering and controlling.

"No," Diaye replies in a clipped tone.

"I can still sort something out for you and get you a great deal if you choose to stay in London. Would be great if two of my sons play for big London clubs."

"No need. Mr O'Connell is handling it." Diaye's tone is flippant.

"Diaye," his father says, his voice a low rumble that reverberates like distant thunder, carrying both disappointment and restrained anger. "I see you've grown comfortable in your defiance."

Diaye stiffens but does not reply. His father's presence alone is enough to reignite the tension in the house like dry wood catching flame. Mr Zambo's gaze lands on me next, a piercing glare that feels like it could strip me bare. I take a step back, but his focus doesn't waver.

"You move away from home, leave your family and your club. Then you supposedly marry this woman," he sneers, his lips curling into a smirk dripping with malice. "I suppose it was some kind of traditional wedding. But I have news for you, jeune fille. Traditional weddings don't count."

"You have no right to speak to Seki like that. Traditional marriages are legal in Nigeria. We have the paperwork to prove it," Diaye snaps, his voice firm but layered with unease.

A dark chuckle rumbles in Mr Zambo's chest, a chilling sound lacking any warmth, more like a growl than a laugh. "Exactly. In Nigeria. You are now in England, and she has no legal rights here."

Is it true? Is our marriage not valid here? Bile rises in my throat, and I fight panic. Why am I panicking? I don't want to be married, right? But if we are not legally married, then Diaye can marry anyone else, including his ex.

"Don't talk to her like that in my house!" Diaye's eyes are as cold as steel, his muscles tighten as his hands clench into fists. I've never heard him sound like this. Not even months ago, when he was angry at Mide's presence at Iye's house.

He's defending me without question. Iye was right. Diaye is protective and will go into battle for me. Does this mean he's in love with—

"Your house?" His father's booming voice destroys my train of thought. "For how long, if you don't have a footballing career. Have you forgotten that I made you what you are today? Spare me your delusions of independence. And as for her..." He turns his gaze back to me, his contempt palpable. "I don't see loyalty or strength. I see a mistake."

Every word is a dagger, sharp and deliberate. My hands tremble, but I ball them into fists at my sides, refusing to show weakness. I open my mouth to respond, but Diaye steps in front of me, shielding me from his father's venomous words.

"You came here uninvited," he says, his tone hardening with a low growl. "It's time for you to leave."

Mr Zambo smirks again, his eyes narrowing. "Leave? She's the one who's going to leave. You know she's only using you to get her papers and then she won't need you anymore once she sucks you dry. Then you will remember where you come from and that your choices have consequences. Diaye, you don't get to run from your family legacy."

"Whatever. Just go!" Diaye orders, pointing at the door.

His father shakes his head as he rises to his feet. "Come on, Liam."

He stomps out and opens the front door.

Liam rises from the sofa and heads for the door. He raises his phone in my direction.

Did he just take a photo of me?

"What are you doing?" I frown.

"Nothing." He chuckles in that weird way. "See you around, bro."

He runs out of the open front door.

Diaye slams the front door and turns to me. "Are you happy now that you've met my father?"

"No. I'm not happy," I retort. "I'm sorry to say this, but your father is vile."

He returns to the living room, and I follow him. "Now you've learnt your lesson. Next time he calls, you'll leave the phone well alone."

I open my mouth to reply and shut it. He's right. I won't be in a hurry to speak to Mr Zambo again. But the thing about the marriage still bothers me.

He opens a drawer under the table and takes out black, over-ear headphones. Then he grabs a handheld games controller, and the screen on the TV changes to a selection screen for a computer game I don't know. Is he going to play games now? After everything that just happened? He can't just avoid the issues. He is withdrawing into himself, and I can't let him.

"Diaye, what about what your father said about our marriage not being legal?" I query.

"What does it matter?"? he says dismissively, annoying me.

"What do you mean, what does it matter?"

"Exactly what I said. At the end of the day, I'm paying you to be my wife. After five years, you're going to leave. You know the way I feel right now? I don't care if you stay five years or five hours. So, if you want to leave, the front door is right there."

He turns, a strange glint in his eyes, and jabs a finger towards the imposing entrance hall. His body language screams of his hurt—his slumped posture, the way his head hung low.

My chest feels constricted, as if a boulder sits upon it, and I struggle to breathe.

"You don't mean that."

"I mean it. My peace of mind is important to me. Yet, today, you decided to smash through it with a hammer. Because in your opinion, I must talk to my father, whether I like it or not."

"I didn't know he was like that."

"You didn't care as long as you got your way. Because in your world, it's all butterflies and roses. What you witnessed was my world, and the people in it are vile. So please just go away. I need to protect my mental health."

He tries to put the headphones on, but I stand in front of him. "But you can talk to me."

He tilts his head. "Talk to you as what? You're not my therapist or my anchor. You're not even my lover. You're just a woman I'm paying to pretend to be my wife. I don't have to talk to you."

His words cut deep. But I know he's hurt and I'm partly to blame.

He puts on the headset and starts playing the game, ignoring me.

I can't leave him alone. I feel guilty, responsible for his current state of mind.

Don't ignore him. Iye's words replay in my mind along with a plan.

Moving, I walk around the coffee table and sit on it in front of Diaye, blocking some of his view of the large flatscreen TV.

"What are you doing?" he asks, irritated, lifting one end of the headset.

"Iye sent me," I say, watching for his reaction.

It's true. Iye sent me to him.

"What?" He puts the controller down on the table, and I have his attention.

"Iye sent me to be your friend and a shoulder to cry on," I say, repeating the words he told me the morning he came to my bedroom after I found out Mide was married.

He's not heartbroken. But he's distressed. He needs a friend, if nothing else.

"Grandma sent you to be my friend?" He huffs, shaking his head with a small smile.

I take the victory because seeing a smile on him seems like a prize. "Yes."

"But you know I fuck my friends."

He meets my gaze with an intensity that takes my breath away.

"I know," I say in a breathy voice. My pulse accelerates, and heat rushes all over me.

"You know. What does that mean?" He takes the head-phones off and places them beside me on the table. Then he shifts forward so his thighs graze mine.

A wave of tingling sensations washes over me. Accompanied by a surge of desire and eager anticipation, my senses heighten.

Maybe I'm not ready for the permanency of marriage. It's been six months since I met Diaye and broke up with Mide. I'm well over my ex and ready to move on to the next stage of my life. But I could use a friend, and I miss the intimacy of having a lover. I'm not saying I'm ready for the full implications of being married. But now that I'm in London with Diaye, we could grow into each other. I'm ready to take the first step. Friend—lover—wife—anchor.

"It means I want to be your friend." I swallow the lump in my throat. "A friend that you fuck."

Eyes bright and twinkling with what I could only describe as lust, he cups his hand around my neck, grazing my chin with his thumb. "I'm going to kiss you."

21

Seki

"Yes," I whisper and lean into him, anticipation skittering over my skin.

It's all the consent he needs as he presses his lips to mine. The kiss is light, a mere touch of lips, but the warmth and electricity it sparks mirrors the intensity of a deep, lingering kiss.

The searing sparks ignite my skin, and a fiery heat blooms in my stomach, like a furnace kindling. I shudder, my pulse a frantic tattoo against my skin, the sound so loud, it fills my ears and blocks out everything else. The coolness of Diaye's lips contrasts with the intense, fiery taste of spice and the deep, decadent sweetness of molten chocolate cake. My longing is to enclose him in my arms and consume him entirely, absorbing every essence of him.

Diaye remains still, the ragged rhythm of his breathing a harsh counterpoint to the soft brush of my fingers against his skin. I press a firmer hand against his chest, feeling the rapid beat of his heart. Run my tongue along the seam of his lips, tasting the faint salt of his skin.

A gasp escapes me as Diaye yanks me towards him, deepening the kiss with a ferocity that steals my breath. His hand, rough and calloused, fists my braids, tugging sharply, forcing my back to arch as his tongue plunders my mouth, hot and demanding.

"You know this is not one of those romantic novels you read. This is real life," he growls, a raw, animalistic possessiveness in his tone.

His grip tightens, making my eyes water. With a forceful spin, he lifts me off the table onto the sofa, the padded arm digging into my back. His hands hoist my legs, wrapping them around his waist. His thick erection presses against my core, the head pulsing with a hot, insistent rhythm as I grind against him, desperate for the friction and the exquisite pressure.

"Wifey, end this now. Tell me to stop," he murmurs.

"Stop? Why?"

My voice is unrecognisable and breathy, a fragile sound barely audible above the whoosh of blood in my ears. The way he touches me is electrifying, and I don't want him to stop. I long for him, in my veins, in my body like a life-saving drug.

The anticipation is almost unbearable as I inch my hand beneath his shirt, the subtle texture of his skin a delightful contrast to the hard, corded strength of his muscles. Every nerve ending screams with need. I'm not even sure his father and brother have left the property because I didn't hear Diaye open the gates for them. They could walk back in and find us.

The potential interruption heightens my arousal to a fever pitch, a delicious illicit tension coiling in my gut. Just like the night at our engagement party being watched by the crowd as he kissed me. The air crackles with unspoken desires, making it feel far more than a simple kiss.

Diaye lets out a groan, the sound thick with desire. His mouth claims mine once more, this time a searing kiss, which ignites a fire within. A ravenous hunger. He invades my senses with a ruthless possessiveness, his touch a brand of fire on my skin, and I surrender without a fight, my body trembling under his heat.

My fingers hover over his belt buckle, about to undo it. He yanks himself away from the sofa, sending me sprawling and leaving me breathless from the unexpected break in our intimacy. A throbbing ache radiates from my core, my nipples taut, and a feather-light breeze sends shivers down my skin. The silence is heavy, filled only with our panting breaths. The hazy fog of overwhelming sensation clears, revealing Diaye's intense gaze burning into me.

"Shit." He scrubs a hand over his head in agitated motion. The scowl twists his features into a mask of agony.

I reach for him. "Diaye—"

"No." He shoots off the sofa. "Shit. I can't believe I'm about to say this, but we can't fuck."

Heat scorches my cheeks. "Is this because of your father—"

"No. It's not about him." He rubs his fingertips against his temples and exhales a slow, controlled breath.

"Then what is it?"

The want in his gaze is undeniable. He wants me, and I can feel the heat of his longing. Not to mention the enormous bulge straining against his trousers.

"I just don't think it's a good idea for us to fuck."

"What?" He fucks other women friends, but he doesn't want to fuck me? Does he think I'm not good enough? "But you wanted to fuck me before, in Sapele."

"That was before we became friends. I don't want to screw up our friendship. Grandma will kill me if she thinks I mess you around."

"But she's the one who wants us to get married."

"As we have already established, you don't want to be my wife. Sex will complicate things between us. Let's keep it simple. We play it up in front of other people. But in private, we're just friends."

The mortification is so intense, I wish for the ground to swallow me up. Uncertainty gnaws at me. Is it worse for Diaye to not kiss me at all? Or for him to kiss me so intensely and then utter those hurtful words, leaving a bitter taste in my mouth?

I can argue with him about the merits of taking the kiss further. Still, a wave of weariness washes over me, silencing my voice. Summoning every ounce of bravery, I finally agreed to have sex with him, a monumental effort, and this is what I get. The sting of rejection is sharp.

"Okay," I concede, straightening my clothes as I rise from the sofa, unable to look him in the eyes. My face burns hot, as if my skin is on fire. "We'll keep it simple. Just friends pretending to be married."

"Exactly." His voice lacks the expected enthusiasm, sounding flat and unconvinced.

I grab the glass of water his father left on the coffee table and walk towards the door.

"Seki, this is for the best," he declares, each word a lead weight, pinning me to the spot, blocking my escape.

"For whom?" Though I won't meet his eyes, the persistent weight of his gaze feels heavy on my back.

"For you."

A hush settles over me as I walk to the kitchen. How can I convince this stubborn man that I can decide what's best for me?

22

Diaye

Two weeks after Seki arrived in London and the start of us living together as a fake married couple, we've settled into a routine.

I'm still waiting to confirm my new playing contract with Viva City FC. The Panthers want to sign me, but my old club bosses are dragging their feet. Mr O says my old club manager is being spiteful because I want to leave the club and is using delaying tactics.

Technically, I've agreed to a salary with VCFC, but they must agree on the fee AKA the selling price Bishampton is demanding to release my contract. VCFC is keen to have me play for them. Worst-case scenario, they'll take me on loan for the rest of the season until the summer break, when my contract with Bishampton will have six months left to run. But then, Bishampton will lose out on the transfer fees because of the Bosman rule. Hence the deadlock.

It's unsettling and frustrating. But I have a good team, and I trust Mr O to handle the contract negotiations on my behalf.

In the meantime, it's a waiting game for me. I keep myself distracted by helping my new housemate, AKA pretend wife, AKA Seki, settle into life in the UK.

The memory of our kiss in the living room is burned into my mind. I think about the warmth of her skin against mine, the way her heart beat a rhythm against my palm as she nestled in my arms. I can still feel her breath on my skin, the softness of her lips on mine. The way she tasted.

I've relived the sensations several times in the shower with my hand wrapped tightly around my dick. Yet, any temporary release doesn't last long. There's no satisfaction. I crave her constantly, especially since we're under the same roof.

Last week, I dropped her off at the university campus so she could register for her degree programme. Afterwards, I drove her around to show her the neighbourhood. We live in a leafy North London suburb on the borders close to Hertfordshire. Well-spaced houses, parkland, and green belt characterise the area. Our neighbours are families with high net-worth, and a few of them are other footballers who play in North London clubs. The area is known for its tranquillity, a retreat from noise and chaos, which is why I love it.

I showed her the local town centre, which had the shops for groceries, clothing, vintage shops, and bookshops. Her eyes lit up as soon as she saw the bookshop. Her love of reading prompted me to install a bookshelf in her bedroom.

I even took her to the railway station and showed her how to use the ticket machine because she will use the trains to get to university and back.

That's how she's been travelling to the campus this week. The train station is about fifteen minutes' walk from here.

However, yesterday evening, Seki was dropped off at the gates by a stranger.

I know this because, out of habit, I review footage from the cameras around the house every day. This morning, I looked at yesterday's images and saw Seki had been dropped off in a bright blue hatchback car. I'm uncertain of the manufacturer from this distance. But it had a white line down the side panels which makes it easily recognisable.

Someone dropped Seki off at our home, and she didn't even tell me.

She walked into the house, same as on the previous day, with a quick greeting before she went upstairs to freshen up. Then she had dinner and went back up to study. I didn't see her again until this morning before she left the house.

Now I'm in my home office, watching the monitor for any signs of her arrival. The evening stretches longer than anticipated, and with each passing hour, my unease grows. It isn't like Seki to be late, and she hasn't responded to my texts or calls. An unbearable silence fills the house, broken only by the occasional groan of the heating system. Each creak is a stark reminder of my isolation and growing unease.

Her schedule is already on my calendar. She forwarded it to me earlier this week. I promised Grandma I would take care of Seki. I'm responsible for her safety while she lives with me.

Her last class ended hours ago. She should have been home an hour ago.

I check my phone again for messages from her. There are none. I call her, and there is no response. I fire off a text message and wait for a reply. None comes. She is usually very good with prompt replies.

Where is she? Has something happened to her?

My pulse rate spikes, and a tightness in my chest is making it difficult to breathe.

I can't stay here. I need to find her.

Unable to stay still any longer, I grab my car keys and shrug my jacket on. My furrowed brow and hurried steps underscore my determination to find her. As I head to the car, I record a voice note for her.

Seki, where are you? I'm heading to your university campus to find you. Call me as soon as you get this message.

With zero patience, I navigate the winding roads towards the university campus. The darkness outside seems heavy, punctuated only by the fleeting glow of streetlights. I blast my car horn at an idiot driver going the wrong way around a small roundabout. Then I overtake a slow-coach doing thirty in a 40-mph zone.

By the time I see the signs directing me to the main campus, my mind is racing with possibilities. Has something happened? Is she okay? My grip tightens around the steering wheel, thoughts turning from concern to frustration. Is she ignoring my messages and calls on purpose? If so, she is in for a shock. On the other hand, if someone hurt her, I'll bury them, and I won't care about the consequences.

After a brief search in the car park, I find a bright blue hatchback car which looks like the one in my CCTV image. Parking nearby, I step out of the car, my custom bay sneakers crunching against the gravel. I spot the student bar—a lively hub spilling music and chatter onto the quiet night. The bar's neon sign blazes into the night, and I can see silhouettes of students moving behind the frosted glass windows.

I enter the establishment, my sharp presence drawing attention from a few patrons. I'm not a man easily overlooked. My tailored jacket and crisp shirt stand out amidst the casual wear of the students milling around. If any of them are football fans, then I'll be recognised soon enough. My eyes scan the room, seeking the familiar figure I came for.

There she is—

I freeze as my gaze lands on Seki.

She is seated at a corner table with a group of students, clad in a body-con black woollen dress with a triangular cutout in front showing off the swells of her breasts.

What the hell! Was that what she wore this morning when she left the house? It must have been covered under her coat. Because I wouldn't have let her leave the house dressed like this for lectures.

My temples throb with a sudden headache.

I've never seen her show off so much cleavage. Not even when we were in the tropical climate of Sapele. She looks so different with her face made up with smoky eyes and pouty, glossy lips. Even her hair is styled loose around her shoulders, softening her features.

Undeniable lust heats the blood in my veins as much as the inexplicable fury that she is surrounded by other men who are lusting after her while she's dressed like this. Yet, relief shoots through me because she is fine, not lying in a ditch somewhere.

Her laughter rings out, unrestrained and carefree, as she gestures during what appears to be a spirited discussion. She's only been in the country for two weeks, but she's already made friends. This is her bubbly personality in action.

Regardless, I'm her friend. Her husband, for goodness' sake. And she didn't think she should call me to tell me her whereabouts. My annoyance spikes again, and I approach the table.

"Seki," I say firmly, my voice cutting through the din of chatter and music like a knife.

The group falls silent, all eyes turning to me—some curious, others wary.

Seki's expression freezes before her eyes widen with alarm.

"Diaye?" she asks, blinking as though seeing me here is the last thing she expected.

"You weren't answering your phone." My tone is clipped although my shoulders relax a little, now I found her safe.

"I'm sorry," she says, her expression softening with guilt. "I didn't realise it was so late. We got caught up talking about the reading list for our course."

"Well, it's late now," I reply. My gaze flicks to her companions before returning to her. "Finish up. I'll drive you home. Right now."

There's no room for negotiation in my voice, but Seki doesn't seem inclined to argue.

"Okay. Sorry, guys, I have to go," she offers as apology to her friends, before standing to gather her things.

"I'll still see you tomorrow, right?" one of them, a male student, says.

I bet he's the one who dropped her yesterday.

"No, you won't," I say through gritted teeth before she can reply.

I yank the coat from the back of her chair and hold it out so she can slip her arms through the sleeves. I'm aware we're in a public arena, and any hassle will end up in the media and could harm my ongoing contract negotiations.

The group exchanges a mix of amused and confused glances.

Seki's jaw drops as she turns to look at me with a frown. She can see my restrained anger because she says nothing. In public, we're a united married couple, after all. But there is a defiant tilt to her chin, and her eyes are blazing with fury.

"Chill, bro. Who are you, anyway?" the male student speaks.

"I'm Seki's husband," I say aloud so anyone in the vicinity will hear it.

There are audible gasps from the table as I guide her towards the exit.

Outside, the cool night air wraps around us after the heat of the bar. Seki walks beside me, her gaze fixed on the pavement.

At the car, I hold the passenger door for her to climb in and shut the door before walking around to the driver's side.

As soon as I shut my door, she turns to me. "Why did you tell my friend I won't see him tomorrow?"

My mood darkens because she made plans to see the man at the weekend, away from the campus.

"Your friend? He's the same one who dropped you off at the house yesterday, isn't he?" My blood simmers.

"Yes, he did. He said he'll take me to a place where I can find part-time work." Her glare intensifies.

"A job? Why do you want a part-time job? You have an allowance and no bills."

"My visa allows me to work for twenty hours a week. And I want to earn my own money. I want to pay for driving lessons."

Exasperated, I scrub my hands over my face. "You know what? If you want a job, get a job. But if that man gives you a lift again, I will cancel our contract and ship you back to Nigeria."

Seki narrows her eyes. "You wouldn't."

"Try me and find out. You obviously have no sense of self-preservation. You will learn it one way or the other."

"You have no right to tell me who I can or cannot see!"

"I have every right. I'm your husband!"

"Are you?" she taunts me.

"What is that supposed to mean?"

Our faces are inches apart. I can hear her breath coming in soft pants.

"It means exactly what it means. Are you even a husband if you don't fuck your wife?" she sneers.

I lose the last of my composure and press the ignition button.

"Put your seatbelt on," I order. "You're about to find out how much of a husband I am."

23

Seki

The drive back to the house was in silence. It's not the first time I've been in a car with Diaye driving in the middle of the night while he's in a dark mood.

This time, he's not just being his usual grumpy self. The air crackles with unspoken desires, a palpable sexual tension hanging heavy in the space between us, making me vibrate with need.

I wasn't expecting him to show up tonight at the student bar.

Last week, he drove me to the university to show me the location so I can find my way. This week, I've been doing the commute myself. It's a fifteen-minute walk to the station, another fifteen-minute ride on the train, and a ten-minute bus ride to the campus. On the way back, I do the reverse.

However, a signal failure delayed yesterday's train schedule, according to the station announcement. I had to sit on the freezing cold bench on the platform waiting for the train to arrive. Gosh, I hate this chilly weather.

On top of it, I was late getting to the campus. Thankfully, I didn't miss my lecture. Later in the day, I was discussing the train delays with other course mates, and one of them, Paul, volunteered to drop me off at home after our lectures. You should have seen how happy I was. I wasn't looking forward to hanging around the frigid platform in the dark. To be fair, the university station is busier and marginally warmer because of the crowds. Still, it was so nice to sit in the warm car on the way back.

That's how I started thinking it would be a good idea if I had a car. Not that I can drive o. Nevertheless, the only way I can get a car is to get a job first.

I asked Paul if he knew where I could find part-time employment. I told him I had experience as a care worker and waiter. He said he would take me to a care home, which wasn't far from the campus. He said he works there, and they were always looking for new employees.

Unsure of how to direct him to the house from the campus, I told him to drive to my local train station. I was going to walk home from the station. But when we got there, Paul said he could drive me to the house. It wasn't a long walk home, but in the cold, it can feel like forever. So, I agreed.

We had chatted about many things on the way. He lives close to the campus and is studying to become a nurse. I was surprised there are so many male nursing students here, about ten percent of the current cohort. In my old college back in Nigeria, there was none in my entire year group.

When we got there, Paul asked if I was sure this was my house. He said I must have super rich parents or married a footballer because they were the only ones living in this postcode. I laughed it off but said nothing because I didn't want to reveal Diaye's identity. He doesn't want his home invaded by paparazzi.

I got out of the car outside the closed electronic gates and punched the code into the wall box. The area was lit by the large black Victorian-style streetlamps which glowed orange on either side of the black steel gates. They slid open, and after waving goodbye to Paul, I walked down the longish driveway, my boots crunching the gravel underneath.

Diaye grunted a welcome at me from the living room when I walked through the door. To be honest, I didn't tell him about being dropped off by Paul because why should I?

Like he says, he doesn't have to talk to me about stuff. So I don't have to talk to him.

We communicate only essentials. Nothing else.

He's not my lover or my proper husband.

But you know, as I lay in my bed last night, under the thick duvet, I was super frustrated. What kind of man did my ancestors match with me?

Two weeks in this house with him, coupled with the previous six months since he entered my life, and I'm almost convinced Diaye is the man for me.

It's an 'almost' because I need physical intimacy to verify if we're compatible. If my affair with Mide taught me anything, it's that I am a sexual person who needs to express my affections through passion and seduction.

Does Diaye believe he can feign ignorance of our bond beyond the friendship he guards so desperately? That every time we are in a room together, the sexual tension isn't trying to set the place ablaze.

Well, I woke up today and dressed with intention. I went downstairs, hoping Diaye would notice the figure-hugging dress showing off my curves. As usual, he was lost in focus, using the indoor gym at the back of the house.

Annoyed, I left for my walk to the station after a quick breakfast. My lectures ended early today, and there were events to welcome the January student intake. So I stayed on campus to celebrate.

One thing I know about my husband, no matter how oblivious he gets, he doesn't like me staying out too late. He volunteered to take me home the second night he was in Sapele when I was working late at the hotel. He showed up when I was stranded in the rain near Mide's house.

Therefore, at some point tonight, he was going to realise I was late coming home, and he would have to do something.

The something I wasn't sure of until he showed up at the student bar on campus.

Guilt niggles at me as I sit in the car on the drive back to the house.

Poor Paul got the brunt of Diaye's brusqueness when all he did was help me. I'm not sure if Paul will have anything to do with me again after the way Diaye spoke to him.

My skin heats with anger at his overbearing attitude. Or it could be from the warm air from the car heater.

Still, I may have an unexpected, much welcomed result.

"You're about to find out how much of a husband I am."

I replay Diaye's words in my mind from when he started driving out of the campus car park.

Stunned, I couldn't say anything, and I still don't want to say anything in case I ruin it. I want what's coming to me—Diaye and I making love for the first time.

If it means I keep my mouth shut when my natural state is to chat, I will put a tape around my mouth to make it happen.

He stops outside the black gates and grabs a black fob from the middle compartment in the car. He presses the fob, and the car headlights illuminate the driveway as the gates slide open.

As he drives in, my heart races in anticipation.

This is it.

He parks in the usual spot, and I sit still, waiting for him to come around to my side. This is a part of our routine I love. It shows his tenderness, consideration. It's a sign of his awareness of my presence in his life, even when other things take up his time.

He opens the door and holds it.

I step out into the chilly night, hesitant to leave the warmth of the vehicle, yet excited about what awaits me in the house.

The lights are on inside, soft and inviting. It looks beautiful through the stained glass bordering the front door. It seems he was in a hurry to come and get me, as he didn't switch them off.

He shuts the car door and presses into me against the side of the car.

I gasp, tilting my head back to look up at him. Away from the light at the front door, his face is shadowed, but his eyes glitter.

He crushes me to his chest, holding me tight, and breathes me in like a starving man, his breath hot against my forehead. His solid, muscular form presses against me, and I feel his strength.

"I know I'm a selfish, grumpy asshole. But you scared me tonight when I couldn't reach you."

His voice, raw with emotion, catches me off guard. I can only stammer, "I'm sorry," my voice trembling.

This is the contradiction that is Diaye Zambo.

The first time I met him, I thought he was arrogant and cold. Yet, he has this side, which is warm and caring and protective, too. Now I've met his family, I can understand why he withdraws into himself. It's a survival mechanism. Like a tortoise retreating into its shell when it senses danger. Diaye is complex and multilayered.

And as much as I have told myself I'm not ready for a permanent relationship, I crave all of Diaye. The good and the bad in him, the darkness and the light, the shadowed soul and beautiful heart. I want to pour all my love into him and light him up from the inside out.

"Promise me you won't do it again. You'll tell me any changes to your schedule daily, every hour if necessary," he says in a gruff voice.

I bury my face in his chest and stifle a chuckle as warmth suffuses me. This is the same Diaye who has ignored me all week. Now he wants hourly updates on my whereabouts. The demand seems excessive. But it's a promise I'm happy to make as long as he's mine.

"I promise," I say.

He holds me, and we stay there for seconds ticking into minutes, outside the car, in the cold, me cuddled against his chest with his arms wrapped around me.

After a while, I say, "Diaye..."

"Yes, Wifey." He runs a hand over my braids gently, and I get another boost of joy.

"You said you will show me how much of a husband you are."

His hand stills, and he stiffens before lifting his head to look at my face. "You really want me to fuck you?"

"Yes," I say without hesitation and lick my lips. Some of the boldness which deserted me when he rejected me the last time returns and I add, "I need you."

Diaye squeezes his eyes shut, his expression pained. "Do you understand what it means to be with me?"

"Yes, I do." I grab his arms. He's trembling, his entire body is quaking, as if he's fighting for control. "Unless you don't want me."

He barks out a laugh, but there is little humour in it. "Want you? I can barely control myself for wanting you."

He moves my hand downward until it covers the bulge straining to burst out of his trousers. He sucks in a sharp breath as my hand moulds him through the fabric and he seems to swell under my touch.

"You don't have to fight it." I squeeze him, eliciting a low growl from his chest.

He pins my hands to my sides. "If I don't fight it, I will be buried deep inside you right where you stand, fucking you against this car while the snow falls around us."

"Wow," I mutter as tiny flakes of white float down from the sky. "Maybe you should fuck me out here."

He groans, closing his eyes. "Grandma warned me you would keep me on my toes. I just didn't picture it would be like this. We're going inside, and I am going to fuck you. But bear this in mind. Having sex with me means you are consenting to be possessed by me and there will be no doubt that you belong to me. Is this what you want? To belong to me totally?"

There's something in his gaze. Something hungry and deviant. Flames burn away the normal coolness of his eyes, and the heat sears me right to my core. My body trembles with lust and with love.

"Yes, I want to belong to you and for you to belong to me, totally." The words tumble out, barely formed, but they're true.

He nods once and takes my hand, walking me to the door.

24

Seki

Diaye unlocks the front door. Light and heat rush out from inside. He waves me into the foyer and follows a step behind. Then he punches the code to disarm the security alarm on the panel. At least he remembered to set it when he left the house.

"Let me take your coat," he says, taking my bag and placing it on the side table against the wall.

I turn, and he helps me out of the long woollen coat he bought me, which covers me from neck to ankle. A shiver passes through me as soon as I lose the heavy barrier. The front door is still open, and the temperature seems to have dropped.

"Are you going to shut the door?" I ask. I can see the steady light flutter of snowfall against the darkness and the glow of streetlamps at the closed gates in the distance.

He's not giving me any space as he looks at me as if he wants to eat me alive.

"Not yet," he says, shrugging off his jacket. He's wearing a button-down shirt and jeans with his stylish trainers.

I'm reminded of how stunning he looked when I saw him in the student bar, compared to all the students in jogging bottoms or sweatshirts. I want to run my hands all over his body.

But he seems to have other plans. "Turn around."

I comply, giving him my back. His hand is warm against my nape as he tugs the zipper on my dress.

"Diaye?"

"No one can see," he whispers in a husky voice.

He isn't wrong. Our house is at the end of a lane and backs onto a field. No one would come down here at this time of night unless they were visiting us. And we don't get visitors. Not since Diaye's father and brother came two weeks ago.

Still, my heart gallops at the thought of discovery, and heat rushes through my body. I am so turned on. It seems Diaye's exhibitionism matches my need for the illicit.

The zipper goes down past my lower back, and he tugs the dress open. The sleeves slip from my arms a little as his hand caresses my shoulder blades, the fabric soft against my skin. His fingers graze my neck, sending shivers down my spine before sliding over my right shoulder, and the dress falls away. Then, with gentle hands, he repeats the process on my left shoulder, the fabric whispering against my skin until the dress falls, pooling at my ankles.

The cold air surrounds me as his fingers slide under my bra strap and he unclips it. I don't stop it from dropping to the porch floor. The cold air is like an instrument of pleasure as my nipples pucker and harden into bullet points.

With the same deliberate motion, he strokes under the waistband of my lace knickers. He wants me naked, right here at the doorstep. I'm shivering, but I also want whatever he offers. My body is a ball of heat because my heart is working overtime.

I push the rest of my clothing down until I'm only in my black leather knee-length boots. Well, I still have the sheer knee-length pop socks, but they can't come off without taking the boots off first. Every item of clothing I wore today, he bought me the first weekend we went shopping when I arrived here.

"Wifey, look at me." His voice is soft and yet like the crack of a whip in the silence surrounding us.

I turn to face him, trying not to feel embarrassed because I've never felt so naked in my life.

Yet, the way he stares at me with total affection and devotion chases my nerves away. Like he wants to bury himself inside me and yet wants to savour every part of me.

I stand tall and proud with my hands behind my back because I'm not sure what to do with them.

"Are you okay?" he asks as he circles me. His eyes devour me, taking in every detail, it seems.

"Yes." I swallow the lump in my throat. "Just cold."

He nods, his eyes sparking with amusement as he steps away and pushes the front door, shutting away the chilly air. "You know, I realised you were an exhibitionist the night of our engagement party when you were dry humping me in front of our party guests."

"You caused it," I say, my cheeks heating. "You were the one who corrupted me."

He chuckles, stopping behind me and pressing his body against mine until I can feel his steel-hard erection against my back. He is still clothed, and the fabric feels rough, yet a welcome warmth against my skin.

"You're so stunning. I could not resist you that night. I had to kiss you. The only thing which saved you from me fucking you against that bar counter was other people."

He presses his lips to my neck, making my skin tingle and sending my pulse in a rapid flutter.

"Wifey, do you still want me to fuck you, to pound into you relentlessly and thoroughly corrupt you? I will erase every lover you've had before." He walks around to face me, his eyes gleam with dark heat.

A whimper escapes my mouth along with my, "Yes. I want it all."

Diaye kisses the hollow of my collarbone and up to my lower jaw. I want him to devour me. To make me forget Mide and wipe him from my memory.

He bites the corner of my neck and shoulder, and I gasp. He bends down and warms my breast with his mouth, sucking on the hard tip, pulling on it with lip-blunted teeth. His attention to my breast makes me moan, awakening the warmth in my crotch.

He trails a wet path from my neck to my stomach with his tongue. When I think I can't take more without falling down from the pleasure of it, he straightens and puts his mouth over mine in a searing kiss. I wind my arms around his neck. His hands warm my back, his touch firm and keeping me upright.

He breaks the kiss. "Go upstairs to my room and wait for me. I'm going to lock up down here."

"Okay," I say, and back up as he watches me. Then, I turn and walk up the stairs.

This is a momentous occasion. I've been in this house for two weeks but never been into his bedroom. My body quivers in anticipation as I turn the handle and push the door open. The room is lit by a single glowing lamp on a side table next to the gigantic hardwood bed. There is nothing else in here. No personal mementos, no photographs. It is another minimalistic haven with its off-white walls and monochromatic bedding. So Diaye.

I need to add some colour to the furnishings in this house.

I grab the comforter at the bottom of the bed and wrap it around my body for some warmth. Then I take my boots and socks off, placing them beside the bed. A quick exploration shows he has a huge walk-in closet and an ensuite bathroom.

I hear him rattling around downstairs with door and window locks. He seems to take forever. Sitting on the side of the bed, I consider crawling under the duvet when I hear him coming up the stairs. He appears through the open doorway, still dressed, with a bottle of water and a glass in his hands. He places them on the bedside table.

"Why were you so long?" I ask, frowning and showing my discomfort.

He kneels in front of me and touches my knee. "I'm sorry, Wifey."

"Okay," I gasp, and tingle as he kisses inside my knee. I didn't know it was an erogenous zone.

He glances up at me with his fiery black eyes and moves his lips up my thigh, spreading my legs. A tingle goes up the inside of my thighs as he runs his hands up them, the edge of his watch making a light scratch on sensitive skin.

He picks my legs up, and I fall back on the pillows as he lightly kisses the outside of my mound.

"Ah, Diaye," I whisper, hand stroking his hair.

He gently pushes my legs apart, planting soft kisses in the space between them. His touch sends shivers down my spine as he slips his finger into my wetness, eliciting a whimper from me. As I gaze at him, his closed eyes convey a sense of focus while he expertly flicks his tongue over my clit.

I say his name again, letting the syllables roll off my tongue. He flicks his tongue, the motion precise and quick, sending sparks of desire through my body. He licks the glistening juices off my skin and flattens his tongue against my clit, the hair on his chin tickling my thighs. He alternates between slow licks and fast flicks.

Heat courses through my body along with tingles. My body primes, winds, chasing the orgasm. He feasts on me like a man possessed, his hand digging into my flesh, fingers curling inside until he finds the spot which makes me buck against his face. He tugs at my clit with his teeth, flicking over the sensitive bud with his tongue, and I explode in climax, my screams reverberating off the walls.

"You taste so good." He laps up every drop until I'm shaking and trembling beneath his touch. "The perfect starter."

Abruptly, he stands, undressing quickly. I don't have enough time to admire his physicality, the plains of hard muscles and perfect angles before he's on top of me. His dick is like a rock pressing against my thigh.

"Are you on contraceptives?" he asks, his beard glistening with my juices.

The unexpectedness of it all jolts me for a moment, a slight gasp escaping my lips. No one except Iye has asked me this question. But I recover and say, "Yes."

I ensured I had a stash to last me for three months before I will need a prescription.

"Good." He kisses me again, tasting of Diaye and my desire.

My yearning for him spikes, and sensation floods me. I want every inch of him. His erection presses at my entrance but doesn't go further. I twist my hips to take him in.

He backs off, lifting his head to stare at me as he slides his dick around my wet folds without entering me.

"You are drenched, Wifey." He continues rubbing his turgid length against my clit, sending pleasure waves all over my body.

"That's because you're driving me insane." I move my body, gyrating my hips, chasing his dick as he rolls the head over my most sensitive parts. My body is primed, and I can climax again like this. But I don't want to. I want him inside me next time.

"Please," I beg, and that seems to do the trick.

He flips me onto my stomach and tugs my hips up. Then he grips the back of my throat and drives his dick into me with a ferocity I've never seen in him. I bury my head in the pillow and sing my moans. He pounds into me, and I feel full to bursting. He tries to slow down as if he's worried I will break.

"Diaye ... Strongman ... don't slow down." I use the nickname he's known by on the pitch and pant between phrases, urging him on. "That's it ... harder ... harder."

"Oh, Wifey, you really are perfect for me."

"Then fuck me like I deserve."

Chuckling, he pushes me onto my back, bends my knees back, and slams into me. I shatter into another orgasm. He fucks me faster and deeper until he comes apart in a powerful climax which shakes his body. He releases my legs, and they fall back onto the mattress. He lowers his head onto my sweat-covered chest, and I watch him catch his breath. My breathing slows, and we come down from the high.

I float, my mind hazy. I could be in heaven as a warm, happy feeling suffuses me.

He lifts his head and brushes his lips against mine. "Are you feeling good, Wifey?"

I take a deep inhale and grin. "Strongman, I feel very good."

"I'm glad." He rolls to the side and takes me with him, placing my head on his chest. Then he tugs the duvet over us.

His warmth, hardness, and smell are comforting, and I feel drowsy.

"Does this mean we're now lovers?" I ask, trying to shake off the drowsiness. There are things I need to ask him. Things I need to tell him.

"Yes, we're now lovers," he replies with amusement in his voice.

"Yay. I love the friends-to-lovers trope."

That's the last thing I remember before I drift off to sleep.

25

Seki

By the time I blink my eyes open again, several hours have passed. I'm sure of it, although it's still dark outside. Heavy drapes obscure the window. Diaye's wristwatch, glowing softly, displays 06:12.

For the first time since I arrived in this country, I've slept through the night. Our lovemaking session last night exhausted me. My body is still achy, but I've never been happier as a smile curls my lips.

Diaye is exactly the kind of lover I need, tender one moment and vigorous the next.

The way he held me lovingly out on the driveway last night while the snow was falling, like I was the most precious thing to him. Yet, minutes later in the bedroom, he was thrusting into me like a locomotive engine.

I love every second of both interactions. They confirm I finally have the husband whose proposal I accepted six months ago.

Diaye is finally mine. He is my friend, my lover, and my husband.

"...But I have news for you, jeune fille. Traditional weddings don't count."

Diaye's father's disdainful words resound in my mind, and my joy diminishes. That man's words are venomous. No wonder Diaye doesn't enjoy talking to him.

But if we're not legally married in the UK, it means the arrangement is only temporary.

Feeling hot and sticky and needing to use the toilet, I roll out of bed. Thankfully, Diaye doesn't move. I'm not quite ready to talk to him this morning. I need to figure out how I feel about our fake marriage arrangement.

Are we still pretending even though we're now having sex?

Feeling grouchy, I find my way in the predawn darkness and walk to my bedroom. Turning on the lights, I enter the ensuite bathroom and use the WC before turning on the shower faucet. I brush my teeth while I wait for the water to heat up. Braids tied up with a black band, I stuff them under the shower cap before opening the enclosure door and stepping under the spray.

I stand under the pinpricks of the hot shower against my skin until my tense muscles loosen. I love this showerhead. It has different settings, and this one works as a massaging tool on my skin. I usually use it after a day at the university. But I didn't shower last night because of Diaye.

I turn to grab my shower gel and loofah from the little chrome shelf in the corner of the wall tiles.

When I turn back, there is a shadow looming on the other side of the glass cubicle.

The gel container slips from my hand onto the limestone floor tiles as I startle. "Diaye! You scared me."

"I'm sorry for scaring you," he says in a gruff voice as he comes closer. "But I don't like not knowing where my wife is."

"Since when?" I ask, flippantly, still feeling grouchy. Thinking about his father ruined my mood, and now, he scared me half to death. Squatting, I grab the shower gel bottle and straighten.

He opens the cubicle door and walks in. Gloriously naked, tall and wide, and powerfully athletic. Even the semi dangling between his thighs is impressive. The shower enclosure seems tiny as he takes up so much space.

"Since the day I picked you up at Heathrow Airport," he says, watching me like a predator watches its prey.

"What does that mean?" I try to pour shower gel onto the loofah.

He fiddles with the faucet, and steam comes out of the showerhead instead of water. I didn't know it could do that. It's like being in a steam room. He takes the bottle from my hand, pours the gel onto the loofah, and lathers it. Then he turns me around and rubs the sponge over my back, scrubbing it sensually, awakening my libido. My body heats as tingles spread through me. I flatten my hands on the wall tiles and present my back to him, bum tilted upwards.

"It means I've known your location since you arrived, aside from last night."

He squeezes my left bum cheek. Hard. My breath hitches. He repeats the action with the right cheek.

My brain is frazzled, and I can't think straight. I don't understand what he's saying. "You can't possibly know where I am when I leave this house in the mornings."

"Are you saying that when you tell me you have lectures at nine a.m. and you leave this house at seven a.m., you don't go to the university?"

"Oh." I suddenly realise where this is going. "No. That's not what I mean."

"Then yes, I know where you are supposed to be, and I trust you to be where you are supposed to be." He glides his finger down the crack of my bum. "Never give me a reason to distrust you."

I part my thighs, and he chuckles as his fingers graze my slippery pussy. I moan, tilting my bum towards him, wanting a deeper connection.

Instead, he removes his hand and rubs the loofah against my legs.

I growl in frustration, and he chuckles some more.

"It's not funny," I grumble.

He removes his hands, and I swivel to face him with a frown on my face.

He straightens and starts rubbing my neck and chest with the loofah. "Then don't make me worry about your whereabouts."

He holds my left nipple between his thumb and forefinger and twists it.

"Ah," I cry out, and molten heat flows through my veins. I push my chest out to him, wanting more of the delicious pain. "But I apologised about it last night."

"I'm not talking about last night." He pinches my right nipple.

I tip my head back against the tiles and moan as electric signals shoot straight to my throbbing clit. Just a little friction, and I will explode in orgasm.

He releases my breast and moves downward, scrubbing my stomach.

"What are you doing?" I grouse. "Are you punishing me because I got up to take a shower?"

Ignoring me, he continues to my legs with the loofah, avoiding between my thighs.

"Fine. I don't need you." I lower my right hand and cup my pussy.

"If you masturbate without my permission, I will tie you to the bed for the rest of the weekend and fuck you in every hole until you realise that your body belongs to me now, Wifey."

My insides clench tight, and I bite my lower lip at the imagery. "You know that threat doesn't scare me."

"Maybe not." He straightens and tosses the loofah aside. "But do you really want to spend the next forty-eight hours physically tied to a bed and only being released for toilet breaks?"

A serious intensity darkens his gaze. He'll tie me up as punishment. No doubt.

"You wouldn't," I say.

Yet, I drop my hand from my pussy as he looms closer, steam billowing around us. I don't want to test him. Not yet.

He takes my hands and raises them above my head, pinning them to the wall. "This is who I am as a lover. I warned you were better off without us having sex, but you insisted. I will make demands that push your boundaries sexually. If it's not your thing, say so now, and we'll go back to being just friends."

Na lie. I refuse to return to a platonic friendship with him. My feelings for him run so deep, I can't imagine life with him as just a friend.

Looking up into his dark, lust-filled gaze, I swallow the lump in my throat. "I'm not going back to being just friends with you, Diaye. No way. Not after last night. I stood naked at that open doorway, freezing my nipples off with the possibility of being caught. I can take being tied up. But I want to know this. No matter how kinky our intimacy gets, if I say stop, will you stop?"

He blinks, and his expression is all serious. "Every fucking time, Wifey. Every time. If you feel uncomfortable about anything, I'm trusting you to let me know. That's the only way this works for us. We must trust each other."

Exhaling a heavy breath, I nod. I trust him, but the whole non-marriage thing is still bothering me. It's a loophole other people can exploit. But I don't want to talk about it here.

"Good. So getting back to this morning," he continues. "Why did you leave the bedroom?"

His free hand cups my left breast, and he bends his head and sucks my nipple. My ability to think straight disappears, and the only thing I can do is moan.

"Answer me, Wifey." He bites my nipple.

Panting, the words are a whisper out of my mouth. "I wanted to use the bathroom."

"There's one in the room. Why didn't you use it? Were you trying to run away from me?" He cups my pussy.

A flash of guilt washes over me. "Run? No. I'm more familiar with the bathroom in my bedroom." I widen my legs, giving him space.

His fingers invade my inner channel, and I clench around him.

"From now on, use the bathroom in the master bedroom. You're moving in with me."

He returns his mouth to my breast as his fingers cause havoc to my pussy.

"Oh," I whimper, canting my body as he plays me like an instrument until my body curls and a wave of orgasm washes over me from toes to head.

Then he lifts me up and impales his rigid dick inside my wet channel, ramming into me and using the wall to hold me up. I wrap my arms around his shoulders and hold on for the ride of my life. Pouring all of myself into the heated kiss we share until we're both climaxing again—me first and then him before he goes still.

My legs wobble when he lets me down and turns the shower back to wet spray. He lets me rinse off, and I step out of the cubicle and grab a towel while he showers.

I'm in the room dressing after moisturising my skin when he comes out of the bathroom, a towel around his hips. I can't stop staring at his muscles glistening with moisture and licking my lips.

"Wifey, if you keep staring at me like that, we won't leave the bedroom." He walks up to me and bends over.

"That's not such a bad idea, *Strongman*," I tease. I'm sore, but a little rest and I'll be happy to go again.

He chuckles and kisses me on the forehead.

"I need food, and so do you." He straightens. "Come down to the kitchen when you're dressed."

"Okay," I say as he walks out.

Minutes later, I'm dressed in a pair of jeans, a long-sleeved turtleneck jumper, and socks before I head downstairs. I can smell the food, and soft music is playing from Bluetooth speakers—Maxi Priest, 'Let Me Know.' It's a soulful reggae track with themes of longing and emotional vulnerability.

Diaye meets my gaze as I walk into the kitchen. His smile is beautiful, and in his eyes, there is a heartfelt expression of how he feels about me, which is augmented by the scene in front of me. He's set places for the two of us at the breakfast bar.

He comes over, cups my cheeks, and plants a kiss on my lips, leaving me breathless.

"Take a seat." He waves at the stool, and I climb onto it.

He pours hot lemon tea from a teapot into the teacup on a saucer.

"Has it got honey?" I ask. He nods, and I pick it up and blow into it before taking a sip. It is perfectly sweetened. Grinning, I say, "Thank you."

"You're welcome." He plates the omelettes and places them on the placemats. Then he brings his mug of coffee over and sits on the stool next to me.

We eat with the music from the speaker filling the silence. This time, the omelette contains sweet peppers and mushrooms. He has perfected the art of making omelettes. I empty my plate with relish.

"I have a surprise for you," he says when he finishes. "Actually, more than one surprise. But here is the first one."

"Oh, really? What it is?" I bounce on the stool with excitement.

He opens the laptop on the table and types something. "Check your email."

I pick up my phone and open the new email notification. My heart slams in my chest.

"What is it?" I glance up at him and back at my phone. "Confirmation of driving lessons?"

"Yes. Our conversation last night got me thinking. You need to learn to drive as soon as possible so you can start driving yourself to uni. I don't want you taking lifts from random men."

I frown. "Is this about Paul, my course-mate?"

"It's not about him. It's about you. You're my wife. You need your own car."

"I agree. I would like my own car. But I was going to pay for the driving lessons myself. That's why I need a job."

"And you will get a job, eventually. In the meantime, you can get started with the lessons. I paid for twenty hours to get you started."

"But I wanted to pay for them myself." I frown. He's unemployed because he's not playing football and therefore not being paid by any club, and he already spent so much money on me. I don't want him spending more than he needs to spend until his new contract is confirmed.

I don't want to mention his unemployed status because it's a touchy subject. His father wielded it as a sword over his head, and I don't want to seem to do the same.

"I know. When you get a job, feel free to spend your money on whatever you like, Wifey. But it is my prerogative as your husband to ensure you have everything you need, here and now. This reminds me. You need to apply for your provisional driving license. You need it for the lessons." He pushes the laptop in front of me. "This is the DVLA website where you can complete the application."

He is right. He promised to provide everything I needed. I don't want to be ungrateful or take him for granted.

"Thank you." I lean over and wrap my arms around his neck and kiss him on the mouth.

"You're welcome." He kisses me back. "Clear up over here and get ready. I'm taking you out for the second surprise."

An hour later, we are at a car showroom. My heart races with excitement as the sleek glass doors slide open and we step into the brightly lit space, our reflections multiplying on the polished surfaces of the gleaming cars on display. Rows of vehicles stretch before us like a gallery of modern art, each one boasting impeccable curves and flawless finishes.

Diaye walks with a confidence matching the vitality of the showroom itself. His hand rests on the small of my back, guiding me forward. A salesman approaches with the practiced smile that speaks of readiness to cater to our every whim.

"Good afternoon, sir and madam. How may I help you today?"

Diaye nods towards the salesman, but keeps his focus on me. "We're here to find a car for my wife. Something that suits her style and needs."

My cheeks warm, and my protests bubble up, but Diaye's firm glance quells them. I don't want to argue—not again, not here. I allow myself to be swept along as he gestures towards a row of compact cars.

"Something reliable, efficient, but with enough charm to match her own," he says, his tone infused with quiet pride.

My eyes roam over the lineup until they land on a Mini Cooper, its vibrant emerald-green paint catching the light in a way that makes it seem alive. My breath hitches. It's perfect.

"That one," Diaye declares, catching my gaze even before I can point it out. "I think that's the one."

The salesman perks up and leads us towards the car, rattling off its features—advanced safety mechanisms, impressive fuel efficiency, and a design that screams personality. But I hardly hear him. My focus is on the sleek contours of the vehicle, the way the stitched leather seats seem to beckon me inside.

"It's beautiful," I murmur, more to myself than anyone else.

"It's yours," Diaye replies simply, his hand pressing warmly against mine.

I turn to him, my lips parting in astonishment. "Are you serious? This is too much—"

He shakes his head, cutting off my objection with a soft smile. "You need a car, Wifey. You deserve the best. I don't want you settling for anything less."

The salesman hands over the keys with the practiced air of someone well-versed in facilitating dreams. Diaye gestures for me to take the driver's seat. I slide into the car, my hands trembling as they touch the steering wheel. The leather is supple and smooth. The cabin filled with the fresh scent of a brand-new car.

"Does it feel right?" Diaye asks, leaning in through the open door.

My eyes cloud with tears in a mix of gratitude and disbelief. "It feels like a dream."

"It's meant to be," he says with a grin. "Let's finalise everything and arrange for them to drop it off at home."

The salesman begins the paperwork, but my mind is elsewhere. Diaye's generosity, his unwavering support, weigh on my heart—not like a burden, but like a reminder of the depth of his commitment. I resolve to repay him in every way I can.

An hour later, the Mini Cooper is rolled onto a truck which drives out of the dealership, heading to our house.

We get back in Diaye's car, and I can't hold back my excitement. I call and speak to everyone who is close to me to tell them the news—Diaye bought me a new car. By the time we get home, I've spoken to Iye, my sisters Imoni and Erhu, my dad. I'm on top of the world.

At the house, we wait for the truck to offload the Mini Cooper and leave. Then I walk around it, touching it, smelling the leather seat. I can't contain my joy. I'm like a little child with a Christmas toy. It's like Christmas came early.

Diaye stands by the front door, watching me with a benevolent grin on his face. The car feels like an extension of me—bright, lively, and full of promise. This compels me to begin driving lessons.

I run up to Diaye and wrap my arms around him. "You are the best."

He places his hand under my chin and tilts my head back. "You know, today was about more than a car. It's about showing you that you'll always have what you need. I'm your friend, your lover, your partner, and your husband. Always remember it."

"Okay. I will." I lean on tiptoes and kiss him. "Thank you, Strongman. For everything."

His smile lights up his face. "You're welcome, Wifey."

26

Seki

Diaye and I spend the rest of the weekend in the house, making love and eating food ordered via an app. We take a break on Sunday afternoon when the groceries arrive from the local supermarket in a delivery van.

Diaye brings in the food boxes from the front door while I unpack the groceries and store them in the cupboards and fridges. We've become quite a team, and we work well together. For example, when he cooks, I wash up and vice versa. Our interactions feel seamless and complementary.

While I stack the frozen items in the freezer, I ask him one question I've been burning to ask since we became lovers.

"Diaye," I say. "I've been meaning to ask you about Beverly."

"Beverly." He frowns. "Who is Beverly?"

"See this man o." I side-eye him. "Have you forgotten her already? The woman who was trying to oppress me because of you."

"Who is she?" He comes around and helps me put away the last of the items.

"You're serious. The woman you met at your welcome party at Crystal Palace Hotel, remember?"

He shakes his head. "I met a few women that night."

"Rukky's friend. The one that came to the house a few times. You made me bring food up to your room for her."

He leans against the counter. "Oh. That Beverly. What about her?"

"Knowing the way you are in bed when we fuck. Everything shakes. It's like the earth moves. So, I'm curious as to why I never heard any loud rattling sounds when she came to visit you."

"Wait? Are you jealous?" He chuckles. "I think I like a jealous Wifey. But you don't need to be jealous of her." He tugs me into his arms. "She wanted sex, but I didn't oblige her. She was a social media influencer and was always taking pictures and posting online. I didn't want to fuck a woman who could livestream it for clicks and coins." He shudders. "I went to Nigeria to avoid scandal, not court it."

I giggle, flooded with warmth that he didn't fuck Beverly. I guess he doesn't fuck all his friends, after all. "Sapele social media was buzzing with news of our engagement party."

"As it should be. A son-of-the-soil proposing to a daughter-of-the-soil is gossip-worthy." He grins. "In any case, it was you I wanted to fuck from the moment I set my eyes on you."

My chest swells with pride, and my heart trips over itself. "Are you serious?"

"Absolutely. Why do you think I was pissed off the next day when Mide showed up and declared he was your fiancé?"

"Ooh." I palm my face. "Now it all makes sense. You were jealous."

"You bet I was. I'm not ashamed to admit it. I couldn't stand the thought of you with him." He waves at the door as if Mide stood beyond it.

"Aww. Mide had no intentions of marrying me." I comb my fingers through his beard and kiss his lips. "It's a good thing I found out about his wife when I did. Otherwise, I might not be here today."

His expression darkens, and he releases me and steps away. "About that. I have a confession to make."

My spine stiffens, and I lean against the counter. I don't like the look on his face. "What is it?"

"The night of my welcome home party in Sapele. After Mide declared he was your fiancé, I talked to Harrison about him. My cousin told me Mide was married and his wife lived in Ibadan. I thought you knew this and were having an affair with a married man."

"Wait." I lift my hand, pausing him. "You thought I knew Mide was married?"

"At first—"

"At first! You think I would choose to have an affair with a married man?"

"What else was I supposed to think? Harrison knew he was married. Why wouldn't you know?"

"Oh, my God! I can't believe you would think that of me."

"I didn't know you then. And Mide came to the house saying he was going to marry you. That he wanted me to help him financially because he wanted to pay to take you abroad."

"What? You gave him money?"

"Of course not. I'm not that gullible."

"Oh. You're implying I am."

He frowns. "Well, you were. You still think the world is a bed of roses—"

"Even roses have thorns. I get it!" I interject, fuming. "I can't believe you knew Mide was married and didn't tell me. I ended up going to his house and meeting his wife. I'd never been so embarrassed in my life."

The memory of that night returns, clouding my eyes with tears. I swipe them angrily.

"Are you crying for that asshole again?"

He steps forward to take my hand, but I push him away.

"I'm crying for you, asshole!" I shout at him. "I asked you why Mide came to the house that week, and you told me to go and ask him. And I went to his house!"

"I thought you would call him or speak to him at work," he retorts. "Why would you go to his house in the middle of the night?"

"He was my boyfriend. I had every right to go to his house at night!"

"Then, I have no regrets. You went there to fuck him. And there was no way I was going to let you two carry on."

I open my mouth to retort. But something in his words clicks in my mind. "What do you mean, you have no regrets?"

"I told Harrison to invite Mide's wife to Sapele. She came to visit, thinking Mide was being honoured for his ten years of service at Crystal Palace Hotel."

"Hey! That was you?" I cry out and pace the kitchen. This is worse than I thought. "So you not only knew Mide was married. You invited his wife to Sapele. And you didn't say a word to me. Not a word. And I went there and received the humiliation of my life—"

His phone on the table buzzes, interrupting me. And I want to toss it at the wall.

He glances at the phone and grabs it. "It's Mr O'Connell. I have to take it."

Shaking my head, I grab my phone and stomp off upstairs. When I enter my room, I slam the door and scream.

I pace the bedroom, and after a while, I sit on the bed, mentally exhausted. I don't understand Diaye and why he did what he did. Iye says he's a cynic, and he sees the worst in people, which makes sense because that's what he did. He saw the worst in me, the me who wasn't even in existence. I would never have dated Mide if I knew he was married. No way.

To think Diaye thought I knew.

And he went to the extent of bringing Mide's wife into the picture to break me and Mide up. Good plan.

Except, I was humiliated. I didn't deserve it.

How can I trust a man who will do such a thing to me?

There's a tap on my bedroom door.

"I don't want to talk to you!" I yell.

"Whatever." Diaye's muffled voice comes through the panel. "I'm going out."

He's going out? I glance at my watch. It's four-thirty p.m. and already dark outside.

I hurry to the door and yank it open. "You're going out, now?"

"Yes," he says in a gruff voice, his back to me as he heads towards the staircase.

He's wearing a different outfit from what he wore earlier. This time, a black long-sleeve shirt and black trousers with black boots. He looks really nice, and I can smell his cologne. Is he going to meet a woman?

"Do you want me to come with you?" I ask, following a few steps behind him as he descends the stairs.

"No."

He's reverted to monosyllabic answers, which means he's upset with me and in grumpy mode.

What right does he have to be upset? I'm the one who should be upset.

"Where are you going? You can't leave the house without telling me where you're going?"

He turns to face me when he reaches the bottom, his expression blank. "I'm going to meet some friends. Don't wait up for me."

He takes his coat from the rack and shrugs it on.

Friends? What friends? I haven't seen any visit him since I moved in. As far as I know, his friends and family are all up north. He doesn't have anyone in the south of England, except me. And maybe his brother, who is now playing for a team with a stadium close-by. But I don't think Diaye has spoken to Liam since they visited over a fortnight ago.

"Where exactly will you be?" I ask, narrowing my eyes at him.

"In a pub in Viva City. I'll send you the location pin when I get there." He enters the code for the locker box next to the security panel in the wall and grabs his keys when the door pops open.

He opens the door and walks out without another glance.

Puffing out a sigh, I enter the living room and turn on the TV. Thirty minutes later, my phone pings with a notification. Diaye sent me his location pin. I look it up, and it's a pub in Viva City, Panthers' Lair.

Another message comes through from him, and it reads: *And BTW, I signed the contract. I'm officially a Viva City Panther.*

Gasping, I cover my mouth. No wonder he went down there. Probably to sign the contract. It's such a relief. For him. For us. He was under such an immense pressure waiting to see if the deal would go through.

But why didn't he tell me this was the reason he was going out? I don't like that he's keeping things from me. It's the same thing he did in Nigeria, which caused me a lot of distress with Mide.

Still, I send him a message.

Congratulations on signing the new contract.

It takes a while for a reply to ping from him.

Thank you.

Glancing at the clock, I stay up to wait for him. I'm still upset with him, and I need to talk to him. But when he doesn't return by ten o'clock, I go to my bedroom, change into my PJs, and climb into bed. I have school tomorrow and need my sleep.

I wake with the light spilling in from the hallway and Diaye striding across my room to my side of the bed.

"Diaye, what are you doing?" I croak.

"We agreed this isn't your bedroom anymore. And yet, here you are." He looms over me.

"I'm upset with you. Don't I have the right to be upset?" I say as he scoops me from the mattress, duvet and all.

"Be upset all you want. You can still be upset and sleep in our bed." He carries me cradled to his chest towards the master bedroom.

Breathing in his scent, I snuggle up to him. I lack the energy and inclination to argue with his valid point. He deposits me on the sheets and covers me. Now, I have two duvets over me.

He goes into the bathroom, and I hear the shower running. I drift off to sleep and wake when the bed dips from him climbing in. The light is off, and Diaye doesn't speak. After a while, I think he's fallen asleep.

I get hot because I'm covered in two duvets and now have his body as another source of heat. I untangle myself, kicking off the one wrapped around me until it falls to the floor. Then I spread my body to cool quickly.

"Are you still in love with him?"

Diaye's voice in the dark gets my heart racing.

"In ... In love with whom?" I stutter a little.

"Your ex, Mide."

"Of course not. God forbid bad thing."

"Then why were you so angry this afternoon?" Fabric rustles as if he's rolling onto his side.

I roll, too, to face him. I can make out his features in the dark. He's watching me.

"I was angry at you for not telling me something that could have saved me some pain. If you'd told me Mide was married. Or even told me he came to ask you for money. It would have prevented me from going to his house. You were being selfish, and I got humiliated because of it."

The sound of a heavy exhale fills the air. "I'm sorry. I was selfish, and you got humiliated. But you have to understand, I saw the effect of my father's cheating on my mother. She was broken-hearted for a long time. Sometimes I feel she died of heartache rather than cancer. It's the reason I could not ignore your ex betraying his wife with you."

The weight of his words presses down on me, along with understanding. The room is charged with unspoken pain and betrayal, his and mine entwined like threads of a barely mended tapestry.

His father's affairs made Diaye distrustful. Turned him into a vigilante of sorts. He punished Mide for his betrayal. But by default, he also punished me. I didn't deserve it.

The silence stretches, thin and taut.

I say nothing because I'm not ready to forgive him yet.

There's sudden movement, and the table lamp comes on. Diaye gets out of bed.

"Where are you going?" I ask.

"I'll be back in a moment." He walks out of the room and returns minutes later with his laptop. He sits on the bed, opens it, and taps a few times before turning the screen to face me. "If you want to understand why I was cynical about your relationship with your ex, watch this."

He taps the keyboard, and a video plays.

"That is my old apartment in Bishampton, and the person there is my ex, Phoebe."

It looks like the interior of a house in the camera shot. The woman goes to the door and opens it. A man walks in. An older man, middle-aged perhaps. He appears familiar. As soon as the door shuts, they start kissing and tearing at each other's clothes.

"Wait a minute. She was having an affair?" I glance at Diaye, eyes widened.

"Yes. Look at the time stamp," he says coolly.

"Goodness! I didn't know. But from what she posted online, she said she left you because you were being difficult. She said she didn't like your sexual demands."

"She said all that after I accused her of betraying me and kicked her out. She was trying to save her own skin."

"But why didn't you tell everyone she was having an affair?"

"I wanted to, but it's complicated. Her father is the head of the FA. He threatened me. Said if any of that came out, I would never play football in this country again. There wasn't much I could do. I couldn't trust my father to have my back. The only one on my side was Mr O. He told me to keep my head down and just play football. So I did."

"Oh, Diaye. I'm so sorry." I scramble across the bed and pull him into a tight hug. "You have me on your side now."

27

Diaye

The sleek black car hums to a stop outside the modern glass façade of Viva City FC's headquarters. The building gleams under the morning sun, its sturdy yet graceful design a symbol of the club's ambition and stature.

I step out, adjusting my tailored navy suit as my eyes take in my new surroundings. Beside me, Mr O'Connell is ever-poised and smooths a crease in his blazer, while giving an approving nod.

"This is it, Diaye," he says with a grin. "The next chapter."

I exhale deeply, my chest rising and falling as a mixture of excitement and gravity settles over me. I'm not just here to sign a contract. I'm stepping into a new era of my career. This one carries a weight of expectation which could crush lesser men. But I'm no ordinary footballer.

I'm Diaye Zambo.

A small smile tugs at the corners of my lips as we enter the building. A receptionist guides us through a corridor lined with framed jerseys and photographs of legends who have graced Viva City's pitch. The scent of polished wood and fresh coffee lingers in the air, and the faint hum of activity echoes through the space.

In a spacious conference room, Carlos Sanchez is already waiting. The stocky manager rises to greet us as we enter, the ever-present waistcoat over his black button-down shirt, a signature style of his. His handshake is firm, his smile broad but calculating.

"Diaye, welcome," Sanchez says, his voice carrying the same booming authority as it does on the training ground. "We've been waiting for this moment. You're going to make a hell of an impact here."

I nod, my face broadening with a smile, betraying the flicker of pride inside. "I'm ready. Let's make it official."

Mr O slides a sleek leather portfolio onto the table and opens it to reveal the contract. I lean forward, scanning the pages—a cascade of terms, clauses, and figures that will make me the third highest-paid defender on the planet. I already know the nitty-gritty as highlighted by my lawyers. Although last night, I discussed the terms again with Mr O in preparations for today.

Still, my pen hovers over the dotted line for a moment, long enough for the weight of the decision to settle on my shoulders. This has been in process since last summer when I was in Nigeria visiting Grandma.

"There's nothing wrong with building something from scratch..." Her words resound in my mind.

At the time, it seemed like too much work to start afresh, especially with a newly promoted club which had never been in the Premier League. However, the Panthers have fought their way up the league and are mid-table in twelfth position, away from the relegation zone. However, they are still conceding too many goals and their back four needs tightening, which is where I come in. If we plug the goal deficiencies, I reckon we could finish the season in the top ten, which is ambitious for a first-time club in the EPL. But I love ambition.

My pulse quickens, and I feel energised at the thought of contributing to the team's success. The weight of uncertainty I felt about this decision vanishes. Spurred on by the idea, I sign the document with deliberate precision.

"Congratulations," Sanchez declares, clapping me on the back. "You're officially part of Viva City."

"Thank you," I say as my lungs expand to their fullest with a surge of pride and a sense of purpose. I'm ready to embrace the challenge of improving the team's defence and striving for a top-ten finish in their debut Premier League season. Signing the contract marks not just a professional milestone but the beginning of a thrilling new chapter in my career.

Just like having Seki in my house was the beginning of a new period in my personal life. Since she moved in with me, I can't seem to get her out of my mind. It got worse since we started sharing a bed only days ago.

She came here as my pretend wife three weeks ago. But it has since evolved into a tentative friendship which comes with the benefits of sharing beds.

Especially after our fight and conversation last night when I showed her the videos of Phoebe having affairs with other men in my apartment. No one else has seen those videos aside from my lawyers.

Sharing the videos made me vulnerable, like I've never been with anyone else as an adult. Yet I had to show Seki so she would understand my emotional state when I landed in

Nigeria six months ago. It's another sign I'm becoming attached to my pretend wife. I know I'm hyper-focusing—

"Diaye, this is Vivian Osondu, our head of comms and media," Coach Sanchez cuts into my thoughts as a woman walks into the conference room.

Her name sounds familiar, but I can't immediately place it.

She is wearing a flamboyant multicoloured jacket over a black blouse, and trousers with matching court stilettos. She stretches out her hand as she beams a smile. "It's great to meet you. Welcome to the team."

Her voice triggers the memory.

"Thank you," I say, taking her hand. "I know you, don't I? You're the host of the Backroom Buzz Podcast, right?"

"Yes, it's a new show I started with my husband, Asher." She beams with a smile as she releases my hand and waves towards the door. "The press conference is this way."

I follow her down the corridor behind Coach Sanchez and Mr O. "I'm a fan of your show."

"Thank you. I hope we can have you as a guest on it as part of your comeback media tour."

"Yes, I would love it. I'm sure we can work something out." I grin as we reach the doors to the media room.

"Wonderful. I'll speak to your team, and we can schedule you in." She waves at the door for me to go in first.

The flashing cameras and the murmur of reporters greet me as I cross the threshold. A long table with microphones awaits us on a raised platform. Behind us, a backdrop proudly displays the Viva City FC crest and the sponsors. The energy crackles as the reporters prepare to throw questions at me and my new club manager.

I take the seat in the middle, flanked by Coach Sanchez and Mr O'Connell. The room falls silent as the head of comms steps up to the podium.

"Ladies and gentlemen, thank you for joining us today. I will read a brief statement on behalf of the club," Vivian begins.

"It is with great pleasure that we announce the signing of Diaye Zambo to Viva City Football Club. Diaye, who has represented England at various youth levels and the senior team, brings a wealth of experience and defensive prowess to our squad.

"He is renowned for his physicality, pace, and strong tackling abilities. His versatility, capable of playing both as a right-back and centre-back, will provide us with defensive stability and enhance our attacking strategies. Diaye is also a natural leader on the field, and we look forward to his contributions in organising our defence.

"His journey to this point has been marked by unwavering dedication and resilience. Diaye's addition to the team is not only a testament to his talent but also a reflection of the club's commitment to strengthening its core. Fans can look forward to witnessing his dynamic displays and tireless work ethic as he embraces this new chapter in his career."

She pauses and glances around the large room. "We'll now open the floor to questions."

A forest of hands shoot up, and the first question is directed at Sanchez.

"What does Diaye bring to the club that convinced you to make this signing?"

Sanchez leans toward the microphone, his confidence palpable. "Diaye is a player who embodies leadership, precision, and resilience. We needed someone who could not only anchor our defence but elevate the entire team. He's that player."

Another reporter turns to me. "Diaye, what does this move mean for you, personally and professionally?"

I adjust the microphone and let my conviction flow steady through my voice. "This is a new chapter for me, a chance to challenge myself at the highest level. Viva City isn't just a club. It's a family, and I'm honoured to be part of it. I'm here to win, plain and simple."

The next hour unfolds in a flurry of questions, flashes, and soundbites. I answer with the poise of someone who has long grown accustomed to the spotlight. I have been in the spotlight in one way or the other since I was a child, so it comes easy to me. My presence here at this press conference cements my arrival—not just as a new player, but as a symbol of Viva City's ambition.

As the session wraps up, Sanchez turns to me with a grin. "You handled that like a pro. Now let's get you on the pitch and show them what you're made of."

I smile as some of the weight of the day lifts. Not totally.

My journey with Viva City FC begins officially.

The world is watching.

While many cheer me on, some can't wait for me to falter.

• • • •

THE SUN BLAZES DOWN on the sprawling training ground as I step onto the pristine grass, my boots sinking into the pitch. I adjust my armband and survey my new teammates, who are scattered across the field, warming up with stretches and casual passing drills. The hum of energy is palpable, a mixture of camaraderie and competitive edge that brews among the players.

It's been a few days since I signed the contract to confirm my transfer from Bishampton United FC to Viva City FC. A few days since Seki and I crossed the line from friends to lovers. The incident on Friday when I had to drive out to her campus to pick her up culminated in my confession of my role in exposing her ex's married status which caused a big argument between us. Our first major argument since the day she arrived.

Mr O's phone call had interrupted it. He'd called to tell me that my former bosses had finally agreed to a fee with the Panthers' bosses. A fee that would make me the third highest paid defender on the planet. Physical tests and press conferences followed the contract signing. Now I am finally on the training grounds with my new teammates.

The coach, a stocky man with a booming voice and a whistle dangling from his neck, claps his hands to gather everyone around. "Alright, lads! Let's make it count today. We've got a match coming up, and I want to see some fire out there!"

I jog to join the huddle, feeling the curious eyes of my new teammates on me. I'm not just any new signing. I'm a name that carries weight in the football world, a name that came with expectations. The whispers and sidelong glances are something I've grown accustomed to, but they still prick at my composure.

"Diaye," the coach barks, pointing a finger at me. "I want you to lead the defence drills. Show them why we brought you in."

I nod curtly, the shadow of a smile tugging at my lips. "Got it, Coach."

The drills begin in earnest, the rhythm of studded boots drumming against the ball, and the air fills with sharp commands. I fall into sync, my every move fluid and deliberate. When a lanky midfielder misjudges a pass, I'm there in a heartbeat, intercepting it with a deft touch and sending it spiralling towards our forward with precision.

The forward, Asher Uzodimma, who plays on the right wing with a fiery streak, claps me on the back. "Not bad for the new guy."

"Not bad?" I grin, flashing my teeth. "That's just the warm-up."

We share a laugh, the tension cracking, and the drills grow sharper, faster, more cohesive. The coaches prowl the sidelines, shouting instructions and offering praise sparingly.

I feel myself easing into the rhythm, my instincts taking over as I navigate the plays with a mix of finesse and grit.

During a break, I lean against the goalpost, my shirt clinging to my back as I gulp down water. A few of the younger players approach, their admiration obvious in their sparkling eyes and tentative smiles.

"Hey, Diaye," one of them ventures, clutching a ball nervously. "Any tips for improving ball control?"

I wipe my brow and crouch down to their level, my tone easy and encouraging. "Ball control is all about connection. You've got to feel the ball, not fight it. Here, let me show you."

As I demonstrate a quick series of touches and turns, the group of players watch intently, nodding at my every word. Somewhere in the distance, the head coach observes, a glimmer of approval in his eyes.

By the time training wraps up, I feel the ache in my muscles and the satisfying weight of a solid session. As I stroll towards the locker room, I catch sight of the old club emblem painted on the wall, its colours bright and bold. For the first time in a long while, I allow myself a moment of quiet pride.

This is a new beginning—a place to prove myself not just as a player, but as a teammate. And as the sun dips lower in the sky, casting long shadows across the field, I know I am ready to rise to the challenge.

• • • •

A WEEK LATER, THE PANTHER'S Lair pub buzzes with the energy of camaraderie and triumph, the air thick with the scent of fried food and the hum of laughter. This is the local watering hole for the Viva City FC AKA Panthers players and supporters.

I sit at a corner table surrounded by my new teammates, the glow of victory still fresh on their faces. Glasses clink in celebration, and the occasional burst of song erupts across the room.

Asher, ever the live-wire, takes centre stage, recounting his last-minute assist with animated gestures that have the table in stitches. "And then—bam! Right between the defender's legs. Poetry in motion," he declares, his grin spreading as the others roar their approval.

I offer a modest smile, nursing a pint as I listen, the warmth of belonging settling into my chest. Next to me, a midfielder, Nonso Chijuka, leans in, nudging me with an elbow. "You, Diaye, that header in the first half—unstoppable, mate. Honestly, thought you'd break the net."

"Had to make it count," I reply, my tone easy, but tinged with pride. "Can't let you lot down, right?"

The table erupts into cheers, calls of "Zambo!" echoing through the pub. Someone raises their glass, and the group follows suit, a chorus of goodwill filling the air.

As the evening progresses, the conversation meanders from the match to life outside the pitch. I about Asher's love for jazz, the left-back's culinary experiments, and the goalkeeper's half-serious dream of opening a coffee shop. I share snippets of my story, my journey to this team, the sacrifices made along the way. With every exchanged word, the bonds of trust and friendship deepen.

By the time the night winds down, the pub quieting as patrons trickle out, I feel the ache in my cheeks from smiling too much. As I step outside, the cool night air hits me, refreshing and sharp. My teammates linger in the doorway, their chatter and laughter carrying on as one of them calls out, "Same time next week after our next win, yeah?"

I nod, my heart buoyed by the promise of more nights like this, more wins, more unity. This isn't just the beginning of my journey with the team—it feels like a homecoming. As long as the team keeps performing like we did today, we stand a strong chance of finishing in the top ten of the EPL table.

28

Seki

The party is in full swing by the time Diaye and I arrive, the soft hum of music mingling with bursts of laughter as we step into the Uzodimmas' elegantly lit garden. Fairy lights stretch like constellations above the crowd, glinting off glasses of champagne and casting a gentle glow over the assembled guests. Tables adorned with understated centrepieces—white roses and sprigs of eucalyptus—line the edges of the space while a buffet of delicacies tempts even the most disciplined athletes.

This is my first formal party since my arrival in the UK. My first party, full stop. It's organised by the club's vivacious head of communications, Vivi, who is also married to one of the players, Asher Uzodimma.

I met her the first time the week after Diaye signed for the club. There was a meet and greet session at the club where I met some members of staff. I was assigned a liaison on Vivi's team, whose job was to help Diaye and me settle by providing information about the local area. Information from the best restaurant to eat to the best schools for my unborn kids. They have been super welcoming.

Tonight's dress code is black and gold, which are the Panthers' club colours. The men are mostly in black suits, tunic sets, or shirts and trousers. The women glitter in various shades of gold.

I'm in a mermaid-style, pearl-sequined, long-sleeved, floor-length evening gown with ruched champagne satin. Diaye bought it as a gift to me, and I feel like a princess wearing it with the strappy gold high-heeled sandals. Even had a make-up artist visit the house to do my face and style my hair. My braids are wrapped in a high bun that looks like a crown with the pearly pins holding it up. I even took a photo and sent it to my sisters. They can't believe it's me looking so glamourous and sophisticated. Inside, I'm still the girl from Sapele via Warri. But for a night, I can be a princess.

This place is a stunning contemporary luxury house near to us. It has modern architecture, set on three floors with a gable roof, a sleek finish, and large glass windows and glass doors leading into an elegant garden with a lawn. It has double-height ceilings and huge open spaces at the front and back.

Vivi approaches us with a welcoming smile, which mirrors the warmth of the evening. She is in an iridescent knee-length, fringe V-neck dress, and her black hair is in a bob. She looks like a film star from the 1920s.

"Diaye! Seki! You made it. Welcome!" she exclaims, her enthusiasm contagious.

"Thank you," Diaye says as they shake hands.

"You have a beautiful home," I say when she pulls me in for a hug. The garden is humongous enough to house a marquee for those wishing to escape the February chill, although there are outdoor heaters at various spots in the garden.

"Thank you. We've only been here a few months, but I love it." She leans back and waves around. "Tonight's all about you two settling in and soaking up the team spirit. Let me introduce you to the rest."

I suppose she's doing it for my benefit because Diaye has been playing for the team for almost a month now. He should know most of the people here.

From what I gather from him, the Panthers are doing well. They haven't lost a match in seven games since my husband joined them. So, he's having a positive impact because their defence is locked tight. They won the match they played this afternoon in Northside Park, which is their home stadium. Hence the celebratory mood of everyone here tonight.

Diaye nods, taking in the scene as Vivi shows us around. Players mingle with their partners, the camaraderie flowing as freely as the drinks. The hum of conversation is punctuated by bursts of laughter—Nonso Chijuka entertaining a small group with his wit, Asher, Vivi's husband, describing a moment from the today's match to a couple of spouses who listen with delight.

Vivi passes two champagne flutes over from the drinks table and steers us to a man and woman at the entrance of the marquee talking in quiet tones, heads almost making contact, his hand around her waist. She clears her throat, getting their attention, and they turn to us with smiling faces.

"Seki, this is Idara, the director of our outreach initiatives. Idara, this is Seki, Diaye's wife," Vivi says. "Excuse me for a moment." She walks away to attend to another guest.

"It's nice to meet you finally, Seki." Idara extends her hand. "I was talking to Diaye the other day about you when he was telling me about the charity events he did last summer in West Africa. That was how you two met, right?"

My cheeks heat, and I smile shyly as I glance at my husband, who is the epitome of composure as always and grinning. "Yes, that's how we met. But he didn't tell me he's been talking about me."

Diaye leans towards me, eyes sparkling and murmurs, "Only good things, Wifey."

"How did this guy sucker you into giving him a chance?" The man who was talking to Idara comes closer with a smile and extends his hand. "I'm Ehizojie, but you can call me Ehi. I know he didn't tell you how I used to run circles around him?"

"Not exactly." I chuckle, shaking his hand. "He told me you two were briefly at the same youth academy, right?"

"That's right. That's where he got the 'Strongman' nickname," Ehi says, stepping back.

"I call him Strongman for a different reason," I murmur.

Diaye chuckles and meets my gaze as my cheeks heat again. I take another sip of champagne to cool down. The alcohol must have loosened my tongue. Then again, I don't need alcohol to speak my mind.

"I'm not even gonna ask what that meant." Ehi grins.

"Good choice, babe." Idara chuckles. The two of them are engaged according to Diaye, and they look it from their interactions. "Come with me, and I'll introduce you to the people in the marquee."

The conversation flows, and I feel at home with these people. It helps that some of them are of African descent, even Nigerians. There's Nigerian food. Diaye went to the barbeque station and returned with beef suya on skewers, amongst other delicacies. Vivi pulled out all the stops with the party. Her charm is irresistible, and she knows how to make an impression.

The night unfolds seamlessly. I find myself sitting in the marquee, ensconced in a conversation with Vivi, Idara, Yinka, who is Nonso's fiancée, and Temi, who is Vivi's cousin and best friend. We are discussing the intricacies of balancing football with family life. It's' a world I rarely think about, but as I listen, I can't help but admire the strength and humour threading through their stories. They are older than me and have more experience living in the UK, so I want to learn as much as possible.

A woman and man walk into the marquee. They must have just arrived because I didn't see them earlier.

"Excuse me a moment." Vivi stands to greet them. "Luca, it's good of you to join us."

"It's always good to attend one of your parties. This is my girlfriend, Phoebe."

As soon as I hear the name, blood drains from my head. It can't be her!

My gaze flies upwards as I look at them. The woman has blond hair and is dressed in a mesh, sleeveless, rhinestone bodycon long dress and matching stilettos. She has her back to me, and I can't see her face.

"It's nice to meet you," Vivi says, but doesn't shake the woman's hand, which is surprising because she is usually warm and welcoming.

"Thank you," the woman says and turns in my direction.

My entire body stiffens, and my ears ring. I don't hear Temi talking to me.

"Are you okay?" she repeats.

Idara and Yinka frown and stare at me.

I turn my face away and wave my hand, indicating for the women to lean closer, which they do.

"That woman is Diaye's ex," I whisper to them.

"Really?" Temi's eyes widen.

"What is she doing with Luca?" Idara glances at them and looks back at me.

"What is she doing here?" Yinka says.

"I don't know," I mutter. "She is the last person I expected to see here."

"The audacity... Do you want to leave? Do you want me to find Diaye?" Temi asks, looking concerned.

"No. Why should I leave? I haven't done anything wrong, and I was here first," I say, tilting my chin up and channelling the inner Warri girl in me.

"That's the spirit," Idara says with a small smile.

I relax back in the chair as Vivi walks back to the table with Phoebe in tow.

"Ladies, let me introduce Phoebe. She came with Luca De Rossi. Phoebe, that's Yinka." Vivi starts with the woman to my left.

"Hi," Yinka says with a small smile but doesn't extend her hand.

"And Seki." Vivi waves at me.

"Hi," I mutter, my hands on my lap, a stony expression on my face. Me, I can't do this fake smile Oyibo people have mastered.

"That's Temi." She waves at her cousin.

Temi just does the finger wave without talking. Her expression is anything but welcoming.

"And Idara." Vivi completes the introductions.

"Welcome," Idara says.

"It's nice to meet you, ladies," Phoebe chimes in a saccharine cheerful voice, pulls out the chair next to Yinka and sits without invitation. Her eyes are glazed and dull. She must be drunk or getting there. "You don't mind if I join you, do you?"

Vivi looks at me with an apologetic expression as she settles in the remaining chair, which is opposite mine. She is sitting between Phoebe and Idara. I'm sitting between Yinka and Temi. Temi is next to Idara. The round table sits six.

Vivi doesn't look happy. It seems she also knows Phoebe is Diaye's ex. Vivi is a journalist by trade, so she would have known when Diaye's scandal with Phoebe broke on the news.

Temi puts her elbow on the table, covering the side of her face as she turns to me. "Do you want to move?"

She is being protective, and I respect it. The ladies have been kind to me today. They've taken me under their wings like a younger sister. They even added me to their group chat. It's nice to have sisters away from home. But I can fight my battles, and I'm not afraid of Phoebe. Far from it.

"No. I'm okay," I say and reach for my drink. If the woman is trying to intimidate me, she's on a long ting.

The air is tense, like one of those episodes of the Real Housewives franchise with the WAGs gathered around the table at an event with smiles on their faces when they really hate each other.

"So, ladies," Phoebe says nonchalantly after taking a long sip of her champagne. "Let's play a game. It's called Name The Spouse."

"What kind of stupid game is that?" Temi says.

"It's just a game. It's fun. Trust me," Phoebe says, batting her lashes coyly.

"Nobody wants to play a game with you!" Temi retorts.

"Ah. Is it because you don't have a spouse? Poor girl." Phoebe flicks her acrylic nails with a bored expression.

"What did you say to me, bitch?" Temi pushes back her chair and looks like she's about to lunge at Phoebe, but Idara holds her back.

People at the other tables turn in our direction.

"Phoebe, I think it's best if you move to a different table," Vivi says, looking annoyed.

"I just want to talk to her." She points at me.

Everyone turns in my direction, and I hate how this woman walked in here and changed the joyous atmosphere. She is so toxic.

I'm already pissed off with her because of what she did to Diaye and how she was the reason he didn't visit his grandmother for five years.

"What the hell do you want to talk to me about?" I snap.

"We have something in common." She does that fake smile again, and I lose my shit.

"You dey mad, if you think I have anything in common with you." I don't even know when I lapse into Pidgin. But it's my natural language when I'm angry.

She jerks back, looking shocked. She recovers, fixing the smile back, but the tightness around her eyes gives her away. "We have Diaye in common, and I wanted to talk to you about the way he is."

"Talk to me as what, exactly?" I glance around the table, and the other women are looking at her with a mix of horror and morbid fascination. "We're not friends."

"But we're both women. And Diaye can be abusive—"

"Shut your smelly, lying mouth up there." I cut her off, shoving my chair back and standing.

She gasps and shifts in her chair, looking offended. "But we know how he gets in bed."

"You mean *you* couldn't handle Strongman in bed." I wave my hand up and down at her, unable to hide my contempt. "Then, you lied against him to hide your betrayals. Now you show up here, practically stalking him. You are being manipulative, and you know it."

I glance around the room and the fire to defend Diaye burns in my belly. "Let me set the record straight for anyone who is wondering. First, there is no law against consensual kinky sex between adults. Second, Diaye would never force anyone to do anything they didn't want to do."

She shifts in the seat, eyes darting around. She didn't expect me to defend Diaye so vehemently or so vocally. Tough.

Diaye has his faults, but she's telling lies. I will defend him against her false allegations.

"I'm only trying to help you." She tugs at her dress, looking sweaty and uncomfortable.

"She doesn't need your help, Ms White Saviour," Temi says.

Phoebe's eyes go wide, and her mouth opens.

Buoyed by Temi's support, I don't let her get a word in. "As for your complaints about my Diaye. Did they come before or after you started having affairs with other men?"

"Why would you say that?" Her face goes red, and the room goes quiet. It seems someone turned the background music off. Everyone in the marquee is watching us.

"I've seen the videos." I emphasis the plural, so everyone will know she did it more than once. People gasp. "You had the audacity to sleep with other men in Diaye's apartment. Much like your audacity to show up here and think you can intimidate me."

Her face rumples, and she looks like she's going to cry. But I don't buy that shit for one minute. I don't trust her motives. Why else would she come to this party knowing Diaye would be here, if not to cause trouble?

"I was only trying to help you—" Are those crocodile tears in her eyes? "—because William said Diaye brought you from an African village and you don't know anything. Like you did a ritual in your village and you think that means you're married to Diaye, but you're not."

She glances around the marquee, lips turned down, as if appealing to the other people that her actions are genuine. Some of them seem to be sympathetic to her.

Her words are like a hammer driving into my chest. Something cracks inside me, and a burn ignites in my larynx and spread upward, putting pressure behind my eyeballs.

I try to hold it together, but it's so intense, I can't form words, and I struggle to breathe. My arms curl around my midriff as if protecting myself.

It's not the first time someone has mentioned my marriage to Diaye with such condescension.

"But I have news for you, jeune fille. Traditional weddings don't count."

William Zambo has obviously been telling anyone who cares to listen that his son and I are not legally married. How many more people are going to make fun of me about it?

When I made the fake marriage pact with Diaye months ago, I didn't envisage I would long to become his wife for real. Our life together since I arrived in the UK has seemed real, especially since we started making love and sharing a bed. It feels like I'm married. We're here at this party and everyone thinks we're a happy couple.

But Phoebe's words expose the truth of it.

"Of course you'll say that, Ms Coloniser." Temi must see my distress because she comes to my rescue again.

"Why would you say this to me? It's racist!" Phoebe whines.

"How dare you?" Temi retorts. "You have the audacity to tell a Black African person her wedding is invalid because she didn't perform it the way the colonisers who invaded her country forced on the indigenes and you have the guts to call me racist? Do you even know what it means?"

A sharp scream pierces the ensuing silence, making everyone jump, snapping me out of my distress about the non-marriage thing.

All the women around the table gape at Phoebe, who just made the awful noise. This woman is mad o.

The men gathered outside chatting around the barbeque platform all rush inside, including Diaye, who pushes his way straight to me.

"Seki, are you okay?" He looks me over for any sign of injury, and I nod, letting him wrap an arm around me.

"What's going on?" Asher asks, standing next to his wife, Vivi.

"I just sat at their table to be friendly, and they were being horrible to me." Phoebe lifts her face, and her mascara is streaked. She looks like she has been crying.

Goodness. This woman can act.

"What did they do?" Luca asks, coming closer with a frown on his face.

"She's being a racist to me and called me a coloniser." Phoebe points at Temi.

"Say that again?" Asher asks, looking bemused.

"She called me a coloniser!" she repeats.

You could hear a pin drop in the subsequent stillness as people stare at Phoebe, gobsmacked.

Diaye bursts into laughter. It's loud and infectious. My anger at Phoebe and her theatrics disappears, and I join in, giggling as he holds me close. It's the only way to react to the madness the woman just displayed. Others try to hold it in and cover their faces. Some people are not laughing, but I don't care.

"Luca, I don't know why you brought this woman here. But trust me, she's not worth the trouble she is going to cause you. Take her home," Diaye says, still chuckling.

"Phoebe, come on. We're going," Luca says in a sharp, angry tone.

Phoebe stands and staggers. Luca stomps out of the marquee, dragging her with him.

I watch my husband, and there isn't a flicker of regret or animosity in his appearance. Not even contempt.

Now I understand why Diaye was adamant about me severing ties with my ex. He went to the extent of ensuring Mide lost his job at the hotel and left Sapele.

It's the same way he's cut Phoebe from his life with precision. She will never mean anything to him other than an ex. He feels nothing for her. Not even anger.

It's a cold and ruthless way to relate to someone you once cared about. Yet, it's the best way to deal with people like Phoebe and Mide.

On impulse, I turn into Diaye, stand on my toes, and kiss him before whispering, "I love you."

He stiffens and stares down at me with a heated gaze. "You mean that?"

"Absolutely. I love you," I repeat, expecting him to say the words back to me. I know it's out of the blue. We've been through our challenges when I first arrived. But the past month with him has been amazing. Surely, he feels the same way.

Instead, his eyes sparkle as he lowers his head and kisses me long and hard, and we only break apart when everyone claps.

"Wifey, this is becoming a habit." He grins and steers me towards the other party guests.

My stomach drops. He didn't say it back. He doesn't feel the same way.

Diaye is not in love with me.

29

Diaye

The glow of the television flickers in the dim living room, reflecting off the edges of the controller I grip more tightly than I should. My thumbs move instinctively, guiding my character through a virtual battlefield filled with chaos and danger—so different, yet eerily similar to the turmoil brewing in my real life.

Something has been off with Seki since the night of the welcome party two days ago at Asher's house, which isn't far from us. She was quiet on the drive home, and I thought she was just exhausted from the excitement and brouhaha of Phoebe's appearance at the event.

We didn't make love that night. Not because I didn't want her. I crave her every goddamned day.

But I've learned to read her cues. When she's quiet, she's either exhausted or upset. Either way, I let her be and give her space. We've been sleeping in the same bed since we became lovers. Whether we're fucking or not, angry with each other or not, we still share the same bed every night. It's a rule that will never change.

Yesterday was an intense training day. I didn't get home until late. She was in bed and reading a book. We greeted each other and chatted briefly. She mentioned she was on campus for classes this morning and in the afternoon, she had a driving lesson. I told her about my training day before I went into the bathroom for a shower, although I'd already had one at the training grounds.

It was an excuse to avoid deeper conversations with her because I think I have an inkling to why she's upset.

She said the three words 'I love you' at the party and I didn't say them back to her.

It was a selfish, asshole move. I know it.

It's not because I don't feel something for her. I do. I care about her. More than I cared about Phoebe.

This makes it so scary, especially coming on the back of seeing my ex giving one of her BAFTA-worthy performances in front of my new teammates and their spouses.

Phoebe told me she loved me first, and look where we are.

It reminded me of all the reasons I don't want to be in a relationship. All the reasons I shouldn't care deeply for another woman. For Seki.

So, I just couldn't bring myself to say those words to her and make myself any more vulnerable than I already am with her.

Seki saying 'I love you' makes no difference. She also told me she would leave me one day.

And all indications show she is preparing herself for such a day.

For one, she got a part-time job. While I understand the necessity of having one to help build her CV and confidence for the UK job market, she doesn't have to do more than a few hours a week. Yet, she is working the full twenty hours she's entitled to on her visa.

Why is she doing this when I'm paying all her bills?

Reasoning with her only turned into an argument. She harped on about wanting her independence, as if I was trying to deprive her of it.

I try to show my unwavering commitment to providing her with everything she wants and needs, making sure she feels secure in our relationship. Still, it doesn't seem enough for her.

See, I get it. She was doing two jobs in Sapele while she was a student. So, getting a job here while at university might feel like child's play, especially when she can save whatever she's earning.

I don't want to dim her shine. Hence the reason I didn't push it.

But I fear her unwillingness to depend on me, to trust me to take care of her is an indication she will leave one day. All she has to do is wait for the two years required to complete her professional certification. By then she'll be qualified as a registered nurse in the UK because she is doing an accelerated course as a graduate. She can then pocket the two million euros she would have earned from me and walk away.

I promised to pay her a million euros for each year she stays with me up to a maximum of five million. Perhaps I shouldn't have been so generous. Then again, she would have so much more than five mil if she stays married to me beyond the agreed time limit.

Forever.

Am I really thinking about forever with Seki?

Have I lost the plot?

My thoughts spiral, unravelling the unease clinging to me. I've tried suppressing it, rationalising everything, telling myself Seki's drive, her ambition, is part of why I fell for her in the first place. Yet, I can't ignore the undercurrent of fear, the nagging whisper all this independence is her way of preparing her exit. And perhaps my silence, my retreat into myself, has only added fuel to the fire.

She's always been assertive, always had this spark of determination which could light up a room—or burn down bridges. But lately, it feels less like an ember of passion and more like a calculated plan. A strategy. A way out.

I don't know whether to confront her about these feelings or keep them buried. Every attempt at discussing our future seems to devolve into tension, a delicate dance of words where one misstep leads to a fall. And so, I stay quiet. I focus on the here and now. On what I can control. Because maybe, just maybe, if I keep showing her I'm here for her, she'll realise she doesn't need to go anywhere. That she has everything she needs right here.

But then, there are moments when her actions feel like a statement, even if unspoken. It's as though she's carving out a piece of herself, which doesn't include me.

And it terrifies me.

The thought lingers as I try to focus on preparing for tomorrow's game, wrapping myself in the comforting blanket of routine and distraction. Yet, the unease remains, an unwelcome guest in my mind.

Today I'm in my pre-match preparation as we have a crucial away game against one of the top four teams. They are challenging opponents, and the last time we met them, before I joined the team, they thrashed us by three goals to one on our home turf. So we—the Panthers—need to bring our A game to come back with any points while playing on their home turf tomorrow.

Playing this video game now is helping my focus and re-laxation. Afterwards, I'm getting an early night in bed. The explosions and chatter coming from the TV are loud, and they drown out everything else.

I don't hear Seki walk into the room, but she appears in my periphery as she comes closer.

My body stiffens as dread slithers down my back. She usually leaves me to my pre-game routine. So her presence must mean she wants to talk about the issue hanging in the air between us.

"What are you going to do about this?" Her voice slices through the air, sharp and unforgiving, a direct hit.

"About what?" Surprised at her tone, I tilt my head to glance at her before looking back at the screen. This is a something in her eyes I haven't seen before.

"Are you really going to pretend you haven't seen this?" she demands, stopping on the other side of the coffee table and crossing her arms.

I blink, shifting my focus from the screen.

"What are you talking about?" I ask, distracted, my char-acter ducking behind cover as if it would somehow shield me from her words.

"Don't play dumb with me, Diaye. You're sitting here, hiding behind a video game as usual. It's obvious you don't care about me or this mess of a relationship."

Her accusation stings more than I want to admit. With a heavy sigh, I pause the game and set the controller down on the coffee table. "It's not hiding, Seki. It's just... decompressing. You know I have a game coming up tomorrow."

"In other words, you are the priority, and I'm just an accessory," she shoots back, her voice raw with incredulity. Her arms fall to her sides, her fists clenching. "Do you think you're the only one who needs to decompress?"

"Seki, seriously. This is not the time for this. We have an agreement. Nothing can distract my pre-match day routine."

"Nothing? Not even my welfare?"

This is not a good night for a tense discussion. Tomorrow's game is too crucial for me to mess up. The nightmare of the last time I had an argument before a match flashes in my mind. The same game where I made a mistake and scored an own goal. No, this can't happen again.

"Is it a life-or-death matter? Can it wait until after the game tomorrow?" I say in a sharp tone because I need to nip this argument in the bud before it screws up my focus.

"No, it's not life-or-death. But it's important to me. And you've reminded me again and again that I'm not important to you."

Her words hit me like a sucker punch. I lean back into the soft teal velvet throw cushions she added to the sofas, running a hand down my face as if it could somehow erase the guilt clawing at me.

"I'm tired, Seki," I admit finally, my voice quieter, carrying the weight of my exhaustion. "I asked you a few days if anything was wrong and you said no. Now you're behaving as if I'm a horrible person ignoring you. When it's not true.

Do you know the reason I don't talk to my father or other siblings so much anymore? Because they make me feel like whatever I do is not enough for them. And honestly, you're making me feel the same way."

The air between us crackles with unspoken words. Seki stands in front of the TV, gripping her phone so tight as if it were the only thing keeping her anchored.

"You're tired." She nods several times, glaring at me. "You know what? It's okay. I'll leave you alone."

Huffing, she walks out of the sitting room, and I slump back into the sofa in frustration. Knowing she's upset makes me uncomfortable. But I've got to keep my mind clear. Otherwise, tomorrow's game could be a disaster. I won't let that happen.

I scrub my fingers over my hair, which I cut when I signed a contract with Viva City to signify a fresh start with my career. Then I pick up the controller and switch the TV back on, getting back to the video game.

• • • •

THE NEXT DAY, I LEAVE the house early to head to the training ground. Seki is getting dressed to go to classes. I kiss her on the cheek at the breakfast table and tell her I'll see her tonight and we will talk. She nods and says goodbye to me as I leave.

Then I head out for the briefing before our trip across to southwest London to play the match.

The match is intense, the kind that gets your blood pumping and makes you forget the world outside the pitch. Victory comes after ninety minutes of relentless effort. As the team celebrates, the weight of the argument with Seki lingers at the back of my mind, gnawing at the edges of my triumph.

The bus ride back to the training ground is a blur of laughter, music, and the occasional chant of "Diaye!" My teammates' cheers are loud enough to drown out every thought except their jubilation. Yet, as I step off the bus into the crisp evening air, the silence greeting me feels heavier than usual.

It would be nice if Seki was here to meet me, like some of the other spouses kissing and embracing the returning football heroes. Seki has a life outside of my career. She is trying to build hers. So I get why she's not here. She hasn't attended any of my other games. This one is no different.

Despite my worry, I console myself with thinking she's calmed down by now. Maybe I'll walk in to find her curled up on the sofa with those teal cushions, her phone in hand, scrolling through something. We can talk—really talk—without the sharp edges of exhaustion and frustration clouding our words. Perhaps we'll kiss and make up and fuck for the first time since the party.

"Diaye, hold up. Hold up." Asher, whose car is a few rows away in the car park, jogs up to me.

"Ash, what's up?" I lean against the car as he reaches me.

"Not much, man." We do the dap handshake. "I just wanted to ask how Seki is doing."

My eyes narrow as a worm of suspicion curls inside me.

"She's doing fine. Why do you want to know?" My voice is sharper than normal.

Why is he asking about my wife? Of course, he can enquire about her wellbeing because he's my friend. But it's the way he asked the question, which raises all my hackles up. He's older than me by five years, and I respect him and his dedication to the team. But I won't hesitate to take him out if his intentions towards Seki are untoward.

"Chill, man. It's not like that," he says in a serious tone. "Vivi mentioned Seki was trending on social media—"

"Trending? What the hell do you mean, trending?" I cut in as my blood runs hot and I try to picture nightmare scenarios. A sex tape, mostly.

Seki knows I avoid social media. I have social media presence, but my personal assistant, who is part of my management team, manages the pages. Phoebe used to manage my pages as my PA. This was how we became involved. After I ended our relationship, she lost the job.

"Something about a less than flattering photo of Seki, which is getting a lot of negative comments." Asher's statement brings me back to the present.

"Fuck. When was this?" I grip the key fob so tight, the lights flash on the car.

Was this the reason Seki wanted to talk yesterday?

"Vivi told me yesterday. But I think the photo was posted on Monday, maybe."

Today is Wednesday. Fuckity fuck fuck.

"Ash, thanks for telling me. But I have to get home now." I move back and yank the car door.

"No worries, man. Reach out if you need help. Vivi is good with the media. She can help. I'm here, too." Ash hugs me before I hop into the car.

"Thanks, man," I say before starting the engine and gunning the car.

The drive home feels longer than usual, the weight of the news pressing down on me as the city blurs past. I curse under my breath, my mind racing with thoughts of Seki, of the photo, of the storm that must be brewing online. The hum of the engine quiets the noise in my head.

By the time I reach the outskirts of the neighbourhood, the familiar streets seem foreign, shadows stretching across the pavement like silent sentinels. I barely register the glowing streetlights as I turn into the cul-de-sac, my grip on the steering wheel tightening with each passing second.

I think about reaching out to Vivi, as Ash suggested. But this isn't just about managing media fallout. It's about Seki—her pain, her silence, and the distance growing between us. It twists uncomfortably in my chest.

Pulling into the driveway, I stare at the house. Its familiar silhouette doesn't soothe me like it used to. Instead, it stood there, still and indifferent. I drag in a deep breath, clutching the car keys, and walk to the entrance. The security lights come on automatically as they should.

"Seki!" I call out, pushing open the front door.

The light in the foyer in on. It's always on when we're out to prevent opportunistic burglars from getting this far. Just like other lights around the house come on at several intervals to project the idea of being occupied.

But the rest of the house is dark and silent—too silent. Like a cold shoulder.

My keys clatter onto the hallway table, and my gaze sweeps through the space. Seki's shoes, which she always kicks off near the door, are gone. Her coat is missing from the rack. The air carries a strange stillness, as if the home itself inhaled and refuses to exhale.

"Seki?" My voice echoes through the house.

No answer.

My pulse quickens as I run up the stairs with my shoes still on. I walk into the master bedroom. The bed is made, untouched from this morning. The part-time housekeeper was in today. She comes twice a week, Wednesdays and Saturdays.

Everything is still as neat as she left it. There isn't even a bum imprint on the bed linen, which means Seki didn't sit on it when she came home this afternoon.

Is she in her old room? She knows not to go there.

I stomp across the longish hallway and throw the bedroom door open. Darkness and emptiness greet me.

Still no Seki.

Where is she?

I glance at the clock on my phone as I pull it out. Five past ten at night.

Where is she?

I dial her number. It rings several times and goes to voicemail. I leave a message.

"Seki, I just got home and you're not here. Are you okay? Where are you?"

Where the hell is she?

My heart is thumping hard against my ribs.

The last time I had cause to look for her was the day she'd stayed back at the campus after lectures and I found her at the student bar. Surely she didn't decide to stay on this late again.

I flick to the location app and open it. I convinced her to install it because she could also track my location in an emergency. Until this moment, I've never needed to use it. The app pinpoints her location to a quiet suburb nestled between the bustling campus and our familiar neighbourhood. It's a saved location—the care home where she works.

Is she at work? At this time? It can't be.

When she accepted the job offer, she chose to work during the days rather than nights. We agreed night shifts were off the table. No matter how busy our days get, we always make time and space for each other at night. It's non-negotiable.

So why is she at work now?

She's deliberately doing this. She has to be. Just like she purposely overstayed at the student bar the other time. This is her way of punishing me because I didn't talk to her last night.

This time, it's so much worse. She is putting a physical barrier between us because I can't stop her from working.

Nah. I'm not having it.

Grabbing my keys, I don't think—I move. Out the door, into the night.

I have to find her and speak to her.

The car snarls to life beneath me, headlights cutting through the dense shadows of the street as I speed towards the care home. The cold air seeps through the slightly cracked window, grounding me amid the storm of my thoughts. The trees lining the road seem to loom closer, their bare branches clawing at the midnight sky.

I don't remember driving. The streets blur past. My knuckles stretched tight as I grip the steering wheel.

When I finally pull into the care home's parking lot, the fluorescent lights above cast a sterile glow over the asphalt. I reverse into an empty spot facing the entrance of the building and park the car.

Then I pull out my phone and see a text from Seki: *I heard your voice note. Work needed an emergency cover for tonight and I volunteered. I'll be home in the morning. Sorry.*

Reading it twists something sharp in my chest.

She doesn't seem sorry at all.

I send a response: *I'm outside your workplace. I need to talk to you. Come outside.*

It takes a few seconds for her reply: *I can't. I'm at work. Go home. I'll see you in the morning.*

"I'm not going anywhere," I grit out as I send the same words to her by text and settle in for the night.

30

Seki

The care home smells of antiseptic and fading flowers. It's a smell you get used to, one that settles into the seams of your clothes and skin, refusing to let go even after you've left. I'm bone-tired. The kind of tired which burrows deep and makes every movement feel heavier than it should. The last notes of dawn filter through the windows, staining the hallway in pale gold as I finish my shift.

I pull my woollen coat tighter against the chill as I step into the lobby. My colleagues chat in low voices among themselves, the mood subdued as always in this place, where loud laughter feels out of place. I'm leaving an hour earlier than my night-shift colleagues because of the restriction on the weekly hours I can work. I nod at them before pushing the door open and stepping outside.

The cold strikes. It's sharper than I expected, biting at my cheeks and hands. The morning air carries a stillness, as if the world hasn't quite woken up yet. But it's not the air arresting me—it's the car parked across the lot, and the figure slumped in the driver's seat. Diaye.

He stayed all night.

I'm not going anywhere.

He said as much in his texts last night, even though I told him to leave.

Hope flared in me last night when I read the text. Maybe he feels something for me.

Yet I squashed the hope because I know whatever he feels is not enough. I will always be second place in his life. He's shown me as much over the past weeks and months.

Last night when I took a quick break and listened to his voice message, I cried at the concern in his voice. He sounded worried, and I felt remorse for not being at home when he returned from his match. At the same time, I felt happy because he noticed my absence and was concerned. How ridiculous that something so simple could make me happy. Luckily, nobody else was there to see the tears in my eyes. I wiped them before sending him a message to explain my absence.

The last-minute request to cover this shift was a godsend, considering the nightmare that has been my life for the past few days.

First was Diaye not telling me he loved me at the welcome party over the weekend.

I can't articulate my disappointment in him.

Then yesterday, I woke to a text from my sister telling me I was trending on social media. She told me not to look, that people were posting horrible things about me. Of course, I checked and was devastated by what I read on Liam's and Phoebe's pages.

The two of them seem to have joined forces to denigrate me online.

I rushed downstairs to tell Diaye about it, and he was playing video games.

He was playing make-believe online while my real life was imploding!

Of course, I was fuming with him.

I still am.

Yet, the reality of his presence at my place of work feels heavier than his words on my screen.

I hesitate, my breath puffing out in clouds as I clutch my bag tighter against my side. For a moment, I consider turning back, slipping into the warmth of the care home until he tires of waiting and leaves. But I know him too well to believe it would work. Diaye doesn't walk away from things—not when he's decided they matter.

In any case, my taxi will arrive any minute, so I should confront him now.

Gathering myself, I make my way across the lot. The sound of my boots against the asphalt feels loud in the stillness. When I reach his car, he stirs, sitting up straighter and rubbing his eyes like someone waking from a restless dream. His gaze locks on mine, and I see the storm he always carries behind him. It's there in the tight line of his jaw, in the way his knuckles grip the steering wheel even though the engine is off.

"Morning," I say, keeping my voice steady, surprised the window on his side is down. I suppose he lowered it so he could hear people coming out of the premises.

He doesn't respond immediately, his eyes scanning me as if searching for something. It's unnerving, this kind of scrutiny, and I shift my weight from one foot to the other.

"Why are you here?" I ask, finally breaking the silence. "I told you to go home."

"I needed to see you." His voice is rough, as though the hours spent parked here have sapped him of warmth. "We need to talk."

I glance around, hoping for some reprieve in the quiet parking lot, but there's nothing to shield me from his intensity. "You've waited all night?"

"Yes."

There's no hesitation in his reply, no apology either. Just a declaration, a stubbornness which makes my chest ache even as it frustrates me.

"You shouldn't have," I say, feeling the weight of his resolve pressing against me. "Anyway, my taxi is on its way. It'll be here any minute. You can head off. I'll meet you at home."

His lips twitch, barely a movement, but it feels like the start of an avalanche.

"Wifey," he says, his voice quieter now. "There is no way I'm going home and leaving you to get a taxi. Unless you were planning to go somewhere else. In which case, you should cancel those plans."

Those words hang heavy between us. I could tell him to leave, to piss off—

The sound of a car approaches and stops outside the entrance.

"If that is your taxi, give him this and apologise for wasting his time." Diaye extends his hand out of the window, flashing cash notes.

It just pisses me off, and I shake my head. He thinks money solves everything.

"Diaye, go home." I ignore him and the money and walk towards the cab. "Is this taxi for Seki?"

Inside is a middle-aged man of South Asian heritage wearing a dark jacket over his shirt and trouser.

"Hi, Miss. Are you Seki Zambo?" He reads my name from the display of the digital device strapped to the dashboard and says it as Say-key rather than the correct Shay-key sound.

"Yes, it's me." Before I can open the back door, Diaye walks up to the car.

"Good morning, sir." He leans over to speak to the man through the window. "I'm sorry we troubled you. My wife forgot I was meant to pick her from work today and booked you instead. Please take this for the inconvenience of coming out this early morning."

I want to strangle Diaye, but I bite my tongue, not wanting to cause a scene. This is my place of work.

The taxi driver eyes Diaye and the money before turning to look at me. "Miss, is everything okay? Is this man harassing you? Do you need the police?"

Diaye's body stiffens as he steps back and his expression shutters.

Shit. He could get arrested, and it will not be good at all.

"No... No," I stammer. "There's nothing wrong. I didn't know my husband would be here to pick me. I'm sorry you had to come out. Please take the money and accept my apologies."

I take the money from Diaye's hand and push it through the open window.

"Are you sure you're okay?" the man asks again.

"Yes, I am," I say without hesitation.

"Okay." He seems satisfied that nothing bad is going on and takes the cash before starting the engine.

Diaye walks back to his car, and I have little choice but to follow him. He holds the car door open and I climb in. The cold air threads through the edges of my clothes as I adjust myself in the seat. Seconds later, he's in the driver's position, car doors shut. His presence is palpable, larger than life.

Outside, the taxi does a three-point turn and departs.

For a moment, we just sit there, the silence stretching between us, taut and fragile.

I steal a glance at Diaye, his hands gripping the dark leather steering wheel, skin stretched tight across the protruding knuckles. His jaw is set, the muscles betraying the struggle within him to say something—or perhaps to hold it back.

He's wearing his trademark shirt and jeans. It's obvious he slept in those clothes because he appears rumpled, which is unlike my husband. He's always immaculate and obsessive about his appearance.

Yet here he is barely composed. Only minutes ago, the threat of arrest hung over him.

He presses the start button, and the ignition kicks to life. But he doesn't drive.

The heater hums, its warmth spreading through the cabin, but it does little to thaw the tension. I know he's waiting for me to speak, to offer some explanation or apology to ease the suffocating weight between us, yet the words refuse to come.

Instead, my eyes trace the frost creeping across the windshield, like delicate veins branching outward, fragile but unrelenting. The silence presses tighter, laden with everything unsaid.

"I waited for you," Diaye finally says, his voice breaking the stillness like a crack of thunder on a clear night. It's quiet, almost a whisper, yet it carries the power of a storm. "I stayed here all night. In the freezing cold. For you."

Something in his tone—a mixture of hurt and hope—makes my chest contract. I close my eyes for a moment, wishing I could rewind time, erase the raw edge of his words, but they linger in the air, unavoidable.

"I didn't ask you to," I murmur, but the response feels cruel, even to my own ears.

I glance at him again, and his expression shifts—guarded, but not impenetrable. His fingers flex against the steering wheel, as though he's searching for some kind of control.

"I know," he says, a bitter smile playing at the corner of his lips. "You didn't have to. I came because I wanted to. Because that's what you do for someone you care about."

The car falls silent again. My heart pounds against my ribs, each beat a reminder of how fragile this moment feels.

He cares for me.

Of course he cares for me. It's not the point.

It's about the intermittent way he displays his affection.

It's about him not caring enough. About me, always being second best.

"I don't know what you want me to say." I stare at the frost-covered grass instead of him. Nothing short of 'I love you' is going to sway me.

"I don't want you to say anything," he replies. "I just want you to listen."

His words hit like a hammer, and I let out a slow breath, bracing myself for whatever comes next.

"I don't understand why you keep shutting me out," he says, and there's a tremor in his voice, anger or pain—I can't tell. "You act like I don't care, like I don't want to help, but that's not true. I'm here, Seki. I'm always here."

The rawness in his tone cuts straight to the quick, and I finally turn to face him. His eyes are fierce, glistening with emotion I've only ever seen once before—the night we first made love.

"I'm not shutting you out," I say, but the words sound weak even to my ears. "I just... I have a lot going on right now."

"You're busy? That's your excuse?" he counters, his voice rising just a fraction. "You came to England to study, all expenses paid. I've fulfilled my obligations to you where finances are concerned. You don't need this job. But you insisted and got the job. I thought you would only do maybe a maximum of ten hours a week. Yet, you chose to be here for twenty. Last night wasn't even your regular shift, and you accepted to work. What is it for if it's not another way for you to build a wall between us? I can't keep pretending I'm okay with being pushed away."

His words are a knife, slipping past the armour I've spent weeks building. I want to respond, to offer him something to ease the sharpness in his gaze, but I don't know how. Instead, I look away again, my hands gripping the armrests.

"I can't do this right now," I say, my voice barely audible.

Diaye's breath hitches, and I can feel the weight of his disappointment hanging in the air between us. But he doesn't move or demand more than I can give. He waits, his presence a quiet insistence I can't ignore.

"I'm here," he says again, softer this time. "Whenever you're ready."

The way he says it melts something inside me. Some of my anger fizzles away.

"I saw my brother's online post last night. Why didn't you tell me about it?" His voice is still soft, almost tender.

"I wanted to tell you." Suddenly, I feel the urge to spill, to share my pain and frustration from the past few days. "But first, I was trying to protect you."

"You were trying to protect me?" He turns to me, his eyes searching my face.

"Yes, I was, because I know how it is important to keep your frame of mind relaxed before a game. But I've been feeling fragile over the last few days, and I didn't know how to express myself without sounding pathetic and needy. Then I came across as selfish and demanding instead." I huff and shake my head. It's been a few hard days. Tears cloud my eyes, and I close them.

"You are the sweetest person I know. You don't have any selfishness in your bones. None at all," he says, giving me a much-needed boost.

I feel his warm hand on top of mine.

"Wifey," he continues. "I know I'm the reason you've felt fragile for the last few days. You told me something very important to you and I didn't respond the way you expected. I was afraid and allowed my fear to dictate my response. It changed something between us and I'm sorry."

His words are a balm which begins to soothe the ache within me, but the uncertainty still lingers. I open my eyes and look at him. The earnestness in his gaze clears away some of the storm clouds in my heart.

"I just... I need to know I can share everything with you, even when it's messy or hard," I say, my voice trembling. "Because I don't want us to feel divided like this again."

He nods, his hand tightening around mine. "You can. Always." He pauses, as if searching for the right words. "I might not always get it right the first time, but I promise I'll keep trying. You're worth every effort."

There's a vulnerability in his admission, making my chest tighten. It's rare to see him so open, and it's exactly what I need. Slowly, I reach out to touch his hairy chin, my fingers trembling.

"I believe you," I whisper, the words feeling like a step forward, like a healing stitch closing a wound.

A faint smile breaks across his face—tentative, hopeful—and I know we'll be okay. Not perfect, not without challenges, but okay. And for now, that's enough.

He drives out of the car park toward home. Low music plays from the speakers — 'I Know Love' by Maxi Priest ft Tiger. I've heard it through the Bluetooth speakers at home. The lyrics resonate with me this time, and I believe love will come our way if we try.

The moving car and the warmth of the heater lull me towards sleep, and I fight it. I've been up for most of the night, and I need sleep. But I also want to talk to Diaye, and I turn my head towards him, watching him drive along the dual carriageway with the early commuters.

"You said you were afraid, and it's hard to believe my big, strong, handsome husband, my Strongman, can be afraid of anything," I say with a sleepy smile. I know he fears not being able to play football. But I don't think it's what he was talking about earlier.

He glances at me with a lopsided grin. "I like it when you call me your big, strong, handsome husband."

"Of course you do." I giggle as my eyes droop. "What are you afraid of?"

"I'm afraid of losing you."

I drift off to sleep and wake from the sound of the gates sliding open.

When did he tilt the seat back because it's now in a reclined position?

"I fell asleep. I'm sorry." I press the button, and the chair moves upright.

"Don't apologise." He pulls into the driveway, and the gravel crunches under the tyres before we come to a stop next to my car.

"Honestly, I don't think I will do a night shift again. I hate not being able to sleep when my body is tired," I say.

He doesn't reply. Instead, he comes around, opens my door, and I step out.

I know why he's saying nothing. I'm the one who insisted on working. Also, I chose to do this shift. He's tired of arguing with me about overworking myself. Even my Imoni was admonishing me the other day.

"Sister, why are you working all these long hours? You go to school. You go to work. When do you rest? Are you not a millionaire's wife, again? Is Diaye not paying for everything?"

Yet, I don't know how to tell her it's all temporary. I don't know how to tell her I'm afraid I'll wake up one day and all the money will be gone, and I'll have no means of earning it because I depended on a man and got used to an expensive lifestyle.

Something triggers in my memory.

"I'm afraid of losing you."

Was I dreaming, or did Diaye say those words to me in the car?

Is it the reason he came out to my workplace and spent the night in the cold, uncomfortable car? Anyone else would have driven home and returned this morning if they were so keen. But he didn't move all night. I know because the frost surrounding the car in the car park showed it hadn't moved for several hours.

I look at his face as he unlocks the front door and pushes it for me to walk through.

Is it possible Diaye loves me but is afraid of saying it because he thinks he will lose me? Why does he think I will leave him?

I stomp my boots on the foot mat and put my bag on the side table so I can shrug off my coat. He's there as usual, helping me take it off and hanging it on the polished metal rack.

"Go upstairs and get some sleep. We'll discuss the online matter when you've had a rest," he says, but something buzzes in his pocket, interrupting him. He pulls his phone out. "Hang on. It's my lawyer. You should listen in to this conversation because it involves you."

My heart skips a beat. "Me?"

He nods and answers the call as he walks into the sitting room, and I follow.

"Good morning, Mr Campbell. Thank you for getting back to me," Diaye says.

"Good morning, Mr Zambo. I got your email and reviewed the attached documents. Everything looks in order." The voice is loud, blasting out of the phone speaker.

"Good. Then I would like you to proceed with the lawsuit."

My heart freezes as I listen. Who is Diaye suing?

"Let me confirm. You want me to file a lawsuit against William Zambo Junior, also known as Liam Zambo, for breach of privacy and damages resulting from the distress caused your wife Seki Zambo due to the photograph and subsequent social media post. Is this correct?"

"Yes." My husband holds my gaze without wavering.

My throat locks tight. He is suing his brother because of me. I can't believe it. He is defending me. I knew he would. But I didn't know he would go to this extent.

"You also want a subsequent lawsuit filed against William Zambo Senior and Phoebe Bristol for defamation and for damages resulting from the distress it caused you."

"That's correct."

"Duly noted. My firm will proceed as instructed, and I will keep you updated with progress. My clerk will contact you to schedule a meeting with you and your wife so we can discuss the next steps."

"I look forward to it."

"Have a good day, Mr Zambo."

"Same to you, Mr Campbell."

Diaye ends the call.

"You're suing your brother," I say in the rush as soon as the call ends. "And your dad and your ex?"

"Yes, you heard the lawyer," he replies, scrubbing a hand over his face.

"Why?" My heart is racing.

"Because they picked on you and they need to know that I will destroy anyone who offends you."

Warmth blooms in my chest because this is the loudest 'I love you' I've ever heard.

"But they picked on me from the first day they met me, and you didn't sue them then," I prod, hoping I will free him from his fear.

"They were foolish and crossed the line this time. Because the evidence is irrefutable. When they did it in private, it was hearsay. He said. She said. Now the proof of their actions is visible online for everyone to see. Even if they delete the posts, the damage is still there for other people to re-share."

I step up to him. "You know you are fearless, taking on your father and Phoebe's father. Two powerful people who can destroy your career. And you still haven't told me why. I'm right here and I'm not going anywhere. I just need you to talk to me honestly."

He sucks in a heavy breath. "I'd walk through Hell for you, but I'm afraid of losing you."

A tremble passes through me as we get closer to the core of the matter. "You are?"

"Yes. Losing you is my biggest fear."

"But why? Our marriage is temporary, and according to your father, it's not even legal."

"What do you mean, it's not legal? My father was playing mind games. Our marriage is legal. We signed a registry document." He looks at me as if I'm losing my mind.

Maybe I am. "I signed so many documents, I can't remember which one was the registry certificate."

"Come with me." He takes my hand and leads me down the corridor into the office space, which we both share sometimes. Then, he moves the painting on the wall to access the safe and punches the code in before it unlocks. He told me the code when I first moved in, but I've never used the safe.

He pulls out papers and holds one in front of me. I take it and read it. Sure enough, it's our marriage certificate with our names on it and our signatures.

"We did this when we were in Yaoundé," I say.

"Exactly. It was the only time we could fit our schedules to be in the same location. I flew the registry guy in so we could complete the paperwork. We are legally married."

"So, you've known we were legally married from the beginning?" Warmth blooms in my chest and spreads to my limbs.

"Yes, of course I know." He grins at me.

"And you have to divorce me before you can marry anyone else."

"Yes." He cups my chin.

The simple answer makes me feel floaty.

"Same as you can't marry anyone else unless you divorce me," he continues, his grin widening. "And I will not make it easy for you to divorce me."

I bark out a laugh, but it chokes in my throat, and I step away from him. "Have you forgotten that there is a prenup agreement that says our marriage ends in five years?"

A frown darkens his expression. "Fine. If that's what it takes to keep you, I'll call my lawyer and tell him to terminate the original agreement."

"Are you serious?" My pulse is racing again.

"Absolutely. The question is, are you willing to give up the five million euros you will receive after five years?"

I scoff. "I've never cared about the money. It was a nice incentive, but the main motivation for me was to make Iye happy. She seemed so adamant that we would be good together."

"Is making my grandmother happy still your motivator for being here?"

"No. I know Iye won't want me to be miserable just to make her happy."

"Are you saying I make you miserable?"

He looks miserable asking the question. I almost chuckle.

"No. it's not what I said, silly."

"Then, what is your motivation? What will make you stay married to me?"

"To love and be loved," I say simply, although my feelings are in a jumble.

His eyes sparkle, and he steps to me, cupping my neck and making my skin tingle. "And if I say I love you."

My breath catches, the air between us charged with an electric intensity.

"Then I would say you're making it hard for me to doubt you," I murmur, my voice barely louder than a whisper.

He smiles, and it feels like sunlight breaking through a storm.

"Good," he whispers, his thumb brushing against my jawline. "Because I don't intend to give you a reason to doubt me—ever."

I swallow hard, trying to steady the flutter in my chest.

"You know words are easy," I reply, though my voice wavers under the intensity of his gaze.

His smile fades, replaced by a determined seriousness.

"Then let me show you," he says. His hands remain steady, grounding me. "Every day, I'll prove it. Not just through grand gestures, but through the quiet ones, too. Through the way I listen, the way I stand by you, the way I fight for us—even when it's hard."

The sincerity in his voice is like a balm to my disquieted thoughts. I want to believe him, to trust this fragile hope blooming between us.

"And what about you?" I ask, my voice trembling. "What keeps you here—what makes you want this marriage?"

He pauses for a moment, as if weighing his words carefully.

"The way you look at me when you're not guarded," he begins, his eyes locking onto mine. "The way you challenge me, make me better without even realising it. And the way I feel whole when I'm with you."

His confession washes over me, leaving me raw and vulnerable.

All I can do is nod, my heart stumbling over itself to catch up. His arms slip around me, pulling me into an embrace. It feels less like a promise and more like an unspoken vow.

"I'll hold you to that," I whisper against his chest, and for the first time in a long while, I allow myself to believe.

We're going to be more than okay.

Thank you for reading Offside Trap by Kiru Taye. Please leave a review on the site of purchase. Do you want more of Diaye and Seki? Sign up for my newsletter to be notified of exclusive epilogues and free short stories. https://www.kiru-taye.com/contact

For more books from the Viva City FC Universe, visit https://www.vivacityfcbooks.net/

Viva City FC Season 1 Books

Game of Two Halves by Unoma Nwankwor

Against the Run of Play[1] by Kiru Taye

---

1. https://www.kirutaye.com/against-the-run-of-play

Viva City FC Season 2 Books

Beyond the Touchline by Unoma Nwankwor
Offside Trap[1] by Kiru Taye
Binge-read the box sets:
Wives and Girlfriends Volume 1

Other books by Kiru Taye

The Essien Series
Keeping Secrets
Making Scandal
Riding Rebel
Kola
A Very Essien Christmas
Freddie Entangled
Freddie Untangled
Bound Series
Bound to Fate
Bound to Ransom
Bound to Passion
Bound to Favor
Bound to Liberty
The Challenge Series
Valentine
Engaged
Worthy
Captive
The Ben & Selina Trilogy
Scars
Secrets
Scores
Men of Valor Series
His Treasure
His Strength
His Princess

Yadili Series
Duke: Prince of Hearts
Xandra: Killer of Kings
Osagie: Bad Santa
Rough Diamond
Tough Alliance
Trophy Wife
Mistletoe Mafia
Royal House of Saene Series
His Captive Princess
The Tainted Prince
The Future King
Saving Her Guard
Screwdriver
Others
Haunted
Outcast
Sacrifice
Black Soul
Scar's Redemption

Don't miss out!

Visit the website below and you can sign up to receive emails whenever Kiru Taye publishes a new book. There's no charge and no obligation.

https://books2read.com/r/B-A-HAGOB-USLYF

BOOKS 2 READ

Connecting independent readers to independent writers.

Did you love *Offside Trap*? Then you should read *Against the Run of Play*[1] by Kiru Taye!

[2]

Soccer player and reformed bad boy, Asher is not having his best season. A spate of poor form and injuries has left him sitting on the bench for crucial games while his team fights for a promotion spot into the league's top division. Frustrated, he falls back on some old habits and gets away to blow off steam, where he meets the vivacious Vivi. She has zero interest in soccer or footballers. Yet, two days with her and his world seems to right itself. She is everything he didn't know he needed in a woman. He wants to spend more time with

1. https://books2read.com/u/brj2xA

2. https://books2read.com/u/brj2xA

her. Yet when he finds out her full identity, she becomes the last woman anyone seems to want for him.

Read more at www.kirutaye.com.